Jess,
To a very special
Earth Angel. Keep
shining your light
bright! I love you!

♡,

Suzanne

Musings
of an Earth Angel

If you are reading this story and are having fun and want to share, please do so across your favorite social media platform using #MOAEAsnippets.

SUZANNE ADAMS

BALBOA
PRESS

A DIVISION OF HAY HOUSE

Balboa Press books may be ordered through booksellers or by contacting:

Balboa Press
A Division of Hay House
1663 Liberty Drive
Bloomington, IN 47403
www.balboapress.com
1 (877) 407-4847

Because of the dynamic nature of the Internet, any web addresses or links contained in this book may have changed since publication and may no longer be valid. The views expressed in this work are solely those of the author and do not necessarily reflect the views of the publisher, and the publisher hereby disclaims any responsibility for them.

The author of this book does not dispense medical advice or prescribe the use of any technique as a form of treatment for physical, emotional, or medical problems without the advice of a physician, either directly or indirectly. The intent of the author is only to offer information of a general nature to help you in your quest for emotional and spiritual well-being. In the event you use any of the information in this book for yourself, which is your constitutional right, the author and the publisher assume no responsibility for your actions.

Any people depicted in stock imagery provided by Thinkstock are models, and such images are being used for illustrative purposes only.
Certain stock imagery © Thinkstock.

Print information available on the last page.

ISBN: 978-1-5043-3960-5 (sc)
ISBN: 978-1-5043-3962-9 (hc)
ISBN: 978-1-5043-3961-2 (e)

Library of Congress Control Number: 2015913990

Balboa Press rev. date: 09/11/2015

My hope is that when reading this book you will escape into a magical and fun world. It will activate parts of your imagination that you didn't know existed! I also hope this story will allow you to view yourself, others, and the world you live in with more love and acceptance.

I would like to dedicate this story to my family and friends. I am extremely grateful for all of the love and support you have given me over the years.

A special thank you to my amazing editing team; Nirmala Nataraj, Lisa Fugard, and Karen Lacy! I am forever grateful for your talent, ideas, and guidance!

Prologue

"Enough is enough, Archangel Michael," said Sam. "These people are never going to get it, and I'm sick and tired of being persecuted. I refuse to continue to torture myself like this over and over."

She'd just transitioned out of her last incarnation in the early eighteen hundreds, and it had been brutal—a journey through the darker side of humanity as she fought for the rights of abused and abandoned children.

"You know what I went through," she said to the angel. "I mean it. I'm done."

Although Sam had a soft spot for helping planet Earth, she was worn out and had to be adamant. Angels were seductive—particularly Archangel Michael—and they could persuade you to do just about anything. Just look at the way he stood there with his wings drooping ever so slightly, peeking down at Sam like she was the only one in the universe who could help him.

"A break. I need a very, very long break. No more pain, no more betrayal. I can't take it anymore . . . not right now. I need to revive myself and just be here." She gazed at the beauty and ever present love that surrounded her.

And with that the angel departed, leaving Sam to relax in an intoxicating atmosphere of grace, happiness, and peace. Here, in the angelic realm, everlasting love permeated every cell in her body, and she didn't constantly have to fight off negativity within herself or from others that the Demon Brigade had sent her way.

Sam's lives had been numerous, a vast array of experiences, romances, and adventures. She was an ambitious woman, living life at full tilt, and she embodied her missions with love and honor. Her favorite experience on earth had been her first, when she appeared in Atlantis as part of a team sent down to transition human evolution. She'd been a bright, beautiful, young girl with the largest smile, the loudest giggle, and the most stunning long blonde curls ever seen; a girl who had a very special and unique gift. Sam embraced her gifts and matured into a woman of the highest frequency, able to perform miraculous healings with crystal energies so intense they usually depleted those mortals of a lower frequency.

She lived high on a hill. A winding road of rose colored stone, broken into gravel-like pieces, led to her home—a modest two story white house with black shutters. In the cellar a secret doorway led to a tunnel that traveled deeper into the earth to a massive cave filled with gigantic crystals of all colors: purple and yellow, brilliant white and smoky grey. Black crystals, streaked with gold, stood three times as tall as she did. This was her sacred room; the crystals were her friends.

Her mission in this lifetime was one of healing and sharing the crystal energy with the people in Atlantis to remind them that they too were filled with divine love. It was their birthright. With her magical powers, Sam transformed pieces of the crystal energy into amulets for guests who travelled far and wide to see her. When she placed one around a visitor's neck, they instantly connected to the love within and remembered their own truth. The amulets allowed the commoners to see their own divinity.

Time is fluid in the Angelic realms—hours, centuries, millennia pass by in what you might consider to be the blink of an eye. After her conversation with Archangel Michael, Sam got her break from earthly incarnations, and she remained in the realm offering guidance and support to those open enough to hear it.

Until, that is, the moment when Archangel Michael realized that she was now ready to return. The stakes were high this time;

the planetary alignment just perfect to allow the earthly beings to raise their vibrations and progress into heaven on earth once and for all. It was time for humans to quit going backward and start moving forward.

Archangel Michael swooped down and gave her a high five. "Hey Sam. I have an idea for you that I think you are going to love."

"Oh really . . . I can't wait to hear . . ." she said in her usual playful tone. "Actually, no thanks. I don't want to be bothered."

"Okay." He swooped a few feet away.

"I'm joking. Come back here."

"I knew it." He approached her again. "The entire crew from Atlantis is heading back down. What do you think? Are you up for it?"

The time on Atlantis had been her favorite incarnation, but it had ended brutally. With mention of the elite team gathering again, the painful memories from Atlantis engulfed her. Her husband, the love of her life, had been dragged away right in front of her. She had been tied to a chair in the middle of the den in her home that had been so safe. The men tried to take her down to the crystal cave below, but the energy was too strong for them without Sam holding and harnessing it. As she pleaded with them to spare her beloved's life, they'd stabbed him brutally and made her watch. They then turned their attention to her, grabbing her by her hair and holding a knife to her throat. They demanded she use her strength and energy to further their path of brute domination. They were the ones in power and they wanted to abolish the Atlantean value of equality for all. They couldn't stand her message of redemption and hope for the commoners, and they promised her riches and an influential position at the royal castle.

She would rather have died than give in to them. She would never take the divine gifts and power she had and use them for evil. These men were in cahoots with the Brigade, and she wasn't going to have any part of it.

When the men realized that Sam wasn't going to cooperate, the blade that had taken her husband's life was wiped clean and held to her throat. As she prepared for her death, she saw the diamond-like crystals flowering where her husband's blood had soaked into the earthen floor of the only home she had ever known.

She floated back to reality and shook her head adamantly. "No," she whispered to Archangel Michael with a sick feeling in the pit of her stomach.

"It will be different this time," he said. "I promise, and you know it. There are more angelic beings down on Earth than ever before, and you know as well as I do that things *have* to change this time. All of your loved ones from long and afar will be there. You will have the human connections with everyone you cherish. Do you want to miss out on this?"

"I find the connections after I forget everything and throw myself into fear and human conditioning and a dysfunctional society. You forgot to mention that part."

"Trust me. All the pieces are divinely orchestrated for your return. But you don't have to go unless you want to. You know how this works."

"Can I have a little time to think about it?"

Archangel Michael sounded convincing, but she was not sure she wanted to go down the road of forgetting everything important and having to relearn in it a new lifetime. How she wished she could simply return with the wisdom of lifetimes. How easy things would be if she could go back knowing it all from the get-go.

"Actually, I am sorry sweet pea, but you can't. It's now or never. If you don't want to go, we have lots of other souls who are willing to take your place. They'd love the chance."

Competition—that always worked. Sam knew that to take on another mission at this time would be good for her, for the planet, and for the evolution of her soul. But still, she felt anxious.

"I won't have time to prepare. For all my other incarnations I had time to prepare, and the Brigade still took me down in crazy, cruel ways. You know how the Brigade works. They get inside your head and screw with you; they push negativity on you through your ego or through the opinions and words of others. I'm not sure I can handle all that again."

"You know as well as I do that you are more prepared than you could ever need to be. This is it Sam, it's your time! You are stronger than they are, and you will win this time. The power of all your kind incarnating will be totally unstoppable. The earth's energy is in perfect rotation to support the vibration you need. You will have a team of people who have your back, not to mention your divine team that definitely has your back. The circumstances have never been better. Now what's the verdict?"

Angels can be very persuasive, and Sam agreed this would be her best chance to finally survive a life in the light against all the attempts of the Brigade to take her down.

So she said yes.

Saint Christopher, Archangel Raphael, Jesus, Ganesh, Archangel Ariel, Goddess Isis, and Archangel Metatron accompanied her to the Akashic records building. They reminded her that in this library she would choose her family and her seven life lessons. They advised her to consider all her options and to choose carefully. Sam stood there in awe of the beauty; it reminded her so much of the Vatican and the Sistine Chapel from her lifetime in Italy. She stared up at the tall towers and noticed the wide open dark blue glass windows. She gave her guides each a hug, and they gave her support and reassuring pats on the back as she entered.

She stood alone in a vast room with nothing but shelves and shelves of books and vases of the most beautiful, lush flowers. She cherished the moment of being alone with her thoughts and the feeling of peace in the realization that nothing is ever lost or wiped away. Here, in this room, all her actions—the reasons she was tortured and maligned on earth—were valued beyond measure. This was the only place where she wouldn't think about the fact that all these memories would soon be foreign to her. It was here that she stepped into eternity and became willing to surrender all that she knew as she dropped through the chute of clouds and formed in her soon-to-be mother's womb.

Chapter 1

I had heard of being possessed by demons, but I never thought I would be so lucky as to get to have the experience firsthand. Once again, I could feel my body trembling and that strange bitter saliva building in my throat. I needed an exit strategy—and *fast*. I'd learned to expect and accept crazy episodes, but I had hoped I could at least enjoy Rose's birthday dinner out with my friends.

Sweat trickled down my forehead, and I pushed my chair away from the dinner table and staggered to my feet. Rose grabbed me by the forearm. She and the others had already enjoyed three bottles of Prosecco; and the night was just getting started at La Lune et La Soleil, the hot new restaurant in midtown.

Rose raised her voice above the clink of glasses and hum of conversation. "Where are you going? Jacob's just getting to the good part. You gotta listen."

With sweat now dripping down my cheeks and the back of my neck, I sat back down as Jacob continued with his crazy story. He'd been over served at a party a few weeks ago and jumped into a parked cop car. The keys were somehow still in the ignition, and he drove through town shouting at random people through the car's megaphone. Then he somehow managed to escape without the local cop tracing him. He'd gotten away scot-free—so far.

The waiter brought over the first course and Ken, a good friend to both Rose and me, proposed another toast. "To the beautiful birthday girl and to another great year of us all having fun together!"

I raised my glass of sparkling water—I could barely stay sane as it was these days and was terrified to think how my body would react to alcohol, at least for now anyway. Woozily, I toasted my dearest friend as best as I could. I fought to keep my eyes from rolling into the back of my head and almost dropped my glass.

"Whoa!" Ken said. "You sure that's just sparkling water?"

The small alcove we were sitting in began to blur and when it came back into focus the flames on the tapered candles adorning our table flickered purple and green. I gripped the table to steady myself. When I glanced down at my hands, they looked ancient, not mine but rather those of something cruel.

The shaman had told me I would be done with the hallucinations and the cleansing after I drank that god-awful drink. He didn't warn me about any of this.

It's in your best interest to get home as soon as possible, my dear, a voice in my head said. I had learned to listen to that voice, especially when I could feel the truth of the words at my core.

"Excuse me, guys. I need to go to the restroom," I said.

As calmly as possible, I made my way past the other tables and out the front door of the restaurant. One of Atlanta's spring storms was about to break, and the air felt charged with electricity. The wind picked up, blowing my hair about my face, and for a moment I felt refreshed. I returned inside and went to the bathroom to splash water on my face. Rose had been there for me through the awful times with Lucas and Honey, and I hated the thought of abandoning her party.

"There you are," Ashley said as she opened the door to the restroom. "They just served the main course. We also asked for chocolate soufflés for dessert. They do this really neat thing where they put a sparkler into the—" She paused and came closer with a look of concern. "Are you okay?"

"Ash, something's not right. I think I ate something bad."

"Here?"

"No, earlier on. I need to go—"

I could barely finish my words. My insides roiled as if something wanted to rise up out of my throat.

"Are you sure? You have been acting really weird and not at all like yourself, Sam. Is there anything I can do?"

She gave me a hug, trying to calm me down. I could barely hug her back; I was so focused on trying to get my bearings so as not to freak her out any further.

"Please tell Rose I'm sorry. I didn't want her to see me, because I knew she would insist on coming with me, and I don't want to ruin her party."

"Ok, sure," Ashley said, "Get an Uber. Text us when you get home."

"I will," I said as I headed out to the street.

It was hailing now, large pieces the size of marbles clattered onto the cars in the parking lot and across the road. Fortunately, because this was such a hot spot, there were several taxis right outside the restaurant. I knew I would not be able to wait for an Uber, so I waved over the closest taxi and opened the door, so grateful to be heading home to safety. It's a strange word to use, but I just knew that in my home, in my environment, I'd be okay. I'd be able to deal with whatever the Demon Brigade sent my way.

"Where are you heading, Miss?" the cab driver asked.

"To Morningside," I spluttered.

I looked at my reflection in his rearview mirror; my eyes wide with my pupils dilated, my face a sickly looking yellowish hue. Sweat continued to stream down my cheeks. Please, please just let me get back home. I did my best to hold in the hideous noises that wanted to escape my body. After Peru I thought the worst was behind me, but now I wasn't so sure. I could feel my organs flailing around inside of me and felt a huge knot of pain on the inside of my throat.

My phone dinged with incoming texts.

3

The first was from Rose. *Hey, what is going on, and do I need to come home now?*

Absolutely not! I texted back. *Stay and enjoy your birthday.*

Ken, sweet Ken, also sent me a message. *I hope you feel better and let me know if I can do anything or if you want company.*

He was the polar opposite from Lucas. Rose had tried to get us together after Lucas and I split up, but I could never see him as more than a friend no matter how hard I tried. Another wave of cramping overcame my body, and I had to lay down across the back seat of the cab in the fetal position. Finally, we pulled up to my place. I threw twenty bucks at the cab driver and staggered out of the cab. The hail had given way to rain, and I was drenched by the time I got into my condo.

I stumbled through the doorway and barely made it into my kitchen, where I began to scream, releasing harsh, wretched noises. The foreign sounds were loud and nasty and came from a place of dark, deep-seated pain. They were unlike anything I had ever heard and did not feel like anything I had ever experienced before. I'd had episodes of uncontrollable sobs, random bouts of back pain, and massive unexplained waves of nausea for a while now, but this was different. This pain was magnified tenfold, as if a strong man had reached inside my chest and was ringing my heart out like a wet towel. I hunched over and a hollow, high-pitched shrill forced its way out of my mouth.

I felt as though I had an entity inside me, something dark and desperate, something that clearly wasn't me, something fighting for its life within my body. I could feel my heart beating faster and faster and faster and even faster. I thought maybe I should have gone to the ER instead of coming home. But I knew that would have given my Uncle Bill all the ammo he needed to prove his theories about me true.

Some days I had truly wondered if I was going insane. The question haunted me constantly: Is all of this real or is it just my imagination?

As I turned, cradling my head in my hands, I saw my reflection in the mirror across the hall. My sweaty face looked contorted with a grimacing frown. My blonde wavy hair was now matted, soaked through from all the toxins leaving my body. This was all the reminder I needed that this was real and not my imagination. Tears flowed down my cheeks and the moans got even fiercer.

A seductive voice wormed its way into my consciousness. "Samantha, you have been such a humble host, and I know you don't want me to leave. Why don't we work together, and you can let me use your power. This should put you at ease, and I will make sure you are very, very comfortable."

"You aren't me and you never were," I gasped.

Despite the pain, I managed to crawl on my hands and knees towards the small altar in the corner of my living room where I kept my crystals and my sage. I grasped my favorite selenite heart crystal and held it to my chest. "You are lucky you lasted this long. You haven't taken me down yet, and you aren't going to take me down now. I know who I am, and I have learned my truth. I will suffer through this and much more to get rid of you and send you to the light."

It's one thing to have a supposed cleansing ceremony supervised by a shaman. But then to return to normal civilization and have some kind of being exorcised out of your body—feeling its screams coming from your voice and feeling it fight with your organs—is totally messed up. I was frozen except for the convulsions coming out of my body, and I couldn't move if I wanted to. Thoughts streamed through my mind.

I must be one tough woman for the universe to think that I can handle this all at once and so quickly.

I am over whatever all of this is and want this phase to be finished and finished for good.

I feel like I am a major piece in one big science experiment, and I am tired of it.

The Demon Brigade has confused me and made me believe things about myself that are not true and have nothing to do with who I really am.

I feel like I am having to relearn the rules of humanity and to figure out things on my own.

This is too much for someone who is only twenty-two!

That oily, dark voice burrowed deeper, trying to break me apart with doubt. "Even if you get rid of me, Sam, the others will never let you be free. You will always have one of me looking to pounce on you. Just remember we will take you down—if not now then at some point. We have taken you down many lifetimes before, and there isn't much that will be different this go around."

With trembling hands, I lit the candles on my altar. I whispered over and over again, "I choose Love and it is always my choice." I mustered the energy to get the words out, because I knew my affirmation of faith would make this thing move faster and allow me to turn within and be at peace with the outcome that I knew to be true.

"Light always wins as long as the intention is pure," I said. "Your cadre knows my intention is pure, and my will is unstoppable."

From my experience in my dream-life, I knew that the more fear I felt, the more power I gave to the demon that was leaving my body and to the whole cadre and army.

The intensity lasted for what seemed to be hours. When my heart finally beat more slowly, I sensed that the monster I had been carrying was no longer inside of me. The reality of what had just happened brought more tears to my eyes, but this time they were tears of gratitude to be rid of that thing.

The logical side of me wondered briefly if I had just had a panic attack, or maybe even a heart attack, but the true me knew better. This was the Brigade at its finest, trying to take me out and make me vulnerable to more of their attacks. I took a deep breath, realizing my life would never again be the same. What I knew as "normal" was gone for good.

With my still trembling hand, I lit another candle and burned more sage, and then I curled up in front of my altar, using my meditation cushion as a pillow. First thing in the morning I'd check in with Bridget to help process what the heck had just happened. Then I'd somehow make it up to Rose for missing her party.

Chapter 2

Ten weeks earlier

Sometimes life hits you with one doozy after another. You come up, you think it's safe, and then suddenly another crappy thing happens. I'd already broken up with Lucas, and I'd totaled my brand new Jetta in an accident that fortunately left me with just a few scrapes. I was safe, wasn't I? Nothing else could happen. Right?

But when I walked into my condo on that cold winter afternoon, I had an odd numbing feeling across my entire body. I knew something was wrong. The air was too still, too quiet.

"Honey?" I called out. "Honey?"

A fifteen-pound bundle of sweetness and unconditional dog-love usually came racing to the door to greet me. And boy did I need that today. Breaking up with Lucas was one of the hardest things I'd ever done.

As I swept through the house, the feeling only intensified. She wasn't curled up on the sofa or hiding in the pantry. Then I noticed my back door swinging back and forth on its hinges. I grabbed my keys and ran outside. My condo was in a quiet complex, a friendly area with big oak trees and lawns where Honey loved to run. However, it was just off a busy road that curved sharply. Drivers flew by, barely paying attention.

I ran through the trees calling her name. No luck.

Panting and out of breath, I reached the main road where I saw my worst nightmare. There was Honey in the middle of the road, lying on her side. The cars slowing down so as to avoid her weren't even making her flinch.

"Honey!" I screamed. "Noooooo!"

I stepped into the oncoming traffic, waving my hands to get the cars to stop. A minivan swerved and honked at me. Suddenly an older man with white sparkling hair and a white beard appeared beside me. He wore a white shirt and khaki pants.

"Don't worry ma'am, I'm here to help you," he said.

He stood in the middle of the road with his hand out and slowed the cars so I could dash to the center to Honey. I knelt beside her. She wasn't moving a bit, and her eyes were dull. I was crushed… Honey was gone.

Again he appeared beside me. "May I help you carry her?"

"You're so kind. But I need to do this myself."

"I understand, I am sorry for your loss," he murmured.

I scooped her up, and while he continued to stop the traffic I slowly made my way across the road with Honey.

I was a few steps down the sidewalk leading back to my condo when I realized I never thanked him. I turned, expecting to see him get into his car, but it was as if he had vanished into thin air, disappearing just as quickly as he had shown up.

I'd had Honey since I was thirteen years old. My parents were going through an awful divorce. At the time I blamed myself for their unhappiness, because I overheard them saying they had stayed together for the last few years for my sake. I was heartbroken at the thought of our perfect family being shattered into pieces, and I was mortified at the thought that I was the one causing my parents, the two people I loved most in this world, so much pain. My dad is now a pilot and is always in a different country, and my mom is back home in Colorado.

Honey, a little fluff ball of love, appeared right when I needed her the most. She was a rescue from the local animal shelter. My mom took me there on a day when I was desperate for some happiness, and I like to say that Honey chose me. I stood in the yard with the puppies, and when I saw her waddling towards me—well, it was love at first sight.

And now she was gone.

Rose had just pulled up to her condo, which was right next door to mine, and when she saw me carrying Honey she dropped her shopping bag and ran towards me.

"Oh Sam, is she going to be okay?"

I shook my head.

Rose gently stroked Honey's silky fur, and I started to cry, the loss finally hitting me. She'd been with me for almost nine years. We sat on the steps of my condo a while, as I cradled Honey, and then Rose gently asked, "What should we do? Should we bury her?"

While Rose went to borrow a shovel from one of our neighbors, I walked behind the condos to the woods where Honey loved to run. I stopped at her favorite spot just under one of the beautiful oak trees and laid her gently on the ground. We took turns digging until the hole was the right size. Honey wasn't very big. She was a Shih Tzu poodle mix, white with brown spots.

"We should pick some flowers and leave them on her grave," I said to Rose with a sniffle.

"I'm on it," she said and dashed away.

Now that I was alone the tears rolled down my face. "Honey, I'm so sorry for what happened today. I just want you to know that I loved you more than anything, and I thank you for all the warmth and kisses and love you gave me over all the years. Because of you I have never felt alone and have always felt loved no matter what. You got me through a lot, and for that I am eternally grateful."

Rose reappeared with an armful of tulips and daffodils.

"Where did you—"

"Shhh." She held a finger to her lips. "I raided Mrs. Warren's window boxes."

Mrs. Warren was our mysterious neighbor who always kept to herself. She lived in the condo catty-corner from mine and had moved in shortly after I did. She drove a purple Mini Cooper and had the most beautiful garden that she quietly tended to. I'd once heard her on her patio in the middle of the night saying "Thank you. Thank you." When I peeped outside I saw that she was all alone. Weird.

We laid the flowers on Honey's grave. I would have stayed for hours but Rose managed to coax me back inside. She suggested we order take out and watch one of my favorite comedies.

"Yeah right, that's really going to help," I blurted out. "I hate my life right now. I hate Lucas, and Becky has zero understanding of how stressed I am and keeps giving me more work. Rose, I can't even get through the day without several glasses of wine and a Xanax."

My anger shocked her. I saw it on her face, but in that moment I didn't care.

I sank into my couch and hugged a pillow. "I don't understand why I have to go through all this suffering. Just when I think it's stopped, there's something else to derail me. Now it's Honey," I said, not even trying to suppress my tears anymore. "And I miss Lucas so much. You know how much I loved him. He didn't even put up the slightest fight to get me back. Not even a phone call."

"Lucas knows you, and he knows that once you make up your mind you can't be swayed. I am certainly not sticking up for him, but I'm trying to help you sort all this out."

"I know, it just hurts, that's all."

We eventually ordered takeout and watched funny reruns of our favorite show. We also reminisced about our crazy adventures as kids. We'd grown up on the same cul de sac until my parents divorced, and I moved to Colorado with my mom. We reunited as roommates in the dorm our freshman year. Rose had always made me laugh, and I was lucky to have her as a BFF and next door neighbor.

"It's all going to be fine," Rose said before she went home.

I wanted to say, *how do you know?* Instead, I soaked up love from the biggest bear hug a friend could get.

The next two days weren't pretty. I stayed in the dark as much as possible and took Xanax so I could sleep or at least feel relaxed and numb enough to watch TV. I called in sick to work and drank too much wine. Rose didn't know what to do or say. When she got home from work she would come over and check on me, and I would just look at her and start bawling.

On the afternoon of the third day my cousin Anna called. We had a special bond. She was seven years older and felt more like a sister than a cousin. She'd married her childhood sweetheart and had three kids under five who I adored. We'd grown even closer since I moved back to Georgia.

"Hey, Sam! What's been going on? I keep getting voicemail when I call. You have me worried."

"Its honestly too painful to discuss over the phone. Can I fill you in at dinner?"

"Yes, sweetie, that will be fine. How is work going?"

"Well, actually I am dreading going back to work, which I know is very odd for me. I can't quite figure out why."

"How about I come over? I can get a sitter for the kids, and the two of us can talk?"

"No!" I said. I didn't want Anna to see me like this, unkempt, with empty wine bottles all over the kitchen counter. "Let's meet for dinner, and I'll fill you in."

"When?"

"I'll check my calendar and text you. I promise."

Before she even said goodbye I hung up and buried my head in the sofa cushions and sobbed. There was something about Anna's loving energy that always cracked my heart wide open.

I woke up the next day and reflected on my convo with Anna. I decided I needed to get back to work. I had landed an amazing internship at a startup software sales company the first summer after my freshman year. I had such a natural ability working with customers that the firm offered me a fulltime position within weeks. I couldn't believe it. The sales poured in, and I continued to be awarded stock options. When the company went public, I knew I had financial security for at least a solid five years.

But as I pulled into the bustling parking deck, things just didn't feel right. The thrill I felt at working at such a cool company was gone. I walked into the sleek skyscraper and waited for the elevator to take me to the 29th floor, and it meant nothing to me—the job, the paycheck.

I freaked a little inside. What the heck was going on with me? My boss, Becky, totally had her stuff together, and I'd been so honored to have her as a role model and teacher. Plus, I'd gotten two major promotions over the years.

Come on, Sam, I told myself, *this is your dream job.*

Just then I saw Claire, one of my favorite people in the company, walking into the lobby. We'd met at corporate training in Philadelphia, and we instantly clicked and stayed in touch even though she lived in New York. Claire had deadpan humor that always had me in hysterics. Not to mention, she had the coolest and most artistic tattoo—an exquisite butterfly that looked as if it could fly off her shoulder any minute. Although I had previously never been a fan of tattoos, hers really piqued my interest.

"Hey, Sam," she said. "It's so good to see you. Are you and Lucas engaged yet?" She flipped back her beautiful, silky, black hair.

I stood there mute, unable to respond.

"Um Sam, do you know you have two different shoes on, and it looks as though you missed a couple of buttons on your shirt."

Oh, crap! I had tried on both shoes to see which one looked better and obviously never made a choice, or even had a second thought about it.

"Lucas and I broke up," I blurted out. "It's been awful. I tried to throw myself into work and was working crazy, insane hours to distract myself, but the quality of my work has been on a downward spiral—in case you haven't heard. Then worst of all my dog, Honey, was hit by a car and killed this week."

"Aww, I am so sorry to hear all of this. I wish there was something I could do to help. Losing a dog like Honey is hard. I know you are devastated too about Lucas, but in my opinion you are better off without him. You can do so much better."

Claire reminded me that after losses like these it takes time to settle back into life. It takes time to trust that we will be okay. She advised me to take it one day at a time and make a commitment to my work. She also suggested that I fill Becky in on all that had been going on. "She's your ally. I promise you, everything is going to be okay."

Chapter 3

Becky was understanding up to a point. She gently suggested that I get counseling or some sort of help to get things back on track. I stubbornly refused. I was convinced I would come out of this on my own.

I started showing up late. I skipped a day and didn't offer any explanation. When I came in the next day the office seemed extra tense, and my coworkers avoided eye contact with me as I walked into my office. I'd just sat down at my desk when Becky walked in with a grim expression.

"Samantha, I am so sorry it has come to this, but we need to talk. I think it is best that we part ways for now, and that you take some much needed time to get yourself put back together and figure a few things out."

What, my job is being snatched from me too? I don't believe this. Even though I knew I hadn't been performing and I was a total mess, I was not expecting to get fired. The next few hours were awful. It was like one of those movies or TV shows where you see the person who has been fired putting their personal belongings into a crappy cardboard box. I felt too embarrassed to walk out in front of everyone, so I waited until the end of the day when I knew most of them would be out. Besides, I didn't want to leave knowing I would never be coming back.

Deep down I knew my behavior must have been really bad if it was coming to this so quickly. I guess I thought with my track record no one would notice my tardiness and frequent hangovers. I shouldn't have allowed my misery to show through without so much as a care, as if I was invincible and nothing could ever happen to me here. I knew Becky felt terrible, but she was doing what was best for me as well as best for the company.

When I returned home that evening I remembered Rose and I had plans to cook dinner together. We usually loved to cook together. We would play music and laugh and dance around the kitchen. This was the first time I had agreed to return back to this ritual since losing Honey and Lucas. She'd let herself into my condo, was playing our favorite iTunes mix, and was prepping the salad. I tried to put on a bright expression as I walked through the door, but my eyes were swollen from crying.

"Oh my gosh, are you okay?" she asked. "What is it?"

"Becky fired me today," I whispered.

Rose actually didn't look that surprised. "I'm so sorry to hear that, but maybe this is for the best."

"What? Why would you say that?" I was pissed she would side with Becky.

"Look Sam, you aren't willing to discuss anything that has happened, and I believe if you really want to get yourself back on track then you need to deal with this mess and move on."

I glared at Rose.

"And guess what?" she continued. "I don't see you doing anything to help yourself. Instead, you seem determined to stay in this miserable place."

I hated what Rose was saying, and I knew she was right. But I felt stuck, truly powerless to shift anything.

"Can I just be alone tonight? I know it messes up our plans, but I'm just not up to it."

"Of course," Rose said. "But I will be back tomorrow, and you are not allowed to grieve the loss of your job the way you did the loss of Honey."

The next morning I forced myself to get out of bed at a decent hour and make myself breakfast. I was finally able to resist the urge to take a Xanax to start my day.

What am I going to do now? I wondered. *Do I go back to school and finish college?* That didn't sound the slightest bit appealing to me. *Do I look for another job?* I walked outside to Honey's grave, wishing she were here to cheer me up. Suddenly, a strange sense of peace came over me, as I watched the sunlight flickering through the trees. I got goose bumps. It was almost as if I could feel Honey's presence with me at that moment.

Claire called me around lunchtime.

"I guess you heard," I said.

"Yes. How are you feeling? What can I do to help?"

"I'm not sure. Even Rose is fed up with me. She actually accused me of wallowing in my misery."

"Ouch. You have been through a lot, Sam. And it's definitely time you get some help with all this. Rose is like me—we hate to see you so unhappy. What if you did another energy healing with that woman you loved?"

"You mean that wacky physic healer or whatever she calls herself?" Just the mention of her had me angry. "That's a great idea. How about I go over there tomorrow and ask her to explain why she fed me all those lies. She made me feel so uplifted and as if everything was going to be great and look how it turned out."

"Sam, calm down. Maybe there is more to it than you realize."

In her usual manner, Claire soon had me laughing, and we made plans to meet for coffee when she was next in town.

After she hung up, I paced my condo thinking about that visit last year with the healer. I'd walked down Fig Street so many times and never noticed her shop until that day last May. Suddenly, there it was on the tree lined residential street—a beautiful tiny white cottage with a purple door. It had an oversized chalkboard on the front porch where the words *Discover Your Soul's Purpose With An Energetic Healing* were written in neon pink. Normally, I would have scoffed at that kind of thing. I believed there was a higher power and forces that existed beyond my knowledge or understanding—but discovering your soul's purpose with an energetic healing? How was that even possible?

I had grown up going to church and always felt a peaceful presence there. We didn't go regularly, but when we did, I liked the feeling it gave me. I never felt scared of God or even believed in a God that you would need to be fearful of. I also never understood the people who needed proof of God. To me it was just undeniable. I certainly didn't have all the answers, but I always had a deep sense of knowing there was more than just what we can physically see.

However, fortunetellers with crystal balls and gypsy palm readers totally freaked me out. But for some unforeseen reason that morning, I couldn't resist that front porch. The words on that chalkboard begged me to come closer.

Before I was even aware of what I was doing, or really even before I had time to give it a second thought, I had knocked on the bright purple door. When the door opened a middle-aged woman with a warm smile, soft brown eyes, and a melodic and soothing voice greeted me. Alongside her was a beautiful golden Labrador.

"Hello, I'm Bridget," she said. "Welcome and come in."

"Umm, hi, I actually have no clue why I knocked on the door," I stuttered.

"Oh, I do my dear. You are exactly where you need to be," she said with absolute certainty. "Follow me."

I sat on a plush white loveseat while she sat opposite me on a green sofa. She closed her eyes, swayed ever so slightly, and when she opened them her smile was even wider.

"Congratulations. You have a lot to look forward to. Wow, I see you have done very well in your professional life. It looks like there may be some changes coming soon in the form of a promotion or change for the better. Your future is so bright, and I can see you going big places. I also see you in a happy and healthy long term romantic relationship."

The reading took about half an hour, and I walked out of there that day with a feeling of hope and excitement. I couldn't wait to see how her words unfolded into my reality. Things had been on the decline with Lucas, so I made the assumption that her prediction meant things between us would end up working out just fine.

Now, the thought of going to see Bridget again had me in a whirl of mixed emotions. I felt an undeniable connection to her, but why had she blatantly lied to me about my future with Lucas? I shivered—she had said something about there being a change at my workplace. How did she know that?

I slowly dialed her number to set up another appointment. I doubted things could get any worse for me, and at the very least Bridget had some explaining to do.

Chapter 4

The night after I called Bridget, I dreamt I was in my childhood home. I grew up in a modest two-story house with a creek that flowed through our open forested backyard. The sound of the water was always soothing to me. I loved the sound of the crows too, that cawed during the day, and I loved the perfect view of the moon while laying on the grass at night. In a clearing amongst the trees we had an old rusty trampoline with creaking springs. This was heaven for me. I'd bounce higher and higher so I could feel the sun warming my face through the leaves of the trees.

My parents showered me with love when I was a young girl, and I think this is why it was so hard on me when they split. It was as if our perfect family—the three musketeers—was crumbling, and with that I lost a major sense of stability and peace.

In my dream that night, I was in my old backyard bouncing crazy high with exhilaration on the trampoline. Up I went, again and again, until I was almost above the tallest tree. Then suddenly I was sitting on the slant of the hill at the far end of the backyard. My feet were buried in the orange, yellow, and brown leaves, and I was trembling with fear as an enormous green snake slithered toward me. I had no idea where this thing came from, and I didn't like the looks of it at all. The more scared I got, the larger the snake grew and the louder the hisses.

"Hello, Sam," it hissed.

This snake is talking?? How does he know my name?

Now it was so close I could make out the individual, diamond shaped, glittering scales on its head. It grew larger and more fierce with every desperate breath I took. Then I remembered a time in high school when a man came to biology class with a snake. He taught us to pay attention to our own thoughts and emotions when around a snake, or any scary animal or creature. "The more afraid you are and the more fear you have, the more power you give the beast. The more fear he senses, the more it encourages him to come after you," the snake guru told us.

I had no clue if that would work, but one thing for sure was that I didn't want this joker coming any closer or getting any stronger, and I definitely didn't want a chance encounter with that flicking, slimy looking tongue.

I did my best to go within, think happy thoughts, and shift the energy in my body from scared-out-of-my-mind to something happy and peaceful

Ugh… this is really hard. I have a freaking gigantic snake about to eat me!

I dug deeper and remembered myself as a child playing right here beside the creek. A sense of peace washed over me. I began to feel at ease and then another memory intruded. Me and Lucas in a screaming match. The snake grew larger and longer and fatter. It wrapped itself around my arm. I could feel the flick of its tongue on my cheek, the chill of its skin as it started to squeeze …

"Ahhhhhhhh!" I screamed as I flung myself upright in bed. I dripped in sweat, and my heart raced. I saw my dresser, my silver jewelry box, and the photos of me and Rose. It dawned on me that there was no snake. It was just a dream, a nightmare. But still, I had an eerie feeling that it had a deeper meaning.

Later that night, I dreamt about some high school friends. It had been years since I had seen most of them, but for some reason they kept showing up in the most random and strange ways.

In one dream I had an interaction with a girl in middle school who I had never liked because she was always mean to me. We were both at an ice cream shop, and she walked over to me and said, "Hey Sam, I just wanted to tell you I am sorry for the way I treated you when we were growing up."

I stood there stunned at her apology, and then before I could think twice words poured out of my mouth. "I forgive you, Jill, and I accept your apology. Thank you, it means a lot to me."

Then we hugged and chatted like besties while eating our ice cream.

The next thing I knew I was scooped up by an angelic creature with broad, white, sparkling wings. The angel put me on a rainbow as if it was a train track of some sort to get me to the other side. She was smiling and laughing with me the entire time on the rainbow, and when we got to the other side she blew me a kiss and vanished.

Then I had the weirdest dream of all. I was at the grocery store and saw the really nice man who helped me retrieve Honey out of the road. I saw him, and I was sure he saw me, but he acted as if he didn't recognize me. I tried to thank him again, but he disappeared, just the same as he had the day Honey died. Next thing I knew I was walking along a long desolate road with nothing in sight other than the road and the blazing sun. Out of nowhere a white Chevrolet with a beat up taillight pulled up and stopped.

Low and behold, the same peculiar man with white hair and a white beard wearing the same white shirt and khaki shorts was sitting in the back seat.

He flung the door open. "Come and get in," he urged.

There was no one driving the car. It was like it was on some sort of autopilot. I hesitated at first, then looked behind me and saw a mass of large and fast gremlin looking creatures running down the road straight for me, and I quickly realized this was my best option.

"What is your name?" I asked somewhat suspiciously as I climbed in the back seat of the Chevy. "I was too shaken up to ask you any questions the day of Honey's accident."

"Don't worry about my name, my dear, that isn't important right now. However, I do have something important to tell you, so

I need you to pay close attention. I come with a message that you need to know and you need to understand. Remember this and keep this message with you anytime you are in doubt or questioning your path."

My path? What path? My life is in shambles. Who does this man think he is?

The man leaned in really close and said, "This may not make sense to you now, but it will soon so listen up. It is your time, and you are getting your wake up call. That is why your life is in shambles, because we needed to get your attention so you would look for us and open yourself up to us. We tried to send you subtle hints, and you weren't getting them, so we had to make them louder and louder until you were finally so desperate you had no choice but to pay attention to us."

"Us, there is only one of you. And who are you that you know anything about the mess my life is in right now?" If this man had anything to do with the way my life had just come crashing down, I definitely wanted nothing to do with him.

"You have a difficult road ahead of you, but remember to trust that there is a bigger plan and have faith. Know this path won't be easy, but focus on the light at the end of the tunnel and stay strong."

"Have faith in what?" I asked, super annoyed.

"Just trust me, my dear, and listen to your heart. Trust your gut and your instincts."

I looked behind me. Way in the distance I could make out a black cluster of angry gremlins. The car kept gliding down the road, and I grudgingly admitted to myself that the man, whoever he was, did sound reassuring. But why? Was it his voice? No, not really. I think it was the way his words resonated with me. I could just tell he was speaking the truth, even though I wasn't sure why I believed him.

I woke up early the morning I was going to see Bridget. I showered and brushed my teeth and still had an hour before I needed to leave. I felt an unexpected urge to clear clothes out of my closet and get rid of some of the clutter around my apartment. I found several tanks and t-shirts to take to the thrift store, including the ones Lucas had given me over the years. I still couldn't shake the eerie feeling of how real that experience with that man in both the grocery store and in the car had seemed. I wanted to find this man and personally thank him for the way he helped me retrieve Honey. And I also wanted to question him about what he knew about my life crashing down.

He'd said I had a path. If so, I was definitely on the wrong one. I knew there was more to life than just going through the motions. I had always been a happy and fun person, and I was now on a mission to get that girl back from wherever it was she went.

Chapter 5

None of what Bridget predicted had come true, and my irritation seemed to grow with each breath I took on the five minute drive to her cottage. How did she get me to believe her and to place so much value on the words she spoke? What was it about her that gave me such a sense of peace? I didn't get it. I thought back to the way she'd done the reading. First, she scanned my body of its energy and cleared whatever negativity needed to be cleared. Then she told me all the supposed "good" things coming my way in the different areas of my life. This was supposedly going to allow me to focus on the good and bring joy into my life via optimism and attraction. Obviously, her predictions were farfetched and anything but true.

I honked my horn, because the guy in front of me was taking forever. Then I had a flash of something totally random Bridget told me during my first session, something that had slipped my mind.

"Sam, it is critical to see all people and animals with empathy and compassion. All animals, even squirrels," she insisted.

This had totally freaked me out. How did she know I hated squirrels? They drove me crazy, and I didn't think there was anything cute about them and no way did they deserve my compassion. I remembered the nasty glares I shot squirrels that hovered around my deck. Maybe I should have taken her advice and been a little kinder.

Within a few minutes I reached her cottage. I parked my car, ran up to the purple door, and knocked as hard as I could.

Bridget opened it with a smile. "Welcome back, Sam."

"Bridget, I have some major questions for you. Honestly, I feel so betrayed."

"Oh, no. What's the matter?" she said in her usual soothing voice.

"Well, for starters you told me that the love of my life and the man of dreams was going to sweep me off my feet and never let me get away. You also told me that I had a life of happiness and joy to look forward to. Finally, you told me that I would be having a change at work in the form of a promotion or change for the better. The truth is that I broke up with the love of my life, I got fired from work, and my dog died—"

"Take a deep breath and follow me. Let's talk about it."

She pulled aside a dark blue, beaded curtain and guided me through a narrow hall into her sacred space, a softly lit room with pale pink walls and bright purple carpet. I gasped. I had forgotten how warm and inviting this place felt. The fireplace tucked in the corner was covered in beautiful crystals and flickering white candles that reminded me of luminaries I saw in my neighborhood as a child around the holidays.

Tears welled up, and I shook my head as if to dismiss them. "You made me feel so at peace, and you gave me such hope for the future when I was here last, and none of it worked out. I'm angry. But it's weird because I feel like you are the only person I can turn to. I don't understand what is going on, and I'm scared."

"It's okay sweetheart," Bridget said. "You're going through a lot, and I'm going to help you make sense of it all. What I was predicting was your future, not necessarily your immediate future. That was only about eight or nine months ago. Sometimes in life we have to hit rock bottom in order to rise up and see what is really important to us. Every human being has a unique and specific purpose in life, and the only way to live a life of true fulfillment and joy is to align yourself with that purpose. Sometimes the universe has to shake things up so you can let go of what isn't serving you and start to make room for what you really do want and for what will serve you well."

I was still confused, but something in my gut told me to trust her and to hear her out. "So you mean all those wonderful things you predicted for me can still come true?"

"Yes, they can and they will. Would you like to try another clearing today? By the looks of you, it seems like you could really benefit from it."

Not knowing what else to do, I reluctantly agreed.

"Just as a reminder, the way I do this is I scan your chakras and clear any negativity as well as tell you what is coming in."

Chakras? Somehow I had totally missed the term in our last session.

"What's wrong?" Bridget asked, as if she could sense I was questioning something.

"Can you explain what chakras are?" I said, feeling a little embarrassed.

"Oh, no worries," Bridget chuckled. "Chakras are energy centers at different points of the body that correlate with parts of our physical body as well as parts of our emotional body. I will explain the basics of the chakras throughout this reading so it will make sense to you."

She then had me lay down on her green sofa and asked me to close my eyes and get comfortable. I felt the warmth of her palm even though her hands never brushed my skin.

"We will begin at the seventh chakra, the crown chakra, which is at the back of your head. Optimism comes through here, and honor and integrity are going to bring in different opportunities for you. There is some effort energy throughout your body that makes you think you have to try harder to accomplish things. I believe this is energy you inherited, and it's on its way out. I can push a lot of it through for you today."

Halleluiah, I thought. I was so sick of trying; trying to gain back the enthusiasm I used to have for my job, trying to get Lucas to see my point of view about the breakup, trying to just be happy again. Bridget could do whatever she wanted with that effort energy.

"Next is the sixth chakra which is located between your eyebrows. This is also known as your third eye. You are bringing healing to mind, and ideas are going to come from the Divine that allow opportunities for you and your journey. Quite huge opportunities."

Okay, now I was starting to think she was a little cray cray with all this, and I was second-guessing my decision to come back here. However, I did like the idea of what she was saying. Although, based on my current situation, none of this sounded even the slightest bit realistic.

Suddenly, I felt a golden rush of energy flowing from the top of my head and my shoulders. It was unlike anything I had ever felt, and my eyes flew open.

Bridget smiled. "You felt that, didn't you? Good."

She then hovered her hands over my throat and explained this was my fifth chakra. "This is where you hold your courage." She paused. "Oh my gosh, you have no idea how much courage you have, Sam. More than enough to get you where you want and need to be. Your courage will bring you perseverance and the ability to have the truth."

"Wait. What do you mean by my truth? I keep hearing the word. On the radio and even at lunch yesterday the woman next to me was talking about 'her truth.'"

"Oh this is exciting." Bridget clapped her hands. "Of course you hear it, because you are being called to do it. Living your truth simply means becoming the woman you are meant to be. Before we come to this planet, we all set a path and a plan for ourselves, and when we as humans can align our personality with the truth of our soul then we are walking our path and living our truth."

Okay, now I really wanted to get up and leave. I had a strong sense that Bridget had more to her then met the eye, and I did believe that each one of us has a purpose, but all this talk of the time before we arrived on the planet was just plain weird. I set my own path? Really? How gullible did she think I was?

Again, she seemed to read my mind, because she said, "Sam, come back. What's going on?"

"Honestly, I don't know why I bothered to come back here after last time. I don't know what it is that keeps bringing me back here and—"

"How do you feel in this room and in my presence?"

My eyes flitted around the room: the ceiling painted with stars, the beautiful bouquet of hot pink flowers next to the turquoise lamp in the corner. "Actually, for some strange reason I feel really good here and like this is where I am supposed to be. I guess that's why I had the nerve to come back again."

"Okay, great. Then trust what you are feeling, and let's continue. You are going to begin to see where negativity is coming from. You will begin to understand when someone shows you anger or rudeness it is from within them internally and has nothing to do with you."

This was a valid point I had never considered before. I had always taken things personally, no matter the situation, if someone was mean or rude to me. As Bridget's hands hovered over my throat I found myself in a vivid memory of being back in Lucas's house. We spent most evenings there because Lucas hated leaving Damon, his twin brother, alone. I'd arrive after work and help with the cooking of the evening meal, and usually after dinner Lucas and I would sneak away for some alone time down in the basement. We had a private signal. When Damon wasn't watching I'd wink twice and nod my head to the right. Silly, I know, but it made the situation with Damon bearable if I threw in these games. On this particular night Lucas ignored me. I felt my face flush. I hated the dependent relationship the two of them had. I cornered Lucas in the kitchen where he was loading the dishwasher

"Not tonight, Sam. Can't you tell Damon needs me?"

"And I don't count?" I hissed. "There's a crisis every day with him. You can't live the rest of your life being your brother's slave because you feel guilty that you were driving the car."

I was treading on dangerous ground, I knew. But I was sick of it. I knew Damon was using him, and I was convinced he would do everything he could to stop our relationship from taking the next step. "It has been over four years. How much longer are you going to be buried in guilt? Damon is lashing out and ruining your life."

"Go to hell," he said.

"You're as sick as him," I blurted back.

Crying, I rushed into the living room and there was Damon ready to hand me my pocket book. "Don't let the door hit you on the way out," he said with a snide smile.

After Lucas and I broke up, I'd racked my brain trying to figure out what I had done wrong. I didn't understand why he didn't come back and why he didn't even fight for me. Now, hearing Bridget's words, it was as if a light bulb went on: I couldn't control what other people did or said, but only how I reacted or responded. But in order to help me not react, I needed to remember the turmoil wasn't coming from me, it was coming from within whomever was trying to dish it out.

My eyes fluttered open, and Bridget, sensing the pain of the memory, soothed me. "It's okay. Trust whatever shows up. This is a process and things will come up that need to heal, so just allow them to and then release and forgive them."

Then she began to move her hands directly over my heart.

"Now we are at the fourth chakra, your heart chakra, which is located at your sternum. Self forgiveness and knowing you are worth being loved will be key for you here. I can see that you love beauty, and that you are great at transforming things into beauty. It looks like there is something holding you back here, that you aren't letting something go. Are you holding onto your old relationship?"

I filled her in about the happenings with Lucas. "It is crystal clear to me that I don't want a future with him anymore, and I know

I am better off without him. But I will always care for him and have feelings for him, so sometimes it is hard to get him out of my head." My eyes welled with tears.

"It looks like you haven't forgiven him. Until you can let go of that you will never truly be able to move on. We often think if we do not forgive someone then it is revenge to them, but all we are doing is punishing ourselves and building up negativity and toxins in our body." Bridget went on to explain that I should say every single day in my head, "I forgive you Lucas, I forgive myself, and we can both be free now."

This sounded totally wacky to me, but honestly at this point I would have done just about anything to get the pieces of my life back together.

"Be sure to send forgiveness to anyone you hold ill will toward, and that will help you clear out this space and open up your heart. It's almost like I see black worms in your heart, Sam. I think it's time we get those out and fill up your heart with loving warmth."

Black worms! I didn't like the sound of this at all, but I knew she was right. This was all the motivation I needed to figure out how to move myself in the proper direction and to follow her instructions. I felt sick to my stomach thinking of black squirmy worms sliding all around inside my heart.

"Your third chakra is your power center. It is located just above your belly button. You have the ability to have truth and happiness," she said elatedly.

Here she went with that truth word again. I needed to do more research to really understand and get to the bottom of what this meant to me.

"You want everyone to have happiness," she said with glee. "Yep, you want everyone to unite and feel opportunity, love, and happiness.

"Your second chakra," she continued, "which is located about three inches below your belly button is your sacral chakra, and it deals with relationships and financial matters. This chakra operates on integrity and honor. You are bringing in vibrations of having someone love and adore you." She gasped. "Sam, you are divinely protected. The angels are your cheerleaders! Jesus is too!"

"What?" I cried out.

"I am serious," she said. "I can see all the Archangels and Ascended Masters, right there on the sidelines of your life, with pompoms in hand and smiles on their faces cheering you on."

I burst out laughing because the image was so surprising. But under the laughter I felt vulnerable and my heart skipped an actual beat. I felt honored by the words she spoke. I had a soft spot for Jesus. Or maybe it's that Jesus had a soft spot for me. I had always been able to sense a certain peace anytime I thought of him, and I had always had a strong knowing that he was with me and supporting me. It made me smile to think of him with pompoms cheering me along.

"Sam, listen to me and hear what I am telling you. The Divine is clapping right now for you. Oh, I just love readings like this," she said. "When you wake up every morning talk to your Angels, and tell them you trust them in career, relationships, and life. Let the Divine lay things down for you and relish it. You have done enough, and it's time to allow yourself to be taken care of."

"You said Angels. There's more than one? Do they have names?" I was totally being sarcastic, I know, but then she named them.

"Oh yes, for starters there's Michael, Raphael, then Azriel and Uriel—and so many more. We all have a team of Angels that helps us on a daily basis. They offer us love and support and guide us on the right path. If you ask for their help they will help you with anything. Also, the more you notice their help and presence the more energy that gives them to help you." She spoke with total confidence as if nothing she was telling me was the least bit bizarre.

Was this really what I needed? It was so easy to doubt her, but something deep inside told me to listen and do what she was telling me. *I guess I need to start talking to my supposed angels every morning;* I made a mental note to myself.

"Can I hear more about bringing in vibrations of someone loving and adoring me?" I asked.

She laughed. "Just know that your true match and the person destined for you is right around the corner." She told me once again of my true primary soul mate who was on the way to get me. She reminded me that I was to trust my instincts; my true love was not Lucas. The man who would be my partner would see the beauty within me from the get go, and he would know how truly amazing I was.

"He will never let you get away and will love you the way you deserve to be loved. He is sexy and everything you have ever dreamed of in a partner, plus so much more. This will be a love and romance like written about in fairy tales."

Every cell in my body seemed to vibrate with happiness as her words took my mind and body into a few moments of the total euphoria of her visions of my future. She was able to give me a glimpse of the potential that lay ahead. I didn't know that you could feel something before it actually happened. I was officially freaked out and confused in a major way, yet also excited and thrilled for what may be.

"Finally, let's look at your first chakra, your root and survival chakra." She continued on as if nothing she had mentioned or said was slightly abnormal at all.

"Listen to me," she said. "This is crucial and so important. You need a ton of rest. Slow down, take it easy, and allow your body to heal. Give yourself extra self-love and care. Do whatever sounds or feels nurturing. Relax, watch movies that bring joy, and take care of yourself."

I had heard the term self-love before but didn't really understand what she meant by it. I had been brought up to think self-love meant you were selfish and only doing things for yourself.

"What do you mean by self-love?"

"Well, just listening to your body and honoring what it tells you."

"Bridget, last I checked my body doesn't actually talk to me."

"Have you ever thought about *asking* your body what you need, or checking in with yourself to see what answer you get?"

She giggled, and I felt a tiny bit exasperated.

"No, I have not."

Since being fired I'd felt exhausted, which didn't make any sense. I wasn't working, and I was always tired. The idea of self-love still sounded ridiculous, but I would take her advice and catch up on rest and sleep.

"Thank you for this reading," I said, not totally convinced I was truly grateful. It was as if she had brought on more confusion.

"Do you trust me?" she asked quietly.

I wavered for a few moments. "Yes."

"Then let's do a visualization exercise. Close your eyes and take a deep breath."

Oh no, what had I just agreed to.

"Imagine a beautiful golden waterfall behind your head. The water is cascading down your entire spine. See and feel it beating down and filling up your spinal cord with this beautiful, golden, loving energy." She gently rubbed her fingers up and down my spine.

I was game. What did I have to lose? Besides, she really wasn't giving me much of a choice.

I started visualizing and soon felt an intense and supremely strong chill leave my body. This release motivated me to visualize a little deeper and harder, and I could almost feel masses of negativity like thick black clouds flowing out of my body.

"How are you feeling?" She spoke with such positive energy and in such matter of fact terms, as if all her predictions were already real.

"Good, I guess," I said shakily.

"You are going to see your life shifting in major ways. You are starting to let go of what doesn't serve you so you can attract what does serve you. Remember to try to keep a positive attitude and stay optimistic. One more thing to keep in mind, just know some unusual stuff may start to happen."

Oh boy, where in the heck is she going with this one?

"Please do tell me what you mean," I said. "You have once again piqued my curiosity."

"You may start to see supernatural things, such as departed spirits or other types of beings, or random spots of light."

"You mean ghosts?" I asked with a giggle, knowing there was no way that was going to happen.

"They aren't ghosts, they're just spirits. Do not be scared, as you are safe and protected. Please call or text me with any questions at all."

I decided to just take the positive pieces of what she told me and roll out of there with that. I thanked her again, and she hugged me goodbye.

When I walked out the world seemed different; the sounds sharper, the colors brighter. I was simultaneously excited and disturbed by what she had told me. Even though my life was at its lowest, I felt like I had a bright future, and more importantly a future that was in line with my truth, even though I still didn't understand what that really meant. I opened the car and sat still for a good minute.

What does it mean to actually live and speak my truth? How in the world am I going to find true love and this soul partner that she spoke of if I am such a mess now? And what had Bridget meant when she said that I was going to experience major changes in my life?

I drove home, and when I opened my front door I once again felt the pain of sorrow at not being greeted by Honey. I picked up a stack of old newspapers that had collected in the hallway over the past few weeks. At least I could straighten up a bit. I took them to the recycle bin, and one strangely and abruptly fell out of the stack. I bent down to pick it up and saw the obituary section. One picture caught my attention. I didn't believe my eyes. As if I hadn't had enough craziness for one day, I saw a photo of the man who had visited me in my dreams; the man who had spoken to me about my truth and who had stopped the traffic so I could reach Honey. Ted Mayfair. His name was stated in bold black print just under his picture. He must have just died in the past few days. I still felt sad that I hadn't been able to thank him.

Then I looked at the date, February 7th, a week before Honey's death. I shivered. *That can't be!* As I read these cold, hard facts, I realized that Bridget had been telling me the truth. I had seen and spoken with a ghost in the middle of the road on the day Honey died.

Chapter 6

Ted - The Afterlife

In room number ten in a skuzzy motel in the impoverished part of town, Ted pulled the shades on the window overlooking the parking lot. He was on his way out to look for trouble and prostitution, per usual. He raised a bottle of whiskey to his lips with trembling hands. One gulp, then another, searching for that sweet, burning oblivion. Instead, a searing pain tore through his chest. He dropped to his knees, gasping for a breath just out of reach. He'd pushed his body to the brink with years of neglect and alcohol abuse. He didn't want it to be like this; a thousand thoughts of regret, a thousand longings. And then he was gone.

He was drifting away from the body, the motel, from everything he had known ... flashes of insight, of knowledge, of power and love. A vast possibility appeared before him. It had always been like that. It had always been there, and in that instant he realized how far he had strayed from his truth.

When he raised his head, he found himself in the presence of two angelic beings radiating unwavering love and grace.

"Welcome Ted," said one of the angels, a woman with a loving smile.

She seemed familiar. Before he could ask her anything the other being, an impressive angel, stepped forward.

"I am Archangel Azrael, the archangel of physical death, and my mission is to meet humans at the time of their physical passing and escort them to the other side to a place of unconditional love and acceptance. Although I normally help newly evolved souls cross over, I am making an exception for you, Ted."

Awed by the angel's power, Ted mumbled, "Why would you make an exception for me?"

"Because of your history," the archangel said. "You have always made us proud in the past, and this is your first miss."

At that moment Ted's previous life flashed before his eyes: visions of drowning himself in alcohol and spitting hatred and abuse on anyone that came across his path. "Get the heck out of my way, or I will beat you to pieces!" he yelled to his innocent seven-year-old daughter. He saw his wife hiding from him in a closet, scared for her life. He dragged her out and hit her with the stock of his shotgun.

Ted sank to his knees in despair. "I didn't know. I didn't know what I was doing. Oh God, I am so sorry. How can I take it back? What can I do, how can I take it back?"

The woman angel spoke now. "Be calm, Ted. Because you are a very evolved soul and you have excellent karma, you may not have regressed as much as one normally would under these circumstances."

Ted froze as he recognized her—Mother Teresa. As if putting together the pieces of a puzzle, he intuitively knew that he and Mother Teresa were in the same soul group and had reincarnated in similar cycles for thousands of years.

"You are deeply connected to each other," said Archangel Azrael. "A soul group is a group of souls that have been together for many, many lifetimes. They reincarnate together to try to achieve the same purpose or to learn life lessons together."

Ted realized his mission was similar to Mother Teresa's: to help bring more love and awareness to the problems of the world. While she nailed her mission plus some, he had regressed and caused so many so much pain. "Look at what you did with your life," he said to her. "Look at all the amazing things you were able to accomplish, and look at what I did with mine. How did I let this happen? How did I end up in cahoots with the Brigade? I let them get to me. I let them inside my head and tell me I wasn't worthy and that I had no real meaning to live for or reason to be kind to others."

"You only missed your wakeup call because you were so buried in fear that you allowed the Brigade to come in," she said. "Your fear allowed them to take over your power and to control your thoughts so they could use your body for evil rather than for love. It was all unconsciously done. You are your own person and shouldn't compare yourself to another.

"It's actually a good thing," she continued, "that your wife and children managed to escape one morning when you were in an alcohol induced coma."

Ted had forgotten that the only reason to come to earth was for your soul's evolution and to learn to love yourself and others. Ted had forgotten that if you can't learn to love yourself, then you have no shot at being able to truly love others at their highest potential.

Ted felt embraced in the ever-present love and support of the heavenly realms, and he began to feel and know his real truth. He knew he was a divine being and in previous lifetimes had brought tremendous amounts of good and love into the world. He basked in the glory of what it felt like to be at God's feet; to be cushioned with so much unconditional love and grace. He had longed for this feeling his entire life, but he'd been unable to even articulate it.

"Are you ready for your life review now?" Azrael gently asked.

"Uh . . . not really."

He knew it would not be good. In his past reincarnations he had worked for the light. This most recent lifetime was the first one where the Demon Brigade had gotten a hold of him.

"Ted, darling," said Mother Teresa. "You know the rules. You have to experience firsthand all the pain you caused, and then we will discuss how far back this is going to put you on your evolutional journey."

"Often times when souls live a life of disgust and humiliation like you just did," said Azrael, "they do not want to depart. They do not want to go to the light, because they are scared of what will happen. If they linger they build more bad karma for themselves and typically end up living in the scum with the Brigade, bringing down the frequency vibration of the entire planet."

"I felt heavy, dark energy trying to hold me down on earth when I died," said Ted. "It told me I would be punished if I went to the light. I hesitated for a moment, as their words were very convincing, but then I trusted my gut which told me to let go and surrender to the loving sensation pulling me away."

"You were smart to follow the magnetic pull all the way up the high tunnel of white light," said Azrael. "Don't be so hard on yourself. You chose a tough family life to enter into for this past incarnation, and those are hard to come out of unscathed. You were abused and battered as a child, so it isn't that far off that you would repeat that behavior as an adult. That being said, unconditional and spontaneous acts of love to others and to any living thing are the greatest gifts you can give to your soul's evolution. Unfortunately, you didn't have very many of those."

Ted remembered as a small child being abused by both his parents and his older brother. A great sorrow filled him as he owned that instead of finding his truth and coming out on top, he had lived the same life of brutality.

"All right," said Azrael. "You know the drill. You will feel the emotions you inflicted upon others at an extremely magnified intensity. The purpose of the Life review is strictly for education, enlightenment, and spiritual growth, so that you will subconsciously remember this going forward and make better decisions. As you know, this can be the deciding factor as to which realm your soul progresses to next."

At that moment, a gathering of men and women appeared. They were bathed in a light so golden it was hard to distinguish their features.

"Wow, who are they?" Ted asked.

"That is the Council of Elders," said Azrael. They are a group of highly evolved, all knowing souls who take compassion in assisting others to see clearly and to feel their mistakes."

"Yes, I remember them from before, but this time, although their presence is so powerful and loving, it feels different to me. I guess because this time I am ashamed, and in times past I have been proud."

"The council is here to make sure your mistakes will not be repeated," said Mother Teresa. "They want to help you with a plan for moving forward."

"Why did this happen?" asked Ted. "In the past these have been such glorious meetings for me. In my past lifetimes I always at least got the gist of what I was on the planet to do. I don't see how I could have gotten so tripped up and regressed so much in this lifetime."

Mother Teresa placed her hand on his forearm. Her touch was soft as a dove, and he began to weep. "Don't be so hard on yourself. This is bound to happen from time to time."

One of the council members stepped forward, and Ted dropped to his knees. She asked Ted to consider several questions while reviewing his life.

What have you done with this life?
How much did you love during this life?
Did you love others as you are being loved now, totally and
  unconditionally?
How much love did you give to others?
How much love did you receive from others?
What did you do with the precious gift of life?
Did you have joy and fun?

"These questions will allow you to reflect on what is really important," said the councilwoman. "And to think about what should be the next steps for you."

"Oh my God, I can't believe how terrible I was," moaned Ted.

Rapid-fire visceral memories bombarded him, and the pain his family experienced at his hands burned within. His three-year-old son lying on the floor with blood running out of his nose; his daughter locked in the burning attic on the hottest day of the year; the prostitute he had beaten up in later years; the shop owner staring at the barrel of a gun and pleading for his life. Ted felt their pain and fear tenfold.

He sobbed with remorse until one of the council members stepped in.

"It is part of the process to move on. You are safe, and you are protected, and we are here in love. We just want to make sure this never happens again. You were emulating what you learned as a child. You did not know any other way to be."

After Ted had finished reliving his life and had seen his missed opportunities to show love, he could not summon the will to look at any of those gathered around him, not even Mother Teresa.

With a flash of light, Archangel Michael appeared and offered his guidance. "Ted, don't beat yourself up," he said. "We all make mistakes. Unfortunately, your mistakes truly impacted your soul's evolution. However, you are fortunate. In previous lifetimes you showed amazing acts of love and service and devotion and courage. Try to focus on those memories; it will help to move you forward. We also have the perfect opportunity for you to redeem yourself."

Archangel Michael then revealed to Ted that there was a lovely girl who needed a lot of help and guidance as she awakened to her truth.

"She only reincarnates for big missions, much like yourself and Mother Teresa. She is going to be scared and lonely, and you can help her. You can offer her guidance and solace and protection. This young lady is an evolved soul and has access to an extremely large amount of Divine power. The Brigade has been after her since birth, and we need to stop them from taking her power. She has been subconsciously fighting them as best she can, but as she gets older and more conditioned by society this is getting harder and harder for her. It is time to help her. It is time for her to wake up to who she really is and to all her magical gifts and powers. She can truly help lift the world up if she is given the right tools and has the right guidance. If you can help her, then you can reshape your karma."

"What is the catch?" Ted asked. "After reliving everything I just put everyone through, I feel like I should have to go back to earth and live a life of struggle and degradation to pay my debt."

"There is no catch," said Archangel Michael. "We just need all the help and mighty power we have to protect her from the Brigade. We think because you are so freshly out of working with them, you will be able to give us more insight. You will be able to relate to her in a way that she needs; in a way that is more human like."

"Yes, I will do it," said Ted, rejoicing in his opportunity. "Show me what I need to know. Show me how I can help. I will do anything I can to make up for the damage I have done. I will be by her side every second and every minute. This will give me a chance to squash the Brigade and give them a taste of their own medicine for taking me over in my last lifetime. I am aware of the shift happening on earth right now, and I want to help those still there to wake up and avoid making the mistakes I just made.

"Oh," Ted added. "What is her name?"

Chapter 7

I needed to figure out what was reality and what was my imagination. Bridget had revealed so much as she worked on my chakras. I knew truths were in there. But it also felt like a total overload—angels and self love and being divinely protected, and most of all . . . me, seeing ghosts. I also had a weird pain in my temples. So I turned to what has always worked for me, a long run. The temperature was a cool 54 degrees, and I put on my favorite Spotify playlist and allowed my feet to hit the pavement one after the other.

Halfway down the block and I saw the first "Bill Shilling For Mayor" sign. Instant bad mood. Bill was my uncle, my mother's brother, but I wasn't quite sure how we could be related. Even as a little girl I'd never trusted him. When my parents divorced, Bill helped my mom sell our home, and then got her set up with a job back in Colorado. Mom adored him, but he still rubbed me the wrong way. Unfortunately, I saw him more often now that I was back in Georgia. There was one good thing about Bill though—Anna, his daughter and one of my dearest friends.

I jogged past several more signs and even a banner across someone's porch that read, *Want to clean up local politics? Vote for Bill Shilling.* Seriously, did these people know anything about him? I tried to focus on my music and clear my head.

By the time I turned down my favorite street lined with oak trees, I was replaying the events of the day I found Honey in the road. I tried to clearly picture the white haired man.

Is this my imagination playing tricks? No, I am sure its not. He was physically there and even patted me on the shoulder as he consoled me. I remember his gentle touch.

Once I began to focus on this memory, I had no doubts. I had saved the obituary and decided that when I got home, I would look at it one more time.

I'd barely run a mile when I started to get winded. Usually I easily could run four miles before getting tired. My feet tingled, as did my temples and the crown of my head. A sudden wave of nausea overcame me, and I knelt in the grass. I was sure I was going to throw up. I heard Bridget's words warning me to take it easy on myself, and I realized that I might need to cut this run short. Walking slowly back I remembered her words. "Focus on self-love."

When I walked into the condo it again felt cold and lonely without Honey. It was times like this when I wished I could explain to my parents what was happening to me. I hadn't spoken to my dad in ages, and I didn't feel like calling my mom, because I knew she would freak out if she knew I had been fired.

I grabbed a cool glass of water and then sat at my laptop and went straight to google. *What is self-love* I typed in the search box. I found several articles, and as I sorted through them I realized there were several common themes. The first theme was that you should notice the reason you do things and who exactly you are trying to please.

In an article I found at mindbodygreen.com I read, "Often we are conditioned by society and our families to think we need to fit some sort of mold. We need to do certain things professionally, or we need to accomplish personal goals like getting married or having babies by a certain age. The truth is no one knows what we need more than ourselves. A major key to self-love is learning to accept yourself just the way you are and in the space you are currently in. Once you accomplish this, you can do an internal assessment. If you aren't happy with what you see then journal about it, and create a solid game plan to start making changes on a daily basis."

When I thought about it, I realized I had spent the bulk of my life doing what others expected of me and what I was "supposed" to be doing. I had never taken the time to ask myself what I actually wanted to be doing, or what I needed out of life.

All the articles suggested that self-love was an easy thing to do once we broke free of our false sense of obligation to others. A few other common threads were to take salt baths, practice yoga, take walks, and meditate.

I loved a good hot bath and would have no problem adding some salt if that was going to help get me back to having fun and feeling normal again. I had been open to yoga but had never actually tried it. Then I remembered a beautiful yoga studio had just opened up a few miles away. I went online and bought a membership. I made a promise to myself that I would do my best to start incorporating yoga into my daily routine. I already took walks and jogged all the time, so this one would be easy. I was skeptical about the meditation though. One article suggested I start with just five minutes, focusing on my breath and a mantra.

That night I sat in bed with the lights low and breathed in and out, slowly and evenly. My mind zipped here and there. "Monkey mind" was the way they described it in the article. I have no idea how long I meditated for, because I fell into a deep and finally dreamless sleep.

The next morning I was stiff and achy. It was time to kick this self-love business into high gear, so I drove to Target in search of bath salts. Because it was mid-morning the traffic was light on the streets of Atlanta, and I was able to cruise to Target within five minutes. The store seemed even bigger than usual, and I swear my eyes were now simultaneously tingling and stinging. I wandered down random aisles. I needed an employee in a red shirt to tell me where the Epsom salts were, but as usual, when you need them they are never around. I headed for the beauty area when my phone dinged with a text.

Hey Sam, I know this is last minute, but do you want to go to Sedona with me next week?

Claire? Oh crap; what will she think if she knows I can see ghosts. But a trip to Sedona or really anywhere fun sounds amazing. I texted back. *Yes!! Sounds fantastic and exactly what I need right now. What's in Sedona and what are the details?*

I have to go there to meet with a client, but I added a few days on because its suppose to be a beautiful town. I know you are always up for adventure and travel, so I was hoping you would be game! Yay, this will be fun!

She then texted me a photo of a beautiful valley surrounded by red rocks and bathed in the glow of the setting sun.

Wow!! I don't know much about Sedona, but based on the picture you just sent it is absolutely gorgeous, and yes as you know it doesn't take much to get me to jump on a plane and check out a new city. J I wrote her back, grateful to have something to look forward to.

Out of nowhere I smacked into a nice looking guy wearing a navy blue jogging suit and tennis shoes. My arm slammed pretty hard into his back, and as he turned around he said, "I am so sorry miss, I wasn't paying attention to where I was going."

"No problem," I replied with a smile. "Clearly neither was I."

"Well, I hope you have a great day," he said.

I felt my stomach drop as he said this, because the brightest, sparkling blue ball of light appeared out of nowhere in his mouth and covered his teeth and tongue. I was sure it was not there when he first apologized. I stood there wide-eyed and dropped my shopping basket.

"Are you okay?" he asked, sounding concerned as he reached down to retrieve my basket.

"Yes," I stuttered. "I'm not sure what got into me."

"Well, I am sorry." This time there was no light in his mouth when he spoke. He turned and walked away.

What is happening to me?

I somehow managed to find the Epsom salts, grabbed three bags, and put them into my basket. I saw a bath pillow that seemed to say self-love to me, so I grabbed it too. I noticed the book section on my way to check out. I never buy books at Target, but it was as if something was moving my body for me and guiding me to a certain area of the section and three books in particular. I shook my head; I wanted something fun to read. *Marie Claire* and *Glamour* looked much more appealing. But as I reached up to grab the magazines, one of those hard cover books literally fell off the shelf and hit me on the head.

Shocked and a little stunned, I picked up the book that hit me and then two more fell at my feet. I put all three books in my basket and then grabbed the *Marie Claire* before I headed to the register. I had always loved to read and loved a good trilogy, but I had never read any sort of self-help books, which is what these books appeared to be.

"Would you like to save five percent today and open a Target card?" the woman at the register asked me.

"No thank you," I said, annoyed that they ask you that every time you check out.

Walking down the stairs to the parking deck, I realized things on this planet might work in ways I had yet to understand. I was now seeing ghosts, the cute guy in Target had a blue light in his mouth, and books were leaping off shelves and knocking me on the head.

When I got back home, I drew a bath with water as hot as I could possibly stand and poured in a bag of lavender salts. It was so cool that they had different scented Epsom salts. I put my stack of books on the side of the tub next to a lit candle. For the first time since Becky let me go, I was grateful not to have a job.

As I waited for the bath to fill, I glanced out the window into the forest beyond my back yard. I opened the bathroom window and heard the blue jays calling to each other. It was as if the bird song unlocked a door that had been blocking memories from my childhood.

I remembered playing in the creek, the water warm and up to my thighs, and I was laughing as the rocks called out to me, "Hey Sam, have a lot of fun today!" This memory was so real and vivid. I also remembered escaping into the forest and running to my favorite hiding place under the large branches of the overgrown magnolia tree, because that was where the glorious angel type beings used to visit me. They were beautiful and mystical creatures made of the colors of the rainbow and had white-feathered wings the length of five trees. They would show up on pink unicorns and take me for rides, and I would feel so at home. The angels loved to be playful and silly with me, and it brought me pure joy.

"Remember, my dear, we all love and adore you so much," they would say to me. "We want you to be happy and to have a fun and joyous life spreading laughter and love. Know we are always with you and supporting you, no matter what, my beloved."

I remembered telling my parents what had happened and them laughing and saying how funny I was and that I had such a wild imagination. Their reaction really stung me. After that I never wanted to go on rides with the angels, and I stopped playing with the unicorns, because I thought my parents wouldn't love me if I did.

It hit me at that moment that Bridget had told me we all have a team of angels helping and supporting us.

Oh my gosh. My angels used to come and play with me as a child. My stomach had butterflies as I realized that everything Bridget said was starting to have quite a bit of merit.

I switched off the faucet and stepped into the warm water. I sunk all the way under, getting my hair wet, and listening to my heartbeat going whomp-whomp, whomp-whomp. Then I dried my hands and reached for one of the books, *The Seat of the Soul* by Gary Zukav. The blurb on the back cover said it was about human evolution.

After a few chapters, I was fiercely drawn in and fascinated by the information. He talked about letting go of anger and choosing to see those that anger you with empathy and compassion. He explained that we all have a specific and unique purpose here on earth, just as Bridget had said.

Oh my gosh, this is so crazy. Why aren't they teaching this stuff in schools? Is this really real? It has to be . . .

I decided to take a break from reading and gently closed my eyes and lay back on my new bath pillow. I'm not sure how long I lay there, but when I opened my eyes again the mysterious "ghost" with the white beard was sitting directly across the tub on top of the sink counter. He was still dressed in a white collared shirt and khaki shorts—either ghosts never changed clothes or this was his uniform.

"Congratulations, Samantha," he said. "You are on the right track, and I am here to assure you that all of this is very real, and it's happening now for you. We are so happy that you agreed to go to Sedona. Listen closely. You will be guided to see a man before you get there. Be sure and see him first thing, as he has critical information for you."

"Who are you? How are you here when you are supposedly dead? I need a reality check." I laughed then, because this was so far from reality as I knew it. Was there any way to decipher what was real and what was my imagination? If this kept going, I'd be the one to check myself into a mental institution.

"I am now serving as support for you on the other side," he said. "You came to this planet with an essence and capabilities that only a few have. You can show the world by example how it is possible for anyone to have love, peace, compassion, and harmony if we can all learn to see things from the perspective of love and not fear. We are doing everything we can to support you through this transition."

"Transition? What are you talking about? None of this is making sense to me. I feel like I am turning into a crazy person."

"Just keep reading your books, and remember that you will get answers in Sedona." He then disappeared in a blink of an eye.

I slid down into the bath completely dunking my head, hoping the water would give me some clarity. When I came up, I suddenly realized the ghost man had seen me nude!

So much for privacy...

I got out of the bath frustrated, wrapped myself in my robe, and fell back onto my bed wondering what in the heck was going on in my life.

Was Gary Zukav's book about humans evolving and people getting attuned and in touch with their sixth sense really true? Does planetary alignment really have that big of an impact on the energy on earth right now? Is this why I am now able to see ghosts?

If I hadn't seen it with my own eyes, I would never have believed any of this was actually happening. But it was happening, and it was happening to me clear as day. There was really no more denying it.

Chapter 8

Two days before my Sedona trip, Anna called me. I'd texted her earlier to tell her I was doing much better and was heading to Arizona for a short visit. We caught up over the phone. She told me how the kids were doing, and I filled her in on how much I loved yoga, and that I'd made peace with losing my job. I wanted to tell her about the ghost man and all that I'd learned from my session with Bridget, but I still felt nervous about revealing the changes in my life.

"I will be happy to look after your place while you're away," she said. "I also wanted to tell you I was talking with Beth when I got your message. She went to Sedona a few years ago and said there is a man there that you must go see. She's going to text you the details."

I thanked Anna, and we made plans to meet up when I returned. It was only when I hung up the phone that I remembered the ghost man telling me I would be guided to a man in Sedona. It was a coincidence. Right?

That night, while I washed the dinner dishes, I glanced at my phone and noticed a text message from Beth. Beth was Anna's best friend from childhood, and she and I had grown close over the last few years.

Hey Sam, Anna told me you are going to Sedona. I have a man there you need to see. He may seem a little out there, but I saw him a few years ago and he was really helpful and gave me some great insight. And then, just for good measure, she had added three lightning emojis and a few smiley faces.

I shivered. Clearly this was no coincidence. I sent back a text with a surprised looking moon. *Thanks Beth!!!*

I immediately went online with my phone and typed in his url. It was fascinating. Hiro was a shamanic astrologer who gave you a blueprint reading for your entire lifetime. He used your birth time, date, and place to get a picture of the sky when you were born. This planetary map served as your life chart. The site explained that this chart could help you answer questions, like who you really were and what was your purpose and pathway to happiness.

My gut told me to go with it. I was learning to listen to my gut, and to trust Bridget for that matter, so I filled out the email contact form and sent it off.

A minute later my inbox pinged.

Hello Sam. I've been waiting for you to contact me. Can we chat now?

Yeah sure…

I quickly dialed the number he had sent me.

"Hello, this is Hiro."

"Hi. I'm going to be in Sedona and wanted to see if you would be available to meet with me?" I half hoped he would be busy.

"Ah, yes. I was all booked up but just had a cancelation, so this should work out beautifully." It all sounded perfectly normal, and then he said, "I had a vision a few months ago that you were going to call me. When I have visions that are vivid like that, they always come to fruition, and they always hold important messages. I have some extremely crucial information for you, so I am looking forward to our visit."

Mind blown and in a tailspin yet again.

I remembered my dream from the car and how the ghost man had told me that "they" needed to wake me up, and that since I wasn't listening the messages had to get louder and louder.

One thing for sure was "they" had my attention now. Hiro emailed me directions to his studio, and I made an appointment for late afternoon of my first day in Sedona.

I really wanted to tell someone about all this. Would Rose think I was crazy? She was concerned enough about me, and I worried this would really freak her out. I missed her though and all the fun we used to have.

Just then I heard a knock on my door. It was nine o'clock, and I was already in my pj's.

"Hey Sam, it's me. Can I come in?" Rose called out to me.

"Hey yes! Want to watch some TV?"

"I would love to!"

We laughed like we always did and enjoyed each other's company. I remembered in one of the self-love articles it said to have a private dance party to boost your mood. Not wanting to think about all that had been happening to me and not knowing what else to do to avoid talking to Rose about it, I suggested a good ol' fashioned dance party. She was thrilled, because to her it seemed like I was my old self again. We rocked out to our favorite songs until we both fell on the couch, laughing.

"That was really fun. I'm glad I came over."

"It was fun," I agreed. "However, I'm exhausted, so I had better get some rest."

"Before I go," she said, "I want to tell you that I think it is my responsibility to at least bring this up."

Ughhhh, I thought with an eye roll. I was so close to escaping this.

"Have you thought any more about what you want to do? Are you going to go back to work or maybe even try school again?"

"Rose, last I checked you aren't my mother," I said with a wink. I wanted to get her out of there quickly now.

She kept going. "Also, this isn't like you to not want to be going on dates or doing more stuff socially. Ken has been asking about you nonstop. Why don't you give him a—"

"Don't even go there. You know I don't see him in that way." I was totally annoyed at her for not understanding that I just needed some me time, some alone time. Why did everyone act as if it was not okay for someone to be single?

"I'm taking my time figuring out what is next for me, so please do not mention it again. In regards to dating, I am learning to love myself first before I get involved in any other romantic relationships."

She looked at me with a crinkle in her nose, and I realized I may have said too much.

"Okay, whatever makes you happy. But I don't get it. Now it seems like all you want to do is mope in solitude. I'm always here if you need me, but just know you sound a little cray cray with all this talk."

"Thank you for loving me anyways," I said.

She was about to say something snippy back, and then she changed her mind. We hugged, and I promised I'd be in touch when I returned from Red Rock country.

I finished packing my bag for the trip and then lit a candle and took some time to reflect on all that had happened over the past few months. I obviously wasn't doing something right or everything wouldn't have come crashing down on me like that. I knew that my choice not to get a job and to drop out of the dating scene seemed crazy, but right now it felt like my only option. Besides, it was all starting to resonate with me at my core. I just hoped everything would become clearer, and I would get some solid answers in Sedona.

Chapter 9

Claire landed in Phoenix about thirty minutes before me, so she picked up our rental car, a sporty red Audi, and came back by to get me from the terminal. I always loved to travel and was thrilled to be on an adventure with her. The drive in to Sedona was pretty magical. About ninety miles out of Phoenix, you turned a corner and it was as if you had entered another world. Suddenly, there in the distance were the stunning red rock vistas. I was blown away by the beauty and filled with excitement. It looked as if someone had spent years carving out the distinct and alluring shapes of the clay red mountains.

"Oh my gosh, Claire, look over there!" To the right was a bright and bold rainbow arching over some of the beautifully chiseled red rocks.

"Wow! It looks like it is right over Cathedral Rock. I love this place already," she said with a smile.

"Cathedral Rock? Of course, you already know all the names of these mountains," I joked. If I ever needed to phone a friend in a trivia game she would no doubt be the first person on my list.

We pulled up to the quaint cottage hotel that was just up a winding road behind town. Already, I was picking up the serene vibe of the place. Sedona was a little off the beaten path, and the feel there seemed open in regard to spirituality. Claire told me the town was filled with people who had dedicated their lives to healing and educating others on what it meant to be in touch with their inner selves.

I was so grateful to be in a place like this at a time when I was filled with questions about my future and about everything I thought I had known about life in general. We got settled into our room, which had two beds with knitted quilt bedspreads and an amazing view of the mountains.

"This place is awesome," I said. "Thank you so much for inviting me."

"I am so glad you could join me," she said. "I'm a little jealous. You get this cool astrology reading, and I'm in meetings for most of the afternoon."

"At least you have time for a tarot card reading afterwards. I saw a sign in the hotel lobby. They'll book one for you."

Claire and I made plans to meet for dinner. I then jumped back into the car, punched in the directions to Hiro's place, and followed the narrow winding road through the town of Sedona. Everyone looked relaxed and happy. It was amazing how such a pretty view could have such a positive effect on your mood. I saw windows lit up with the neon signs of fortunetellers and tarot card readers. There were shops selling crystals and dream catchers and signs for tours to Sedona's famous vortexes. I laughed to myself thinking how not that long ago I would have thought this seemed absurd, but now I was sort of eager to explore it.

Following Google maps, I began to distance myself from town. Hiro's place was a lot further away from civilization then I had expected, and my feeling of peace and ease was drifting away. I was feeling a little nauseated as well. I didn't like thinking of the unknown that lay ahead.

I drove along the twisty road and felt like I had been in the car for an hour. I looked at the clock. It had only been fifteen minutes. Then the road started to narrow even further as it wound its way up a steep mountain. I didn't like driving on cliffs like this, especially not alone in a new and strange place. There were no houses for what seemed like forever, and then finally I pulled up to a gravel driveway. According to the GPS, this was Hiro's place.

I looked up at a small, rickety house that seemed like it could crumble with the slightest gust of wind. I got out of the car and was stopped in my tracks by the view from this high up the mountain. I didn't think it was possible to get any prettier a view than from our hotel room, but this blew me away.

I noticed a sign that said to go around back. I hesitated, as I wasn't sure I wanted to go through with this anymore. This scary, abandoned looking house wasn't exactly what I had been picturing in my mind. When I heard from Beth I was envisioning a safe looking office in town with a nice polite secretary to greet me. What kind of "studio" was this anyway?

I peered around to the back of the house and saw a light on in what looked like a gloomy basement with bars on the windows.

Bars on the window? I need to get out of here, now!

No. Beth wouldn't have told you about this guy if he weren't safe. You have come this far, don't chicken out now. I heard this as a whisper in my head with a tone of certainty.

A cool breeze brushed softly across my skin, and I was met with a comforting shiver. A skinny, older Asian man, who looked like the happiest person on the planet, came around the corner. He was smiling from ear to ear and waved me over. "Hello my friend, you must be Samantha."

I let out a sigh of relief. "Hiro?"

"Do not worry, my friend, it will not be scary in there," he said with cheer as he looked toward his prison-like, underground apartment.

He was dressed in head to toe purple, including a purple turban wrapped around his head. He had a long, cherry-red silk cloth strewn over his shoulders, round wire rim glasses, and a gray beard that had grown into a point. He twirled the point of his beard with his fingers and grinned as he waited for me.

I entered a small room with red walls. There was a mattress on the floor with a light blue sheet and one pillow on it, and a small table with a TV with an antenna coming out of it. I hadn't even known those things existed anymore. Along one wall was a floor-to-ceiling bookshelf stuffed to the brim with all sorts of books that looked as though they had been read and used more than their fair share. Along another wall a small step led up to a platform with a table that had some beads, crystals, and a few candles on it. Soft Egyptian type music played in the background.

"Sit my friend," Hiro guided me. "I do not need much, you know. The view outside and the animals are all I really need to be happy." He said this as though he knew what I was thinking about his living quarters.

"Thank you," I mumbled, as I perched on a fragile chair I thought might break any minute.

"I am so honored and happy to have you here with me today." He opened our session with a prayer inviting the guides and angels of the highest good to come and join us. Shortly after the prayer, he jumped out of his seat and began pacing the tiny apartment while talking ninety miles a minute. When he paused his pacing, he made sure to look me deep in the eyes and let me know he was serious and that he meant business.

"I want you to know there is no such thing as coincidence," he said. "And there are no accidents here on this planet. You are here for a reason, and it is really important that you understand what I am telling you." He laid his hand on the table to be sure he was holding my attention.

"I give readings that are good for a lifetime," he continued. "The way I would typically do this is to do the reading in front of you and explain what I am saying as I go. However, with you my friend, because you are so special and unique, I have already done the reading and recorded it so you can listen to it on a regular basis at home. You will get something out of it every time you do so."

Now this was just too bizarre. Was he some kind of con man? I had always considered myself rather ordinary. Especially compared to Claire, who always seemed to have all of the answers; and to Anna, who had the perfect family life; and to Rose, who was just a natural blonde bombshell and beauty queen. But one thing that did strike me was what he was saying sounded awfully similar to what Bridget and the ghost man had been telling me.

"But how did you do the reading before you even met me?" I asked.

"When we spoke on the phone you gave me your birthday, time of birth, and city in which you were born. What happens is when we decide to reincarnate on earth, we choose the right birth chart for what we want to accomplish in this lifetime."

I remembered Bridget telling me how supposedly before I got here, I chose my own path. According to her and Hiro, I was making a lot of decisions about my life when I wasn't even on the planet!

"What do you mean before we get here?" I asked warily

"Well, you see, we all come here many many times before we get it right. We arrive in all different races, genders, and situations for the purpose of learning lessons and evolving our soul to a deeper and more meaningful realm. It is important to know where we have been so we can know where we are going. In my recording, I tell you about the woman you are here to be. And let me tell you my friend, you are here to be a true powerhouse." This time he slammed his fist onto the table for emphasis.

"You are here to be a leader and a mover and a shaker who will be recorded into history. You are here to master self-love and then go out and teach self-love to the world. You are here to radiate and ooze this self-love so it will inspire others to do the same for themselves." Hiro was wearing his ear to ear grin again and hopping up and down with excitement as he spoke.

Listening to his words, it began to hit me clear as day that I had never really valued my worth. It was as if I didn't think I deserved to be any of these things he was telling me that I was. I'd been practicing self-love recently, and I was getting better at taking care of myself, but the one thing that was hard for me was actually believing I was worthy of all this.

"I'm just going to be really honest," I said. "You lost me way back, buddy. The truth is I am now more curious, but I'm also really confused with all this new knowledge you are dropping. Even though I want to understand it, I am just learning all this stuff, and who knows how long it will take me to master it. So how do you expect me to teach it to the whole world? Don't you think it's a lot to ask of an average girl?"

Hiro chuckled. "Oh my friend, you are anything but average. You are so much more than you realize. You will see what I mean in time. What you are feeling is totally normal. You see, the beautiful thing is that we are always a student at the same time we are teaching. It's like Maya Angelou said. 'When you learn, teach, when you get, give.' She pretty much nailed it with that one," he said with his charming grin and laughing eyes.

"If you want a good example of radical self-love, look at Lady Gaga. Listen to the words of her songs. 'I am on the right track baby, I was born this way.'"

He danced with his hands on his hips, and I couldn't help but let out a giggle at his silly and funny imitation.

"She owns who she is and embraces her authenticity, and you can like it or leave it. When she performs she motivates the audience to go after their dreams. She may seem like a clown to some, but she is doing some really great work here on this planet, my friend."

He is comparing ME to Lady Gaga? I couldn't believe it, especially when he told me I would become a master of radical, radiant love and become my own Samantha Gaga or whatever it was I chose to do.

"I know this is a lot to take in," he said. "And you will never get it all in one sitting, so this is exactly why I have this CD for you. You need to listen to it multiple times to digest and really hear the words I am telling you. Then you can see what resonates with your inner being and go after your dreams. I didn't want to overwhelm you with too much, so I recorded it so you can hear the true message I need to give you today."

"Well, this should be interesting, and what is that message please?" I asked with a little more attitude than I probably should have given this nice man.

He walked over to the table in a much more serious mode. "Samantha, listen carefully. This is really important. You are here to help transition the planet. Humans are evolving, and you are a key part of getting things rolling. You are going to lead by example."

Now he really had my attention. I had just finished reading *The Seat of the Soul*—the book I had started in the bathtub—about human evolution and where the planet was heading.

"I was just reading about this," I said. "And it did resonate with me at my core. But what am I supposed to do to help with this transition? I really don't see how me, a twenty-two year old regular girl, can mean that much."

"That's what I need to tell you, and it is crucial that you HEAR me when I say this. You are anything but regular, my friend, and in fact you are extraordinary. You are here with a lot of magical capabilities to help lift up the world."

"Hiro, you aren't the first person to tell me this, and I am honored and flattered by what you are saying. But I just don't see it. What you are saying seems so big, and I just don't see how in the world all of this is going to go down."

"Ahh, have patience. It will all unfold in due time, but first we all have to heal. Travel, adventure, laughter, and music are all going to be healing and soothing for your soul and spirit. The trick for you, my friend, is to go deep within and learn to listen to your intuition and find these adventures that your soul has laid out for you. At each place, you will get an answer to the puzzle you are trying to put together." His eyes were now quite serious looking, almost fierce. He stopped pacing and sat directly across from me. He laid his hand gently on top of mine.

"The sooner and faster you get to these seven power spots, the more quickly you will be able to walk and stand in your truth. They can be anywhere in the world. You set them up for your path before you got here. Only you know where they are, and the only way you can find them is to listen to your gut and follow your intuition."

"But I don't think I have a very strong intuition. How do I learn to listen to it?"

"My friend, you have one of the strongest intuitions of anyone on this planet. You have always listened to it; you just thought everyone else was like that too. Start to pay attention to your gut feelings and your hunches. This is the key to your success and to your freedom."

"How in the world am I going to know where to go or what to do? Can't you give me some clues?"

"Do what feels natural and good. Do not limit yourself, and if you feel called to take a trip or visit somewhere, then do it. Follow and trust any Divine guidance that comes your way. You have your own answers, you just have to learn to unblock them so you can hear them."

"How do I do that?"

"There are a lot of ways, but the first is to eat a healthy diet, limit your alcohol intake, and meditate and pray, meditate and pray, and meditate some more." He sat on the floor with his legs crossed and his hands in prayer position.

Well, he sure is entertaining!

Hiro opened his eyes and jumped off the floor. "Then listen to your gut and follow your intuition. Ask for help, and you will always be guided and always get answers." And with that he threw his clenched fist into the air.

"I have said enough. You are in Sedona. Go have some fun and adventure here, and when you get home listen to my recordings at least once a month around the new moon. This will help guide you and keep you on the right track."

"Holy crap, that is a lot of stuff to pile on me at once, Hiro," I said with my thoughts spinning yet again. "I only attempted to meditate once, and my mind was all over the place. And then I think I fell asleep."

"Learn to trust and surrender your fears."

"Surrender to who?"

"To the Divine. They are always with you and are always willing to help. Ask the Divine to show you how to meditate, and they will help you."

"They? Who do you mean by they?"

Hiro didn't answer. Instead he gave me a CD of my reading and led me back outside. "The drive back will be beautiful. Look, the moon is coming up."

An almost full moon was cresting a ridge of red rock, while on the other side of the valley the sun was about to dip below the mountains.

The drive to Hiro's that had seemed so long now felt short as I made my way back down the mountain.

Claire had made a reservation at one of the local Italian spots that everyone raved about, apparently they made their noodles from scratch. As we walked into the dimly lit restaurant with white tablecloths and a man playing the piano, I knew one thing was for sure—after the day I had, I was going to need a glass of wine and a bowl of delish pasta to tide me over.

I decided to tell Claire bits and pieces of what Hiro had told me. Of course, she thought the power spots thing was super cool. I left out the parts about my apparent super strong intuition and potential for this "lifetime."

Chapter 10

I slept for what seemed like an "eternity" that night. Only joking, but that's how it felt. Deep and restful. I woke up feeling so peaceful, snuggled under the covers of the comfy quilt, tucked in the warm bed. Claire was waking too, and we grinned at each other. Over dinner she had told me about her wild reading from the tarot lady. She'd drawn the ten of Pentacles, one of the best cards as it signifies abundance and material wealth. She joked and said that when she got her new Prius she'd get me one as well.

We heard a soft knock at the door, and a man called out, "Room Service."

"Sweet!" I said to Claire. "I forgot we preordered breakfast."

We wrapped ourselves in the white fluffy bathrobes the hotel provided, and then Claire opened the door.

A handsome, young guy walked in with a tray piled high with our orders, and Claire asked him to set it up on our porch. Fresh squeezed orange juice and a fluffy veggie omelet for me, and organic granola and fresh berries for Claire. Hiro would have been pleased with my healthy order.

"It's tough to have a better view than this for breakfast," I said, enjoying my surroundings and soaking it all in. "I can't wait for our hike today."

"I know it is going to be so beautiful," said Claire. "We had better hurry up and eat."

After breakfast, we suited up in our hiking gear, grabbed some water, and headed down to the lobby to meet the guide. It was a little chilly outside, so we had decided to layer up in case we got warm while on the hike.

Christy, our bubbly tour guide, was tall, had strawberry blonde hair, and was in fantastic shape. "Are you guys ready for the best hike of your life?"

"Yep," we said in unison, both wearing smiles.

Two other couples that seemed to be up for an adventure joined us. We all loaded up in a silver hotel van and headed to the trail. The concierge had explained that the van did a loop every thirty minutes, so hotel guests could take advantage of all that Sedona had to offer throughout their stay. This loop included stopping at several popular hiking trails.

We drove for about ten minutes, until we reached the trailhead. Once the van stopped, Christy slid the side door open and jumped out, welcoming us all to Sedona's magnificence up close and personal. The lower slopes of the mountain in front of us were awash in early spring flowers.

"Alright guys, as we walk I encourage you just to take it all in. If you need to veer off and check something out, feel free. The hike is tagged with yellow flags, so if you get separated from us you can always catch up by following the yellow flags. It's too early for the cactus bloom, but as you can see the poppies are coming out. We had fantastic rains this winter. I'll point out other interesting plants and birds along the way. And don't forget— keep yourself hydrated. Drink that water."

An overwhelming sense of peace came over me as we set out on the trail. Christy led the way, followed by Claire and the two couples. I dawdled in the back, wanting a little time alone. I kept hearing Hiro's advice for me to seek adventure and ask for help. It came easily as the sun warmed the rocks, and I smelled the desert sage.

I don't know who is listening or who I am talking to, but the Divine, Jesus, the angels, whoever you are, I am ready. I want to heal and I want to walk in my truth, so please help me and please bring me the messages Hiro told me I needed to share.

We hiked for about half an hour until we reached a plateau with views of the valley and Sedona below.

"This is a good spot to stop for photos," said Christy. "I can take pictures if you want to hand me your phones."

"Sam, let's get her to take a picture of us," Claire said. We linked arms with the mountains in the background, and Christy took a couple of shots. She moved on to the couples, and we fooled around and took some selfies.

When I saw a red porta potty that blended right in with the mountain, I told Christy to go on ahead, I'd catch up with them.

"Do you want me to wait on you?" Claire called from the front of the group.

"No thanks. I'll be fine."

After I came out of the bathroom, I took in the view once again. For the first time, I noticed some blue flags and another trail that led in a different direction. That trail seemed to go all the way to the top of the mountain, while the yellow flagged trail looked as if it wrapped around the side.

Follow the blue flags for answers, I heard a familiar whisper in my head tell me. I thought for a second, and then, just like Hiro said to, I followed my intuition. Besides, it would be so cool to get to the top.

The climb was steeper and rockier than the first one, and I was soon winded. I stopped and chugged as much water as possible and waited until I caught my breath. I noticed I was almost half way up and gave myself the encouragement I needed to keep going. As I focused again on the trail, I noticed a carving in one of the large nearby rocks. I moved closer and read it. *Only love is Real.*

Despite the heat, I shivered a little. *Was this a message for me? Is this what happened when you trusted your intuition?* I felt my phone vibrating and pulled it out of my pocket. Claire had sent me a text.

Where are you? Are you ok? It's been over an hour since we have seen you and we are getting worried.

Yes! I'm sorry! I ended up on the blue path. I'll just catch the shuttle on my own and will see you back at the hotel. Tell Christy I am fine. Getting a great workout!!

Cool. I thought you may have been kidnapped by a coyote ;)

Not willing to give up now, I pushed through my remaining resistance and powered my way up to the tippy top of the mountain. When I got there I felt so proud. I had a panoramic, 360 degree view of red rock country. Climbing the mountain felt symbolic, a first step on my journey.

I'm following my path. How about that!

I did a little happy dance up there all alone, and then decided that I needed to document the moment. I took a photo and then turned to take one from the other direction. I was adjusting the setting on my camera app, when a golden sensation of warmth, unlike anything I had ever felt before, came over me. I looked up and my phone slipped from my hand. My knees began to shake and tears filled my eyes, as I stood in the presence of pure peace, grace, and love.

"Hey Sam, welcome to the team," said the most magnificent angel. Tall and handsome, he looked as though he was a warrior for God. He wore beautiful golden sandals and carried a golden shield and sword.

Stunned and overcome with grace, I stood there speechless; this presence and this glory felt so soft and comforting and oddly familiar. I didn't understand the familiarity, but it was too strong to deny. This beautiful being stood there smiling in a way that let me know he was so proud, and that this was a very special moment for me.

"I'm Archangel Michael," he said. "I am the leader among all the archangels, and my name serves reference to he who is like God. I will do anything I can to protect you, as we are very close and have been together for eons. Literally." He winked and smiled broadly.

"Before you came here, I promised to protect you and help to see you through fulfilling your divine mission."

His presence was so amazing and blissful, but I didn't know how this could be really happening. *Was this real??!* I didn't think I could have even dreamed up anything quite like this.

"I have to be honest with you," he said. "I had no idea how hard it would be for me to watch you suffer this go around."

"This go around?" I stammered, still wondering if the altitude was playing mind games with me and this was all my imagination. I took a deep breath and peered down at the valley to remind myself of my whereabouts.

"Don't worry about your previous lifetimes, as they aren't relevant at this point. I am here to welcome you on your spiritual awakening, and to tell you that I am always here and you can call on me anytime you need anything. This path will not be easy at first but know you have much Divine support. If you can stay strong, the tough part will be over before you know it."

"The tough part? You mean there's more? Would you say my life has been a walk in the park until now?" I still couldn't decide if I was making all this up or if I really was talking to an angel. I turned away from him, or it, or my imagination, and sat on a rock and stared hard at the valley below. Surely I was hallucinating. "Honestly, right now I'm not buying any of this."

"I understand your confusion, but know I am here for you. It is important that you learn to love yourself. Learn to notice your thoughts and your words, because what you think today and the words you use today will shape your future and map out your tomorrow."

There it was again, the notion of loving myself. The voice in my imagination or the angel—I still wasn't convinced—kept speaking. "You did it Sam, your intuition led you here to me. So you got this."

"I got what?"

"Following your bliss. Finding the road that is your truth." He walked over and lifted me into the most loving, gentle hug. I felt the lightness and the purity of his wings as they wrapped around my shoulders. For the first time since I could remember, I felt safe. No, it was more than that. I felt whole and complete.

I loved feeling supported by this angel, this being. I didn't want him to go. So he sat with me and embraced me for what seemed like hours.

Then he said, "Hey, kiddo, there is something we need to discuss. You have a few energetic attachments that I need to release from you, but I can't do it without your permission."

His wings were tickling my nose a bit, and they smelled of roses. "Okay, go ahead. But what do you mean by energetic attachments?"

"They are actually five earthbound spirits. These are simply spirits who perhaps had an unfortunate life or death on earth, and when they died they did not want to go to the light because they were scared of what the consequences would be." He spoke like this was everyday chit chat. "They have no place to live, because they don't have bodies. So they attach onto people who do have bodies. This happens if a person becomes vulnerable enough to allow them in. These spirits often travel in groups."

"Should they be scared? And what are they scared of? And how in the world are they attached to me without my knowing?" I was totally freaked out by all that he was saying.

"No, they should not be scared, they just do not understand. There is no such thing as hell, and humans do not ever die. They just move from realm to realm depending on their karma and what was accomplished in their most recent lifetime. You became susceptible when you were so down and out with everything that had happened with Lucas, and they attached to you. You have been feeling a lot of the symptoms they carried in their bodies while on earth. That happens when you pick up a spirit."

Well, that would explain a lot of all of these crazy symptoms. Ugh, I felt as if I had been super violated.

"Don't feel bad," he said. "You couldn't control it. It is nothing to be embarrassed about. It is just something that happens sometimes. I also want to let you know that some of the physical symptoms have been from these spirits—the depression, anxiety, and the urge to medicate yourself. But something that is also happening with you is that you are having the physical symptoms of a human spiritual awakening. Your energy is ascending fast, and your physical body needs to catch up. You may still feel some symptoms, but they will pass quickly as long as you honor your body's needs and get rest. I am removing the spirits now and sending them to the light."

With his palm outstretched, the angel gently ushered these beings off my energetic body and sent them to what he was calling the light. As he did this, I instantly felt lighter and freer.

"When someone comes here with a mission such as your own, the Demon Brigade gets busy. They will try to grab your energy and use it for dark instead of light."

"Demons? That sounds awful."

"Don't be scared. This is normal. Most people don't even know this can happen. The Brigade has been after you since you were a girl, but you have been subconsciously fighting them off."

He must have sensed how this was freaking me out big time, because he said, "You are divinely protected, but you do need to be aware that the Brigade exists and to know you will be tested. Make sure you don't react or feed the negativity."

His wingtips rustled as a warm breeze crested the mountain. He leaned in to me. "You are free of these attachments, and I am going to make sure this can never happen to you again. Would you like a shield?"

"YES! Please!"

"Here goes." He guided his hands around my body, and a most beautiful rainbow colored shield surrounded me, studded with mirrors that glimmered in the sun.

"This will protect you so spirits can no longer attach to you. It will force them to look into a mirror and see their own souls and be drawn to the light. By wearing this shield you are helping to clean the earth of unwanted energies causing havoc. When I go you will not see the shield anymore, but trust and know it is always there and will always protect you."

"Thank you," I gasped, stunned by the beauty of the colors in the shield. A deep certainty came over me, and I knew I had not made up any of this extraordinary meeting with Archangel Michael.

"I have to go now," he said. "But remember I love you, I am proud of you, and I am always here." He gave me a reassuring smile. "Sorry, too, about the phone."

Then he disappeared as quickly as he had shown up.

I bent down to pick up my I-phone and saw there was a lightning bolt shaped crack zigzagged across the screen. No way was I going to replace it. This would be the perfect reminder for me to trust my intuition.

Chapter 11

Two days and nights were not nearly enough time in Sedona. The morning of our departure, Claire and I each had a massage and then walked the town for some shopping. She found a beautiful pair of turquoise earrings, and I bought a dream catcher—a willow hoop decorated with feathers, thread, and beads. I loved the way the woman in the shop explained how they work. The good dreams would slide down the feathers while the bad ones would move on, fearful of being caught in the web woven within the hoop. I never wanted that snake dream again. Claire and I said our goodbyes at Sky Harbor Airport in Phoenix with promises to return for another visit. She was heading west to another client meeting in Las Vegas.

On my way back, the plane flew north over the red rock country and then skirted the rim of the Grand Canyon. An odd but intense feeling of loneliness washed over me. I already missed Claire; my friendship with her was so easy. I also didn't quite know what I would find back home. Self-love, self-care, my truth, my mission . . . angels? It all started to seem unreal again. Not that long ago I thought I had my whole life mapped out. I thought I was at the company I would be at throughout my career, and that I was on the fast track to where I wanted to be in the corporate world. I thought I had met the love of my life and that one day we would have a family of our own.

I remembered being scared but excited when I decided to make the move back to Georgia for college. I was born in northern Georgia, but after things got so sticky between my parents, Mom and I moved out west to Colorado. I loved the opportunity to ski and be outdoors, and of course that was where I met Honey. I ended up feeling safe in Colorado. I thought I had everything I needed. Something shifted though, when I came to Georgia. Suddenly I wanted to see the world. I wanted to travel. Maybe that's what happens for a lot of kids when they leave home and break out on their own.

At my college orientation, I reunited with Rose who would become my roommate. A week later, I met Lucas. With his shaggy blonde curls and a smile that would melt any woman's heart, he caught my eye immediately. He was a senior, and when he asked me to go to a football game with him I was so excited. I knew Lucas was a ladies' man; he wasn't ready to settle down with me right away. But still, I felt a strange internal pull toward him that I couldn't put my finger on.

At the end of every year the college did a drawing for a trip to an exotic locale that only the freshman were allowed to participate in. It was a way to welcome the freshmen, and for those in my year the trip was to the Maldives. I had a pretty good record with winning things of this sort, and for days before the drawing I visualized my name being pulled out of the eight-foot glass bowl filled with thousands of entries. I knew this trip was a once in a lifetime opportunity.

I went to the football field along with hundreds of other students for the drawing. The college president was on a stage in the middle of the field, and the bleachers were packed with students. All of us were filled with anticipation as he dipped his hand in the bowl and pulled out a ticket

"Samantha Kingston, you are our winner!" he announced.

I was stunned—my dream was coming true. I turned to Rose right away. "Will you go with me? It will be such a fun adventure."

"Yeah! Umm, are you kidding? This is freaking AWESOME!"

A week before we were to leave, Rose's mother was hospitalized with pneumonia, and Rose just didn't feel right about making the trip. I knew who I wanted to invite to take her place, but I felt shy and awkward. Go alone, I told myself. But that would be so sad. This trip was meant to be shared. I was going to paradise.

YOLO, I thought as I finally summoned up the courage and dialed his number.

"Hey Sam, what's up?" said Lucas.

"Hey," I said quietly.

"Are you stoked about your trip or what? You girls are gonna have a blast."

"Um, well . . . actually Rose can't make it. Her mom is really sick. I'm sure she's going to be okay, but Rose still feels like she needs to stay. She's bummed and worried."

My heartbeat sped up, and my palms shook.

"Sorry to hear that. But you're still going, right? Want me to take her place?" He laughed, but I knew that he knew that was the reason I called.

"Actually, yeah, that is exactly want I want. Are you game?" I sputtered out the words and held my breath, waiting to hear his reply.

"Hell, yeah! Are you serious? My bags are packed, and I am ready to go. When do we leave?"

The biggest grin possible rolled across my face, and excitement shot through my entire body.

"Next Friday. Our flight leaves at four, and get ready because this place looks totally freaking amazing."

"Sounds perfect. I am thrilled to be joining you, and I promise you won't regret inviting me."

"Thanks Lucas, and please know this is a no strings attached invitation. We can just enjoy each other's company in paradise."

After the first football game date, we had gone out a few more times, and I became even more convinced he was not the type to settle down. Not to mention, I had never been in love before, and I wasn't sure if that would ever be possible for me. So the day before we left to go to the Maldives, I was overwhelmed with excitement and giddiness.

We had twenty-four hours of travel ahead, but it was anything but miserable because of the happiness I felt with Lucas by my side. It was like I was living an actual fairy tale. I had told myself to keep things PG with him on this trip, but I knew my will power probably wouldn't hold out very long. We spent our first night at a hotel on one of the islands before heading out the next day to the luxury resort for the week. We checked in at eleven at night island time, and I was both wound up and exhausted. "Lucas, you go to sleep, I am just going to rinse off before I get into bed."

"Okay, I am sure I'll still be awake," he said with his heart melting grin and a wink.

As I stepped in the shower, I realized it had no door. I was standing there totally exposed with only the blinds over the tub separating me from Lucas. I couldn't help but let out a little giggle as I saw him peaking through the blinds trying to catch a glimpse of me. He then turned and relaxed on the bed.

Man, I am in for it. Through the blinds I could see him laying on the bed, his head propped up on one hand. He looked stunning as usual. My heart skipped a beat, and my stomach filled with butterflies.

I stepped out of the shower and covered myself in the black, lacey silk robe I'd bought for the trip. Shyly I entered the room.

"You look beautiful, Sam," he whispered.

I was so nervous I wasn't sure what to do. So I blushed and peered down at my feet. Lucas slowly strolled toward me and loosened the tie on my robe. He caressed my body in a way that made me feel like I was his and he was mine. He gently guided my robe to the floor and scooped me up into his arms. I couldn't resist his alluring gaze and touch. We had a loving and magical night together, and it was the beginning of a life-changing trip for both of us. That night Lucas seemed to hold me at a level of honor and respect that he had never held for me before.

When we woke the next morning, we gathered our things and walked out to the beautiful water's edge to wait for our boat to pick us up and take us to our hotel for the week. When the boat came everyone who set foot on it smiled from ear to ear. You could feel the beauty, peace, and happiness in the air. When we pulled up to the hotel I couldn't believe my eyes. I was in true paradise with a beautiful man who was now treating me like a princess.

The obliging hotel staff escorted us to our luxurious glass bottom hut out in the clear blue ocean. I honestly felt like I was on my honeymoon, with days of love and laughter and ever deepening intimacy. Our room was pristine with elegant furnishings. The flooring near the bathroom had been replaced with glass tiles, and we soon became obsessed with watching the tropical fish. Burnt orange, fuchsia, neon green, and every shade of blue—they darted beneath us like a constantly shifting kaleidoscope. Our biggest thrill was seeing a toothy barracuda glide by one evening.

We took jet ski tours and found coconuts to crack open and eat; we swam with sharks; we sailed across the beautiful blue sea all the while brimming over with happiness to be together on such an amazing island. One afternoon we skipped the arranged snorkel trip and went skinny dipping in a private lagoon near our cabana. It was as if Lucas and I were the only people in this tropical paradise.

On the fourth night we snuggled on the deck outside our suite for a night of stargazing. A sliver of moon lay just above the horizon. I'd never seen so many stars; including shooting ones that raced clear across the velvet sky. I felt as though I were staring into infinity. I knew that I had fallen in love with this beautiful man, and I didn't want to let him go. I'd seen a side to Lucas that I didn't know existed; he was so kind and gentle and loving and made sure my every need was taken care of.

For our remaining three nights we relished the local flavors and laughed and danced to the local bands. We picnicked on a private island, had a couple's massage, and walked incessantly hand and hand everywhere we went. We spent hours in the beautiful hot tub, which sat on a ledge with an open, ten foot high window overlooking the crystal clear water.

"Wow, you two are such a cute couple," said a friendly man staying in the cabana next to us. "We can see the love between you."

On the plane back home my heart ached. I tried to be mature about it and act as if I was prepared to let him go. But deep inside I knew I would be devastated if all it came to was a week of love in paradise.

I was overcome with joy when on our return we began dating seriously and started to know each other in our own realities. Lucas and I didn't see eye to eye on most things. We differed in politics, religion, and many other topics, but I had a love for him that went deeper then I could ever understand. Our highs were very high, and our lows were very low. In fact, our relationship was quite tumultuous.

Lucas lived with Damon, his handicapped identical twin brother. Damon was in physical therapy and getting the feeling back in his legs, but he wouldn't let Lucas forget that he was the one in control of the car when they had the wreck. As the months went by, I saw how intertwined the brothers' lives were. Lucas had such a magnetizing and sweet energy, and Damon, well . . . let's just say he was the complete opposite.

I understood at first and tried to be as compassionate as possible. I could only imagine how it must be for Damon, to constantly be looking into a rear view mirror of what could have been. I knew that Lucas felt guilty, and that he often wondered what twist of fate left him uninjured and Damon's life so changed. I tried and tried to include Damon in our plans and to be sweet to him, but all he ever did was try to tear Lucas and me apart. I saw how guilt drove Lucas, and how Damon used that guilt in increasingly manipulative ways as our love deepened.

Lucas couldn't make a decision or do anything without running it by Damon and getting his approval. Damon would use these opportunities to drive wedges between Lucas and me. Once I realized these circumstances were never going to change, I started to wonder if I could deal with this the rest of my life. I always put

Lucas first, and I needed him to show me the same respect—at least some of the time. But he could never do it.

On the evening of the second annual company awards gala, I was stoked because I had another killer year with my job and was going to be recognized and awarded for my success. I had bought a fancy new Nicole Miller dress in celebration of the event. I zipped up my dress and was putting on my sparkly stilettos when my doorbell rang. I opened the door to see Lucas, unshaven, and still in his workout clothes.

"I can't go with you tonight," he said. "I'm sorry. I know I promised, but Damon is in pain, and he doesn't want to be alone tonight."

I was stunned. I would have to be alone at yet another work banquet because Damon was in need? I was decked out to the nines, and Lucas didn't so much as compliment me. For the first few years, I was understanding when this type of thing happened so often, but my patience had grown thin, and I was at my wits end.

"I am sorry that things have to end like this," I said, as tears filled my eyes. "You know I love you more than anything. All I wanted from you was for you to put me first for once, and you obviously are never going to be able to do that."

Lucas got eerily calm and walked around my condo collecting all the things he had there. He had his stuff packed in about twenty minutes, and my heart was stung by his silence. I sat there sobbing as he went to the door in seething rage.

"That is it? Aren't you even going to say anything?" I said in a panic.

"I know you threatened to do this the next time I had to bail, but honestly I never thought you would go through with it. You are the one calling it quits, so why are you asking me if this is it?"

"I thought you would at least say something." I looked up at him, as tears streamed down my cheeks.

"This is un-effing believable that you are breaking up with me after telling me how much you love me and how much you want a future with me."

"Don't you get it? With you! I want a future with me and you, not a relationship run by your brother. You don't even make your own decisions. You handed your voice and your life totally over to Damon. Don't you see it?"

"I can't believe you Sam!"

He slammed the door and left just like that. I did my best to hold it together and walked up the stairs to redo my makeup. I was not going to let Lucas, and especially not Damon, ruin this evening.

Looking back, I realize this situation was particularly hard for me because I had such strong feelings for him. But I knew I deserved better, and I knew I deserved to be put first. I longed for Lucas in a way that I never believed possible, but I had reached my limit on what I could handle and tolerate from him. Lucas couldn't ever see it. He would never see things the way I did.

In the weeks after the breakup, I acknowledged that we weren't the best long term match for each other. But that didn't explain the connection and the glue that held us together for so long and that made it so hard for me to let him go. I couldn't get him out of my head, and now here on the flight back from Sedona I found myself revisiting the love we shared and all the hurts. I'd thought that after we split I would be able to let him go, and even though physically I did, he was still always on my mind.

When we landed in Atlanta, I was exhausted. My heart felt so heavy. I made it to the baggage claim on auto pilot, and then once I got to the parking lot I couldn't remember where I had parked. I looked on three different floors before I realized I had actually parked in park-n-ride and not in the deck.

I finally found my car and slipped into the driver's seat. I started the car, and a favorite song of mine came on the radio. One that I listened to with my parents when I was growing up. The beat got to me every time. I just loved it, and this time it was as if the words from the song spoke directly to me.

I'm starting with the man in the mirror. I'm asking him to change his ways, and no message could have been any clearer. If you want to make the world a better place, you take a look at yourself and make the change.

That's deep, Michael, I thought. *How come I never really noticed the true meaning of these words before now?*

I blasted the song on repeat on my satellite channel until I was back at my condo. Each time I heard the words, I realized the song was telling me that everything starts with me internally. I couldn't help myself for longing to see Lucas. I missed him so much some days and longed to lay beside him at night. Knowing that I needed to do my best to repress these feelings as best I could, I lugged my bags up the stairs and fell directly onto my bed. I was exhausted and needed a good night's sleep to clear my head.

Chapter 12

The next morning, I hung my dream catcher above my bed and renewed my commitment to self-care. I went out for breakfast and ordered an acai bowl from the new juice bar and organic restaurant next to the yoga studio. I took an awesome vinyasa flow class and then stocked up on fresh fruit and veggies at the organic market before heading home.

I still felt super tired, so I had another relaxing salt bath and then settled down on the couch to reflect on my trip. It seemed like something from a dream—a visit with a crazy astrologer; a conversation with an angel. *It's all true*, I told myself. *Trust it—all of it.*

I must have drifted off, because when I opened my eyes an elderly but familiar looking man greeted me with a cheery, "Well hello there, sleepy head."

I sat up slowly and wondered if I was still dreaming. He had an infectious energy about him and was all smiles.

"Hi," I said cautiously.

He was about 5'10" and had a thin frame with a pudgy belly. His black hair was thinning on top, and he had the softest brown eyes.

"You don't recognize me." He chuckled. "I am your grandfather, Papa Jack."

Now I understood why he looked so familiar even though I had never met him: he looked just like my father. My father's dad had passed away young because of an alcohol addiction and an unhealthy heart. My father seemed to remember him with fond memories though.

I once again wondered if I was hallucinating, and then it hit me that this was now my reality, and I might as well embrace it.

"Hey, Papa Jack. Even though I admit I am a little disturbed at all of this, I am really happy to meet you."

To my surprise, his eyes filled with tears. "Samantha, baby doll, I am so proud of you, and I want you to know that. I have been with you your entire life, through thick and thin. I've seen the joy you give to so many people with your smile and your infectious laughter. Don't you dare ever lose that. Please tell your dad that I am doing great, and I am with his mother, and we are so proud of him too."

"I will tell him," I said, wondering how in the world I would ever actually be able to explain this to my dad. "Papa Jack, why are you here?"

With that he sat in the comfy chair across from my couch. "I've got a mission, sugar. I've got to explain something important that you need to understand in order to move forward on your path. Now you realize you are clairvoyant, right?"

"Hold up. Sorry to interrupt, but what's clairvoyant?"

"It means that you can see spirits, energies, and angels."

"Well that does explain a lot," I said with a smirk.

"I have three important messages. The first is to not be scared as we are always with you in love. The second is I want to explain to you about soul contracts. Before we come to this planet, we all make agreements and contracts to help each other based on what we want or need to accomplish in this lifetime. For instance, you and I made a contract that I would serve as your guide and help you along your way. I'm to help you get to the point where you can spiritually awaken."

"Hang tight, Papa Jack. People keep telling me this, Bridget, Hiro and now you. But I still have a hard time believing that I asked for all of this."

"Well, you didn't really know how it would all fall into play, but yes, you did ask. Your one human lifetime is just a tiny blimp in eternity. We all see things differently when we aren't in bodies. Wow, do we ever." Papa Jack paused as he was getting a little choked up. "You are helping me so much to heal with your willingness to move forward. This is helping with the evolution of my soul, and for this I am forever grateful."

Oh, man, now I was getting all teary too. "You are welcome. I am honored to be able to help you." I could feel the love and the connection with this man, even though I had never met or seen him before.

"Samantha, you had a soul contract with Lucas too. It's why you always were drawn to him and why you are having a hard time letting him go. You two have more of a history than you realize."

"So what does that mean? What do I need to do?"

"You just need to understand that the agreement was to see if the two of you could come together in this lifetime as equals. You also both wanted to learn about love together."

"So is the contract over now?" My heart sank a little, but then I felt a sense of relief as I understood the depth of what Papa Jack was saying. It made me think of our relationship as a stepping stone to move me forward, versus before when I felt like this break up was holding me back from happiness and true love.

Papa Jack explained that the contract would be over as long as I could truly forgive Lucas and send him love. He told me that we often make these agreements with others when we have unfinished business from lifetimes past. We also come together to learn things and to help heal one another. If we have been with someone in lifetimes past, or have contracts with them, then we often have an unexplained pull toward them. He told me that now it was definitely time to let Lucas go.

Then he grew more serious. He leaned forward in his chair and took my hands in his. "Listen sugar, my third message is about the Demon Brigade. They don't want you to grow and move forward.

They are trying their best to get inside your head and make you long for him. They are constantly trying to remind you of him. They do not want you to forgive him or let him go, because that is how you will grow and evolve."

I shuddered remembering Archangel Michael telling me about the Demon Brigade. I'd tried to push this out of my mind because it sounded scary, like something from a horror movie.

"Don't worry, though. You have several options for love. You have a true primary soul partner that you will be with in this lifetime if you will just be patient and get started on your divine mission."

"Divine mission? What in the heck is that? Archangel Michael mentioned it as well, and I was too slow to ask about it before he left."

"Uh oh, I have said too much," said Papa Jack. "I am getting the call to return home. Listen, I am always here. Don't be scared. Just ask for what you need, and I will do my best to get it for you. I love you, Samantha."

Poof! He was gone just like that.

Honestly, a girl could get annoyed by all the random visitors dropping these truth bombs and then leaving in the blink of an eye. Now I had seen the ghost man, a.k.a. Ted, a few times; I'd seen a man with a light in his mouth; had a beautiful encounter with Archangel Michael at the top of the red rocks; and now was able to meet my grandfather and have an enlightening conversation with him.

I knew all of this seemed out there, but at this point, it was too much for me to deny. I knew this was way more than just my imagination.

Chapter 13

Three days went by, and I didn't see any angels, the mystery man in the white shirt, or cheery Papa Jack. It might sound crazy, but I was missing my supernatural beings, and I wanted another visitor. My dreams were peaceful, and each morning I looked at the web in the center of the willow hoop of my gorgeous dream catcher and wondered what was in there. Just to be safe, I hung it outside on my patio every morning so nightmares could flap away. I was transitioning to all organic food, and I'd given up caffeine completely. Instead, I was experimenting with essential oils that promised to relax, revive, restore, and rejuvenate. Who knew these little oils could do so much so fast. I'd also found the channel with Oprah shows, and I was addicted. Her guests were so inspiring, and this morning was no exception.

I found an episode where people were talking about near death experiences when they were saved or visited by an angel. I couldn't believe it! This was exactly what I needed to see right now. I was glued to the TV as the angel expert, Sophy Burnham, began to describe these events with angels.

"We all have at least one angel," she said cheerily. "But many of us have teams of angels that watch out for us and support us on our way. Everyone has at least one, and they are available upon request. You can always ask for more angels at anytime."

Bridget had told me the same thing, but I was still resistant to inviting them in every morning. I needed to do better with this. I jotted a note down on a pad. *Remember to talk to the angels!!! The more you call on them the easier all of this will be for you!* The words flowed effortlessly onto the paper.

Just then I heard my phone. It was the ring I had designated for my mom. I had still been avoiding her, but yet I really wanted to hear her voice about then too. I decided to answer.

"Hey, Sam! How are you sweetie? I miss you so much."

"Hey, Mom," I said as my heart ached a little. "I miss you so much too."

There was a weird silence, and then she said, "Are you okay? I know you have been through quite a lot lately. Do you want to come home? I would love to see you soon."

Now it was my turn for silence, as I imagined how it would go over if I said to my pragmatic mother— *You're right. It has been a lot. I've discovered I have a strong psychic ability. Papa Jack paid me a visit, and I met an Archangel on top of a mountain in Sedona.*

"Sam? Are you still there? I spoke to your Uncle Bill, and he told me about the job. Why didn't you tell me you were let go?"

"Why did he do that?"

"Because he cares."

Yeah right, I silently mouthed. "There is nothing to worry about, I promise. I did really well at work. You know that. I saved a lot, and I'm fine for a while."

"It's not the finances. You broke up with Lucas and then Honey's death. Now the job, any mom would be worrying about her daughter."

"I'll come home soon. I promise."

I swear I could almost hear her heartbeat quicken when I said I'd visit. I also realized how much I missed her. My mom was always so loving and supportive. Maybe she could be there for me through all this spiritual craziness. No way was I going to mention my Archangel Michael encounter, but maybe, just maybe, she would believe or at least be curious about what happened when I met Papa Jack.

"Did you ever meet Dad's dad?"

"What? That is a weird thing to ask me. You know he died before your father was a teenager. So no, I did not."

"I mean, did you ever see him after that?" I held my breath waiting for her response.

"What on earth are you talking about, Sam? Who in the world have you gotten mixed up with? No, of course not, and why would you even ask me?"

"Well . . . umm . . . I'm not really sure how to say this. I . . . uhh . . . I think I may have seen him for a second."

Another awkward silence, and then she asked me dead serious and with concern, "Sweetie, are you medicating yourself?"

"You mean drinking or taking pills to numb my pain? No, I mean I was earlier, but I haven't been doing that in quite some time. Why?"

"You did not see your father's father. That is just plain nonsense. I was right. This is too much for you, and you need help. I am going to get Bill to take you to that doctor he suggested you see."

"Mom, trust me. I'm fine. And it wasn't like I spoke to him," I lied. "It was probably just a dream or something."

"Your Uncle Bill and I had an Aunt who thought she saw crazy things like this. She even told us she spoke to angels. She disappeared, Sam."

"What aunt? What do you mean she disappeared?"

I could hear the anxiety in my mom's voice when she said, "I don't know where she is. Maybe she's homeless, or in an institution somewhere. Maybe she is dead by now. Sam, please. I insist we get you help before you go down the same road."

"I'm fine, Mom. I promise you will see me soon."

I hung up before more of an inquisition could begin. Besides, Oprah was back on and I needed a distraction to get Mom's words that I was crazy out of my head. I also wanted to hear more from the angel expert.

Sophy went on to explain that there are three things you do to get more angel support and help.

"First, you have to ask for help. We all have free will, so if you don't ask for help then they can't help you. Second, you have to notice when they are helping you and trying to communicate with you. Third, you must thank them."

At the end of the show I switched off the TV. The entire conversation with my mom had me feeling jumpy. And who was this mysterious aunt?

My dream catcher was swaying in the breeze outside, and I went to bring it in. As always, I glanced at Honey's grave beneath the oaks. And then, because really it couldn't hurt and it might even help, I whispered, "Michael, and any other angels who might be listening, it's me, Sam. I just wanted to say hi, where are you guys, and that if you want me to go through with this then I need help. I feel alone and scared and now my mom thinks I am crazy."

A few hours later I heard an unexpected knock on my door. These were not the surprise visitors I wanted to see: my Aunt Mary and Uncle Bill, Anna's parents.

"Hey Sam, we were just in the neighborhood and thought we would stop by," said Uncle Bill.

"Campaigning?" I asked. "Do you have any bumper stickers for me?"

Bill laughed and slapped me on the back. Since I'd moved back to Georgia we barely managed to cover our dislike for each other with good old southern courtesy. I couldn't understand it, because I could usually get along with just about anyone. However, there was something about him that I couldn't ignore that absolutely drove me crazy.

"The campaign is going well, and I'm counting on your vote. But that's not why we're here. Your mom asked us to stop by. She's worried about you."

"We are too," said Aunt Mary, as she stood meekly beside Bill.

"Thank you for checking on me," I said to Mary. "I have been going through some stuff, and I don't really want to get into it right now."

"I don't want to get too personal," said Uncle Bill, "but rumor has it you've been seeing the psychic healer on Fig Street. This is mumbo jumbo, Sam. We know you have been feeling lost, but the road you are heading down isn't what the world is all about."

I was shocked. Had he been spying on me?

Aunt Mary just stood there quietly looking uncomfortable, like she didn't know what to say—as she usually did when Bill was overbearing and rude, which was basically all the time.

"Uncle Bill and Aunt Mary, I appreciate your concern, but you can report back to my mother that I am fine. Mission accomplished. Now if you will excuse me, I have something to do this evening." I was about to shut the door on them when Bill elbowed his way in.

"I didn't want to have to tell you this," he said, "but one of my buddies is good friends with your old boss, Becky. He asked about you, and she told him you weren't doing well and needed some help. I've got a number of a psychiatrist—a good one. He can help you." He handed me a card and then excused himself and went to the restroom.

The second Bill was gone, Mary whispered, "Bill doesn't mean to be harsh. He's under such stress with the campaign."

"So what? Is he worried I'm going to ruin it for him?"

"No, that's not what this is about. He also genuinely cares about you."

Why do you stay married to him? I wondered for the umpteenth time. I could tell Mary didn't necessarily agree with what she was saying.

A moment later Bill was back, and I turned to him. "I understand you don't want your crazy niece tarnishing your reputation or your career. I hear you loud and clear. Don't worry, I will not screw up your stupid election."

I held up the card he had given me and tore it into little pieces. "I'll stay out of your business, and I suggest you stay out of mine." I kept my eye on him as I sprinkled the pieces of the card on my coffee table, and then something strange and totally unexpected happened. I could hear his voice, but his mouth wasn't moving . . .

I'll tell the family it is best that she is locked up, but really the only way to control this girl is to get rid of her for good.

Ahhh, wow! This must be one of my special powers! I was excited for a second until the reality of his harsh words came crashing down. My uncle wanted to get rid of me? Then a loving whisper in my head urged me to keep it together, to not let on that I could hear his thoughts. I stood there frozen trying to get my bearings and figure out how to react.

"Our family went through this once before," he said. "And if we think you are in any way mentally incapacitated we will get you help. It's what family does. No one in their right mind sees dead people."

I walked to the door and flung it open. I felt betrayed that my mother had told him about our conversation. "Please leave and do not come back unless you are invited."

With a shake of her head and a pitying glance in my direction, Mary walked out toward the car. Bill stepped out the door and then turned back and glared at me. "You better watch yourself and your attitude girl, and you best be careful what you do. I do not want to have to come back here and check you into an institution. Do you understand?"

"Loud and clear," I said and slammed the door. Tears streamed down my face, as I crossed my arms and slid down the door.

Maybe they are right. Maybe this is crazy. Am I making all this up? Is my imagination that wild? Do I trust what I have known to be true all my life, or do I trust what I know is true and is happening for me right now?

Chapter 14

The Demon Brigade

It was a dark, low corner of the earth where the leader of the Demon Brigade, Sneeth, held his headquarters. He and the massive team he had created sat on hard, cold stones near a pond filled with black snakes, scum, and pure filth. You could smell the stench of this place from miles away.

Sneeth was not a pretty sight. His skin was leathery and foul, as if it had been burned beyond recognition. His body was rotund and heavy, with rolls of fat dripping grotesquely off his bones. His eyes glowed bright red, and his mouth resembled a sunken cave that stretched into a toothless tunnel of vile odors and unknown darkness.

"Listen up and now," he said. "Those angels think they have this girl covered, but they do not know what they are in for. We have taken her down in hundreds of lives before, so I don't know why they think this life will be any different. She may have made some progress in the past, but in the end we always win, and she leaves this planet more beaten and battered then she was before she got here. Too bad she is so dang evolved that it never sets her back, but at least we keep her from being able to move forward.

"This time her mission is even bigger. She has the power to lift up a large percentage of the planet as she grows into the power of love. What a load of malarkey." He circled the scum pond, scratching off puss from large boils that covered his shoulders.

"Who wants this challenge?" he continued. "They haven't sent someone down with this much potential in ages."

A dull roar rose from the horde of demons as they jockeyed for position in front of Sneeth.

"Who wants to take her down and push her out of her body?" Sneeth growled. His eyes settled on a young, sickly looking man who had bare skeleton bones, a hunchback, and grey crooked teeth. "Skanky, come here."

Skanky limped forward to grovel at Sneeth's feet.

"You go to that girl, and you make her think she isn't worthy. Confuse her. Get deep inside of her head, and make her think she can't do any of this, that it all is her imagination. Twist her ego so she will work for us. Get inside her entire body and screw with her as much as possible. She is new to all of this, and she will not know how to control herself, so we must pounce now. Do you hear me? Get out of here and go NOW!" Sneeth shouted in disgust.

The demons dispersed, and Sneeth remained at what appeared to be a cesspool. Even though Archangel Michael had given the girl the shield, Sneeth still had the Key of Splendor. It could penetrate anything, but it could only be used once. He needed to be strategic. Skanky was part of that plan, and Sneeth had every confidence his henchman would be able to suck up her light. He would return larger and darker and would be able to take on even more powerful beings fighting for love. He would be stronger and able to help the demons and their ultimate goal of a fear-based world full of lack and hate.

"Love!" Sneeth spat the word into the fetid pool and watched the waters writhe.

Chapter 15

In the week after Uncle Bill's visit, I realized my sleeping patterns were changing. I woke up consistently at 3:33 am. I found this odd, and I couldn't understand why I woke up then, but I was always able to go back to sleep. I'd sleep till nine or ten in the morning and still I'd wake up exhausted. I took afternoon naps, but they rarely recharged me. Bridget was correct when she told me I was going to be tired.

Determined to fight my fatigue, I headed out to run some errands on a Friday morning. It was a gorgeous March day. I absolutely loved early spring in Atlanta, and all of the beautiful flowers blooming brought a smile to my face. I drove past the flowering trees, and I was filled with gratitude that I had won all those stock options back at my job, so I was able to take this time for myself.

After going to Whole Foods to pick up some coconut water, (I had read it was really good for you), I decided I would go check out Lululemon and see if I could find a new pair of yoga pants. I found the perfect pair and then left the store to bask in the bright sunshine. I was looking in my purse to grab my keys, when a powerful but gentle force seemed to take over and directed my body away from my car and down the block.

It was like a loving but insistent nudging, and it felt so strange not to be the one making the decisions for where my body was going and what it was doing. I tried to stop, but couldn't, and as it felt weirdly good, I surrendered and found myself walking into

Paper Source, a stationary store I'd never noticed before. I was instantly drawn to the journal section. For some reason, I bought four journals, and it was as if I instinctively knew which ones to choose. There was no doubt in my mind.

"Oh wow, you must love to journal. These are my favorite ones," said the girl at the checkout, and she pointed to the bright pink journal I had grabbed.

I nodded and smiled.

Nope. I have never really journaled in my life, and I have no idea why I am in here or why I am buying these books.

Back home I sat on my back porch watching the blue jays and cardinals chirping and playing with each other. I took a sip of coconut water and wondered what I was going to write about. I reached for the bright pink journal, then decided to flip open the one with the gold and white polka dot glossy cover instead. Before I could even take another glance, my hand grabbed a pen and was writing fluidly across the page.

I'd done some writing in college and written reports and several business plans for work, but this was different. The words were flowing out of me. It was as if I had been writing for years, and yet also like I had never written a word and felt compelled to write every thought I had ever had down at this very moment. I wrote down all my feelings for Lucas, and how I was lucky to have had a love like that even though it didn't work out. I wrote about gratitude for myself and how proud I was, because I was trying to discover my path. The writing was fun and exciting, and I became eager to "learn" whatever it was my subconscious wanted to tell me.

After writing about ten pages I got up to get some water, as I had had enough of the coconut water. I decided it must be an acquired taste.

Afterwards, I still felt the urge to sit back down with my pen, and this time I chose the pink journal. My hand seemed to move with a little more force. After writing a few sentences I sat there staring at the paper with my mouth wide open. The sentences were written by me but in a different style of handwriting.

> *Hello my dear, this is Archangel Michael. I am so proud of you, and you are doing great. You have the capability to do automatic writing, which is what you are doing now. This is a way we can communicate with you. When you feel like writing it usually means we want to tell you something. We are all so proud of you, and you are very strong and brave.* ☺

I couldn't believe it. Shocked, I wanted to get to the bottom of this. I immediately got up and googled "automatic writing." I found out that automatic writing is considered to be a psychic ability that allows a person to produce written words without consciously writing. The article said the words arise from a spiritual, subconscious, or supernatural source.

Man, this is absolutely crazy, I thought. *So let me get this straight. I not only see dead people and angels, but now I can channel them onto paper too?*

Feeling more intrigued, I decided to experiment. I wrote whatever came up in my head. This is what came out on the paper:

> *My spiritual awakening - I am so happy that I have finally seen the light! There is so much more to this world we live in then what actually meets the eye. I am living my purpose by discovering all of this and by sharing this information with those that cross my path.*

I wrote until late afternoon, page after page, and then all of a sudden there was some sort of shift. I didn't like what I was writing this time, and it seemed as if the grace that had pushed me into the stationary store and that was with me earlier had abruptly disappeared. I felt physically odd, as well. My head ached, I was nauseated and dizzy, and I had an odd, bitter taste in my mouth. And still I continued to write, gouging the words onto the page.

I am so important, and no one can ever take that away! Never!! One day the world will wake up and see this. One day people will wise up and realize that I have special powers, and that no one can touch me. One day they will realize how lucky they are if I even consider calling them a friend! And those who judge me now had better watch out. The time is coming when people will see the real Samantha Kingston.

Even though the words flowing from my pen made me uncomfortable, I could not stop.

This feeling and this force that had taken over my body lasted for a few days. I had no control of not only what was being written on the paper, but also over how long or how often I wrote. I felt as if I was in an uncontrollable trance and no longer calling the shots. When I "came to," I read the writing and felt sick all over again. I tried crossing it out, but it was as if I lacked the willpower to do so. At one point I ripped out a few pages to burn them, but instead I lay on my couch and wept.

When I stopped to eat or to watch TV, my wrist would start to twitch. The twitches were slow at first, but then would get faster and more noticeable. The more I ignored these symptoms, the worse they got. If I tried to fight it for too long, my arm would start to flail as if something was picking it up and throwing it around.

You better get back to writing or else! A voice screamed inside my head. My arm literally smacked me in the face in one of the flail fits. Not knowing what else to do, I wrote some more. At this point I had filled up all the journals I bought and was writing on a yellow legal pad. About that time I also started hearing more voices in my head.

"This is your job now Sam," said a wretched, dark, high-pitched voice. "You came to this planet to write and deliver our messages.

You better do as we say and get back to it. Who do you think you are taking a break? You wanted this, and you asked for it. You decided on all of this before you even came to this planet. You have a lot of lost time to make up for, so you better keep writing."

The voices wouldn't let me take breaks, rest, or ever really give me much time to eat—except when Anna stopped by. I'd forgotten I'd made a date with her, and because I hadn't texted to confirm she showed up to check on me. I answered the door, and the voices inside silenced. I must have appeared normal to Anna. I apologized for not checking my phone.

She saw all the journals and legal pads on my coffee table. "You're writing? That's so great. I wish I had the time to journal and write down ideas for stories."

Too ashamed and not yet fully understanding what was going on with me, I put on my best fake smile and said, "Yeah, I needed to take the time to do some personal work. We'll have that dinner when I come out of this. I promise!"

Anna left, and the moment the door closed the voices started up again. They grew stronger and louder. After the fourth day of this, I was ready to check myself into an insane asylum. I had bruises on my cheek and my upper arms—self inflicted from an hour when I seemed to have lost all control and smacked myself repeatedly. I felt more scared and alone then I had ever felt in my entire life.

Maybe Bill was right. Maybe I do need serious help. How am I going to be able to stay one step ahead of him and his plan if I can't even keep my own sanity?

Rose was out of town, and I was terrified, lonely, and scared for my life. I didn't know how I would explain any of this to her, but I desperately needed her support. I was getting to a point where I didn't feel safe being alone. After initially giving me a hard time for not getting back in the job market, Rose had become supportive of me. She had patience with my crying fits, and when I explained that they were serving as some sort of release she seemed to believe me.

Somehow, in the midst of a break from the crazy writing energy, I found myself flipping through the journal with the hot pink cover, and I read Archangel Michael's words.

We are so proud of you- you are so strong and brave!!! J

Of course! There were angels to help me. I felt an overwhelming sense of grace come over my body the second I remembered this. The angels were with me, and even though I couldn't see them, I could now feel them. Acknowledging their divine presence allowed me to snap back into my body and into control. But then, with a sick feeling, it dawned on me that maybe I was being tested. I remembered Archangel Michael telling me about the Demon Brigade.

This was far worse than I had anticipated. I thought I'd have some kind of warning, but I wasn't able to see them coming or even to control myself when they entered my body. How was I supposed to fight something if I did not even know it existed or that it was within me? I had thought I was at my lowest point a few months ago with the loss of Honey and Lucas and my job. Now I was supposed to be on the up and up, making myself a better person and aligning myself with my soul and my purpose. This wasn't supposed to be more sorrow, uncontrollable sobbing, headaches, and body pains. I literally felt like I was in a battle between heaven and hell; between good and evil.

I called the one person who I hoped would be able to help.

"Bridget, I am desperate," I said, almost hyperventilating. "Can you please help?"

"Yes, of course. What is going on?"

"I have started hearing voices in my head, and they are mean and Archangel Michael told me I can automatic write, but the writing won't stop, and some of the things coming out of my hand onto the paper are ugly and mean. I can't have a thought, or do anything really, without hearing a million voices, and I honestly think I am going crazy, this has been happening for several days. I'm totally loosing it over here!"

"Why didn't you call me sooner?"

"Because the voices in my head told me not too. This part of the test was seeing how I handled all this on my own." My voice cracked and the tears came.

"Oh dear, listen to me. Put your hands on your belly and take a deep breath. Anytime we start to grow spiritually and move closer to the light, there will always be dark forces such as the Demon Brigade that will be after us. The key thing is to remember that you are always in control, and they have to listen to you. You need to speak to them firmly. 'You are not me, and you are not welcome here, and you must leave now.' If you do this they have to go. You can also call on Archangel Michael to take these beings and bring them to the light." She spoke calmly.

"I thought he shielded me from all this when I met him in Sedona," I said, feeling betrayed and not knowing what or who to believe.

"Okay, let me take a look at you. Wow, it is beautiful. He did shield you, but he shielded you from that day moving forward. There could still be some energy you let in from years past that you have to clear all on your own. Also, it can take our bodies a little bit of time to adjust to the shield and allow it to fully develop.

"This is a process," she continued. "And it's important that you understand how to manage this and that you have time to do it. I have just the place for you. Agape Resort. I'll send you the info, and let's get you there as soon as possible. I actually have a casita there that just opened up for next week, and it's yours. You are welcome to bring a friend with you, as well."

Claire was the only one who would want to do anything like this and not think I was crazy.

Bridget then explained that all I had to do was book the flight to Mexico. She would take care of the rest. "The Agape resort has so many wonderful practitioners who can help you with healing and direction. It is near the water, and there is special energy there from crystals that have been in the ground holding space for thousands of years. I will email you the brochure so you can call and get your appointments set up. Be sure and choose services and practitioners that look good to you. Listen to your gut, because that is how you are going to get your answers."

As she said that I felt a flutter in my heart, the same way I had the day I decided to take the blue path instead of the yellow path in Sedona.

Follow fun, adventure, and your gut to get to your power spots, I remembered Hiro saying. *This has to be a power spot for me, and I bet I will for sure get answers at this place.*

After the phone call, I lit some candles and some white sage that I brought back from Sedona, and then I did as Bridget suggested. Loudly and forcefully, I said, "Whatever is taking over my body, you are not me. I demand that you leave my body this instant, and you are not welcome back. I also demand that all voices inside my head be shut off at once."

A calm seemed to settle over my condo, and I breathed in the earthy scent of desert sage. I felt safe and relieved. Without even opening them, I instinctively knew which journals to throw away. Then, listening to my inner guidance, I decided to burn them in the grill outside. A gentle light was filtering through the oaks, and I could feel Honey's presence.

As I was getting ready for bed that evening, I felt an urge to write again. This was a soft urge, and it seemed like my choice and I wasn't being forced. Still a little nervous about writing, I tried to ignore it, but the feeling just wouldn't go away. I sat on the side of my bed with my pad and picked up the bright pink journal that I had forgotten I put in my bedside table. I was grateful that I still had one of the pretty journals that was unused. My pen began to fluidly move across the page, and I felt grace and at ease during the writing.

You will get answers at Agape, my dear. There is a man named Jimmy there who will be able to give you answers and help show you the ropes on your journey ☺

There was no name signed on this one, but there was a smiley face, and it seemed to be coming from the good and not the bad. I needed human validation more now than ever, and I couldn't wait to go to Agape and get answers. I scribbled a title on the front cover of the journal. GUIDANCE FROM THE ANGELS

I texted Claire, and just as I had expected, she was totally on board with joining me yet again for an adventure. I really wanted to tell her all that was going on, but so much of it was just so out there. I wasn't ready to tell her yet. Then I sent her the brochure that Bridget had emailed me.

She texted me right back. *Yes, I definitely want to join you but will probably have to miss the first night as I have some deadlines for work. It looks amazing!*

I stayed up late looking over the brochure for Agape, and I was filled with peace as the resort looked like a place of healing and hope. I viewed the services, and one in particular jumped off the page at me—a Blast Rocket. The brochure explained it as one of a kind, run by a practitioner who had been apprenticing for over thirty years with his elders. During the ninety minute session he would take you to a state of pure bliss and propel you onwards in your spiritual journey.

When I searched in the index for the practitioner's name, I saw it was Jimmy and got goose bumps. I immediately flipped open my GUIDANCE FROM THE ANGELS journal, and there it was, a message to search for a man named Jimmy. It was close to two in the morning when I emailed the resort and booked a Blast Rocket for my first session. I was now counting down the seconds to check out Agape.

Chapter 16

After passing through customs, I saw a friendly looking older man holding up a sign with my name. I'd learned a few Spanish phrases on the plane, but he welcomed me in perfect English. He helped me get my new red suitcase I'd bought for this adventure and then escorted me to the resort shuttle. The other passengers were laughing amongst themselves and seemed to be in such good moods. Who wouldn't be with a view like this of the ocean and palm trees? Curious about just who would come to a resort like Agape, I introduced myself to a charming older couple from Florida who were celebrating their fortieth wedding anniversary; a woman from Nebraska who was the CEO of three companies and had come for a detox; and two young women from Germany who were taking six months to explore some of the world's spiritual hot spots.

After a fifteen minute drive, we turned onto a curved road lined with palm trees. The reception area was a thatched roof building, and as I stepped off the shuttle I could feel a shift. It was as if the palm trees and the huge, pink and gold hibiscus flowers were pumping happiness into the air. A woman in a bright orange shirt greeted us with a tray of fresh juices. A papaya and mango blend was the resort's signature arrival drink. It was delish! As I sipped and looked around at the gorgeous surroundings, the positive feeling in my gut was so strong and distinct. I knew this place would be significant for me, and that I would get answers here.

"Hello, I am Samantha Kingston," I told the man behind the counter, whose nametag read Javier. "I am here to check into cottage 333."

"Wonderful, welcome to Agape resort. Mrs. Smith let us know you would be joining us in her casita."

Mrs. Smith? In the months that I'd know Bridget, I've never asked about her last name. I smiled. Smith was such an ordinary name for such a remarkable woman.

Javier handed me a folder with a list of the appointments I had booked. "You made some great choices, Ms. Kingston. Jimmy is in high demand. He books out months in advance and just happened to have a slot open up right when you emailed us. You are fortunate to have a session with him. Follow me, and I'll give you a tour of Agape."

We rounded a corner beyond the lobby, and I gasped at the expansive view: to my right were purplish mountains topped with wispy clouds, while straight ahead, beyond a green pasture where horses grazed, was the sea. It's odd, but for a brief moment I thought of Lucas. For that moment I wished he was the one joining me instead of Claire.

Next, Javier walked me through the most glorious spa I had ever seen, with plush lounge chairs and a ten foot wide stone fireplace. On each side of the fireplace were floor to ceiling windows framing the mountains. Beyond the spa terrace we followed a path that led through the pasture to the ocean. We stood on a small cliff and looked down at the waves thundering onto the black rocks.

"That is where the gigantic quartz live," he said. "We are blessed to have them here, as they hold the healing energy we need in order to serve our guests to the highest level."

I was intrigued by the fact that the crystals were in the ocean, and especially that they could "hold" energy for the resort. I felt so serene standing there, that I knew it had to be true. I made a mental note to do some investigating about this before I left.

In the meantime, I continued to enjoy the vista. To my left were palm trees, pasture, and a beautiful mountain, and to my right were the dark blue ocean and the warm ocean breeze. I was officially in heaven!

We left that gorgeous view and walked back through the pasture to my accommodation. Each of the guests had their own casita. They were painted a neutral color to blend in with the landscape, and they each had a quaint sitting area in front with a view of the mountains or the ocean, depending on which side of the resort.

"Here you are, Ms. Kingston. Number 333."

Inside, my luggage was already on the luggage rack, and I could feel Bridget's loving energy in the room. The window was cracked open, and I could smell the ocean breeze. I touched the crystals on the mantel above the small fireplace. I found the rose quartz incense and lit it and then read the note on the small bedside table.

> *Dear Samantha,*
> *You will find so many answers here.*
> *You will leave a changed woman in so many ways.*
> *I can't wait to hear about your adventures.*
>
> *Love,*
> *Bridget*

After I unpacked, I still had a few hours to chill before my Blast Rocket treatment. Bridget had mentioned that Agape had a cool little bookstore, so I bought a copy of *How to Hear Your Angels*, by Doreen Virtue and headed for the pool. Apparently, she had great advice on easy ways to connect with the angels. I read for a while and then decided it would be better for me to make a list of the questions I had for Jimmy, as I didn't want to forget them while I was in front of him during the session. I pulled out a note pad and wrote:

Questions for Jimmy

1. *How do I learn to control these voices in my head?*
2. *I need help knowing that I am not hallucinating.*
3. *Is there a way that I can identify these voices when they are coming from the Brigade?*

I laid there thinking how ridiculous these questions seemed, but I knew I had to ask him if I wanted to get my sanity back. I still felt a little nervous about picking up a pen to do any kind of journaling. I'd experimented on the plane, and of course the pen took flight on its own and wrote:

> *You are an empath my dear, ask Jimmy to help with this also.*

I added question #4 to my list.

What the heck is an empath?

The room where Jimmy performed the ceremony was at the far end of the resort beyond a reflecting pool where huge blue dragonflies buzzed above the water lilies and lotus flowers. On the door of the casita where Jimmy gave his session was taped an orange piece of paper. In purple marker he had written, *Running fifteen minutes late. Thanks for your patience.* ☺

I giggled as the smiley face reminded me of the faces I had been drawing "to myself" in my writing. I sat down in one of the two chairs located just outside the door and soon heard loud and baffling noises coming from inside. It literally sounded like a chicken was clucking for dear life. Following the chicken shrieks and clucks were chants and smacking sounds.

Was he beating his client?

For the first time since booking this supposed treatment, I felt alarmed and wondered what I had gotten myself into. My heart started racing and my palms were sweating. I stood up to go for a walk around the pool, because I knew that if I sat there and listened to those noises for much longer, I wouldn't go through with this. Then I heard an even louder cluck and some sickening moans. Hiking trails wound their way up the slope of the mountains, and I seriously thought about cancelling the session and going for a hike.

Remember your note about Jimmy. He will have your answers. Do not be scared, a loving whisper said in my head.

I watched the dragonflies dance above the water for a while. Then I mustered up the courage to go back to the casita, take a seat, and wait for Jimmy to finish up. All of a sudden things got really quiet. Then the door flung open, and it was like a flash, or a burst of bright sunlight, came flaming through. A smiling, youngish looking, and super hot man popped out with a big smile and a ton of happiness. "Hey!" he said. "Give me just one more minute please, and thank you for your patience." The door slammed behind him just as quickly as it had opened.

It was all I could do not to smile from ear to ear. His energy was contagious and inviting, and I wondered what in the world I needed to do to capture that energy within myself. The Blast Rocket was going to be fun! This made me happy and grateful that I hadn't run off like I wanted to only a few minutes earlier.

Something in my gut told me this was a big moment in history for me. It would be like an official rebirth for me and my journey into the spiritual world. I realized that although all of this was new to me, I had learned quite a bit in a short time. Because of my unexplained obsession with researching and learning, I was beginning to understand a lot more of the new age lingo.

Not long after Jimmy's brief appearance, an older woman with long, strawberry-blonde hair came stumbling out of the room looking like she had just had the best lay of her life. She had a happy but woozy look on her face, and when she looked at me with her bright, wide eyes, she said, "Whoa!" Then she turned around and scurried off as though on a mission.

About a minute later, Jimmy appeared in the doorway and calmly said, "Thank you again for your patience. Welcome and please come into my sacred space." He was dripping wet with sweat, and I wondered how he could seem so at ease and happy when he was clearly physically depleted.

"I am not depleted, sweetie. This is just what I do, and I love it!" he said with a wink.

Oh my God, did I say that out loud? Is he reading my mind?

The room was steamy hot with an unfamiliar, intense smell about it. On a table appeared to be Indian "tools" and feathers, and I remembered that Jimmy was trained by a long lineage of Cherokee Indians. I smiled, wanting to embrace this wild ride I knew he was going to take me on. All of a sudden the bright smiling man I had just seen seemed to slip into a serious trance, and his eyes glazed over.

"Hello, Samantha. This is not the first time we are meeting," he said in a deep voice. He looked me straight in the eye. "You and I met long ago on a different plane, many, many lifetimes and hundreds and hundreds of years ago. We made an agreement that has brought us here today."

I felt a little freaked and wondered what in the heck he was doing.

He is channeling the Divine. Listen to him, said the loving whisper in my head.

I heard drumming music playing in the background. Jimmy continued on with his ritual as if I wasn't even there. He talked and chanted as he burnt what appeared to be sage but to me smelled like marijuana. After a few minutes of his carrying on and me standing there trying to calm myself with slow, steady breaths, he walked over to the table set up in the middle of the room and started shaking what appeared be an ancient carved *maraca*. He looked at me with a blank stare and whispered, "Please say your name loud and with intention."

"Samantha Kingston!" The scream escaped me before I knew what I was doing. It was as if some larger force was catapulting me forward into the session.

Jimmy lit some oil in a little bowl, then put the fire on his hands and on his belly. He then smashed out the fire on his belly with the fire on his hands. My head was spinning and my mind blown for about the millionth time. After about five more minutes of dancing around, he came over and sat in the chair next to the one I had somehow made my way into.

"Think about it," he said. "It takes most people until they are fifty to get into this room. This is no accident, and I am so happy and honored that you are here." He spoke in that same deep voice, obviously back in the trance/channel mode.

I registered what he was saying, and it did make sense—Hiro and Bridget had said similar things to me. It gave me an odd sense of reassurance getting the same message from various sources; especially human sources as I had begun to second guess myself when listening to the messages from the ghosts and angels I was seeing.

"This is so weird," he said, now as the normal, smiley version of Jimmy who had escorted me into the room. "I normally don't go in and out like this, but for some reason I can't quit channeling with you."

I felt almost embarrassed with my list of questions. I also took note of how far I had come. It wasn't that long ago that I wouldn't have even known what channeling meant. If I wanted answers, I needed to be honest.

"I guess if you are channeling, I don't need my list of questions then," I giggled and stuck my list back into my bag.

Although what was going on seemed totally wacko, I was super drawn to Jimmy and found him extremely attractive. I felt myself blushing. *All I can think of is how hot he is, while all of this other stuff is going on, and meanwhile he is reading my mind . . .* I focused on a wall painting that reminded me of the snake in my recurring dreams. Ugh, that snapped me back to reality, and I was finally able to think clearly and remember why I'd booked the Rocket Blast.

"I really need your help," I said. "I have had a massive spiritual awakening, and I really don't understand what is happening to me. I have been hearing all sorts of voices in my head, and I don't know how to control them or how to know who is trying to communicate with me. I have been having "visitors" that are dead, and Archangel Michael showed up one day. Can you please help me and explain what is going on? Oh, and one other thing. It came across to me in my writing that I am an empath, and I don't even know what this means really or how to deal with it either."

"Oh beloved one, you are in the right place." He was back in a trance. His eyes rolled back into his head, and his voice was a much higher pitch than before. "Just so you know, all of this is very normal, and it is a process that you will figure out for yourself. Remember that you are always in control, and that you are always safe."

Quick as a flash, smiley normal Jimmy was back. "Okay, here is the deal. This is the way to be in control of how you communicate with the angels. You pick someone on the "other side," and they serve as your gatekeeper. You set up a business plan and make an agreement with the Divine."

Business plan? Now he was speaking language that I could actually understand.

He continued. "You need to figure out what exactly you want to do, and what you are willing to do to get there."

"What do you mean?"

"You have very special gifts that you came here with, but it's up to you as to which gifts you use and how you use them. This will become clearer to you in time. You can rewrite your business plan whenever you want to. For now, maybe you don't want any voices in your head, because they are making you feel crazy. Then set that rule, and tell your gatekeeper to get all the information you need for the highest good and to communicate with you via thoughts or gut feelings.

"Once you are clear about what you want, write it all down and then read it out loud and pick your gatekeeper. Maybe Archangel Michael since you have already met him. If you do not make it clear that you only want to work with the Divine and be protected, there is a chance the Demon Brigade can come in and use you for darkness instead of light. I am not saying this to scare you, but so you understand."

"Can you go into more detail about the Demon Brigade?" I wanted to know everything I could about them.

Trance Jimmy now reached over and gently touched my hand. "You came here on a very special mission," he said. "Anytime one of us, like me or like you, comes here to open a window of bright light to share with the world, we will face adversaries. Do not be scared. You just have to learn to protect yourself from them. Always ask the Divine for protection and help. Sam, you need to understand how much potential you have."

I felt frustrated. Just like Hiro and Bridget, Jimmy was being so vague about what I was here to do. Obviously, it was big, but it wasn't making sense to me. I wanted specifics.

"After I make this business plan, what do I do?"

Normal Jimmy took over. "You sign the paper and make the agreement official. You tell Archangel Michael that he is to act like a bouncer at your crown chakra, and when you are working the only ones allowed to come through must be for the highest good for all. You have to be very specific, and you need to learn to create sacred space with a prayer of protection before you begin. This should help with the voices. You can stop them totally if you want. If it is too much, tell Archangel Michael exactly what you want, and ask him to stop them altogether for now."

It seemed a bit odd to be making a business plan with an angel, but at this point I'd do it. "And after that? What's next?"

Jimmy had no answers for that. Instead, he told me that I was indeed an empath, and he assured me it was a gift. "You have the ability to know how others are feeling simply by tapping into their story or hearing them talk. You can also feel their pain physically, which is why you have always had back and hip issues. You have been feeling the emotional and physical pain of many other people. You then unconsciously take on their pain to heal it, because that is what you decided to do before you came here. You wanted to have this gift and ability to help those you loved."

A tear rolled down my face at the realization of what he was telling me. I had spent my entire life with tightness in my hips and lower back, and I never knew why. My mom took me to several doctors when I was in high school, and they all came up empty handed. I was told I must have fibromyalgia or chronic fatigue, and there really wasn't much they could do. The main thing that seemed to help was daily exercise and being in nature. If I wasn't moving or being active the pain would always be so much worse. If after skiing or hiking I still felt bad, then a hot bath or a massage would often help.

"I no longer want to feel the physical pain. I have suffered enough." The words flowed sharply out of my mouth, as if they weren't even my own.

"We will take care of that today," said Jimmy. "When you leave this room you will still be able to tap into the feelings and emotions of others, but from here on out you will be doing it by choice and consciously. We will totally remove any physical aspect of this. I will get rid of every pain in the butt you have ever had," he said with a chuckle and a really cute wink.

"Thank you," I said quietly.

"One other important thing is to know you can curse with the Divine, and a sense of humor is key. If we don't have laughter then what do we have? You have recently had a relationship that didn't work out, right?"

Man, he really does know everything about me.

"Yes, I did. It's sort of a part of the trifecta that 'woke me up.'"

"Well, they want you to know that this was karmic and something you needed to do in this lifetime. I am also getting a big hit for you that you need to listen to the tape of your reading from the astrologer you saw in Sedona."

"Okay," I mumbled, kicking myself for not taking the time to listen to it yet.

"Now, I need to get you on the table," he said with a Cheshire cat grin. "We have a ton of work to do, and this is only the beginning. I'll step outside and you can change into a robe and get on the table.

While Jimmy was outside, I quickly undressed and slid onto the massage table in the middle of the room. He knew exactly when I was ready and walked back in. He turned the music way up and began to walk around the table shouting different names, many of which sounded unfamiliar to me. I did notice, however, that he was inviting in several Archangels. He placed acupuncture needles strategically throughout my body and at certain points in my ears. He then started clucking like a chicken. This time I felt totally calm and wasn't even aware of how odd this was. It didn't take long before a feeling like pure and utter grace filled my body. The music in the background got louder, and Jimmy's voice changed pitch and register several times. He was speaking a couple of different languages and saying all sorts of things about my past, my family, and my future.

Before I knew it, I felt like my body had risen off the table. I opened my eyes and realized I was standing outside of myself and watching my physical body on the table. Out of nowhere, a green flash of light appeared around me, and a spectacular angel in a green gown and a golden flaming headdress swooped into the room.

"Hello, darling Samantha, I am Archangel Raphael. I am the archangel of healing, and we have worked together since your conception my dear."

I stared down at my physical body bathed in a luminescent emerald green light.

"How do you feel?" Archangel Raphael asked gently.

"I uh—actually, uh, I feel amazing."

"Jimmy is helping you clear away old toxins and cellular memory from your old, limiting beliefs. This will help you on your journey to communicate with us. Agape is your second power spot, so congratulations."

"Will I go back into my body? I'm not sure I like not being in it."

"Yes, you will return soon after our conversation. Just know there are many other archangels and members of the Divine that are here, cheering you on and supporting this healing. You are strong and brave, and you are making all the right choices, so stick with your guts and remember to trust us."

I felt as though I had known this beautiful, loving creature for quite some time. Next thing I knew I was back in my body on Jimmy's table.

His voice got louder. "You are the first in generations! Your lineage is full of potential and ability, and you are the first in generations!" He then got the oversized feathers out and started to smack me up and down my body while continuing to chant that I was the first in generations.

"I usually never change my music," he said. "But every time I touch you, your body screams the name of this song to me." He walked over to his stereo and switched the CD.

I recognized it instantly, although I knew that I had never heard it in my twenty-two years on this planet. Tears seeped down my face, and my body convulsed in sobs.

May the Long time sun shine upon you,
all love surround you, and the pure light within you,
guide your way on.

Something about that song touched my soul and brought forth emotions assuring me I was in the right place and this was in fact my path and my truth. I felt more grace in that room then I ever knew possible.

Jimmy came over to me and gently laid his hand on my forehead. "Remember, you will find the others. You are like a butterfly. When the monarchs come out of their cocoons they will travel for many,

many miles alone. You will do the same. And then instinctively one monarch butterfly will naturally attract other monarchs and they gather together. Just like you will. Remember, Samantha, there are many others like you, and you will not be alone for long."

Even though this was supposed to be only a ninety-minute session, I was with Jimmy for another few hours, but it felt like a blink. I didn't want this to end, as I didn't know one could feel this much pure joy and bliss without any help from external substances.

"We are all done," he said eventually. "Every decision you make from here on out will be considered conscious. Take your time getting up. I put a robe on the bed for you, and I will step out. After this you need to submerge yourself in water and surrender to the Divine, so they can propel you forward on your mission."

As I woozily sat up on the table, I realized why the woman before me had looked the way she did when she left. Still in a complete daze, I did my best to slip on a robe. No longer intimidated by his good looks and loving warm energy, I gave Jimmy the biggest hug imaginable. I walked out in a state of bliss, happily disoriented and wondering what exactly just happened to me. Half way to the lotus pond, I turned around as I realized I had forgotten my bag and my clothes.

Jimmy was waiting at the door for me. He had my bag in his hand. "Don't worry about it sweetie. Everyone leaves their baggage in this room." He gave me another Cheshire grin and sent me on my way.

Busting out with laughter, I went back to my casita, followed his post ceremony instructions, and immersed myself in the tub for a long soak. I then collapsed in bed, as I didn't think I had the energy to move a limb or do anything else.

Chapter 17

That night in my sleep, I had another visit from the venomous giant green snake. This time it slithered up my leg and started to wrap its huge body around my ankles and knees, so I couldn't move. I was standing in the middle of a deserted playground with not a soul in sight. At first I panicked, my breathing ragged, and the snake almost doubled in size. I gasped for air—

Out of the blue a small fairy with black hair and red lipstick zipped around my head and perched on the snake's glistening coils. "Fear feeds the demons, sista! Remember to control your thoughts and think of loving and positive things."

With that she lifted into the air and vanished in a flash.

Breathe, Sam, breathe, I told myself.

I focused on Honey, remembering how she loved to catch the Frisbee with me in the backyard, and this instantly slowed my heart rate. Honey could have played that game for hours. I saw her bright questioning eyes as she dropped the Frisbee at my feet. The memory was so great I started to smile, and when I opened my eyes I couldn't believe it—the snake was half the size.

Way to go Sam! I felt encouraged by my success and proud of myself. Determined to shrink that hideous snake to the size of an earthworm, I imagined wading in the creek with the cool water flowing around my legs. The angel-like beings who showed me the unicorns were there, reassuring me everything would always be okay. Then the sound of my alarm woke me. Not fair!

"I'll get you next time," I muttered to the snake.

I reached for the phone to shut off the alarm and saw I had a voicemail from Lucas. I pressed speaker.

"It's me. Listen, I messed up, and I really want to see you. Give me a call."

My heart ached. Why hadn't he said this three months ago? Part of me wanted to call him right back, and part of me knew that wouldn't be a good idea. I did still long to see him and to feel his touch, but I remembered Papa Jack's warning to me about the Brigade. They would do whatever they could to keep me wanting Lucas, so I'd look backwards instead of having the courage to move forward with my life.

Firm in my resolve, I switched my phone off and dressed for an early morning, guided meditative walk along the path to the ocean. Afterwards, I ate the most delicious breakfast frittata and sipped a decaf latte in the restaurant near the spa, followed by a great yin yoga class to settle into my body. I was officially blissed out when Claire arrived on the noon shuttle.

Over pineapple smoothies and fresh quinoa and prosciutto salad, we caught up and then treated ourselves to a facial and a hot stone massage. I still felt hesitant about revealing the full extent of the amazing things that had happened to me—the episode with the writing, the Blast Rocket session with Jimmy—because it was as if a small part of me still doubted it all. I did tell her about the snake, and how I'd managed to shrink it. Claire knew something about lucid dreaming, and we talked about how meditation and stilling the mind—both of which I had been doing—could allow you to face fears, heal unwanted issues, and problem solve as you slept. She even told me that dreams are one of the most underused ways that people can get messages from their subconscious mind. Of course she would have known that.

Over the next few days, we hiked the mountain trails where we saw roadrunners and flowering cacti. One five mile hike took us to the highest peak with views of the ocean and the dark glittering quartz rocks on the jagged shoreline. We also spoiled ourselves with lengthy and luxurious spa treatments. Body scrubs with essential oils, mud wraps, watsu massages in the pool, cranial sacral therapy, and reiki—Claire and I tried it all.

The day before our departure, I spent an hour exploring the resort's boutiques and shops. I found an amazing blue, spaghetti strap sundress that matched the color of the ocean water. I felt like a princess wearing it, twirling around in the dressing room. I bought hot pink sarongs for Anna and Rose, and on the spur of the moment I chose some beautiful turquoise earrings for my mom. I saw a really cool visor and immediately thought of Lucas. I gently reminded myself I was done with that and moved on, feeling quite sad. I'd spent the limit I had set for myself, but as I walked back to our casita I felt a strong urge to enter a boutique filled with crystals.

"May I help you?" said a woman with pink hair.

Mesmerized by the energy and beauty of the crystals, I stood speechless and in awe.

She smiled. "Take your time. See which one speaks to you."

With a sense of purpose, I walked toward an exquisite purple amethyst crystal. It was smaller than some of the others and not as extravagant looking, but when I picked it up I felt it's energy. It was mine. It was almost like it had been waiting on me.

The woman then went on to tell me about the powerful healing effects that crystals can have. "You chose amethyst. It's a calming stone that provides balance and patience. It's also known to increase your intuition."

After browsing some more, I also chose a smoky quartz for protection, a beautiful selenite heart she said would help me connect with my angels, a green aventurine that was supposed to help with manifesting, and a beautiful chakra set that I could use to help balance and cleanse my chakras all on my own.

"You seem to have quite a connection with these crystals," she said. She watched me intently as I handled the smoky quartz. I remembered what I learned on the tour with Javier and decided she would probably have an answer for me.

"Yes, I do feel very drawn to them. I also love the huge crystals in the water. Is it true that they hold the energy for the resort, to allow ultimate healing?"

She came over to me with a soft smile. "I am Maria, by the way. Yes, it is. Do you want to hear the legend of those crystals?"

"For sure."

"Thousands and thousands of years ago there was a magical island named Atlantis. Obviously, there was no such thing as electricity back then, so the people operated off crystal energy. The crystals offered the people of Atlantis a sense of peace and helped them to remember their truth. The society flourished for millennia and then something happened to bring about their demise. No one really knows why.

"But what we do know is that the island sunk. No one has ever found artifacts from Atlantis, but the crystals remained. Their energy is eternal. We think there was an underground centrifugal force, a giant maelstrom from the depths of the ocean, which dispersed large chucks of the crystals. Rumor has it that the divine beings that live in the sea followed the crystals as they erupted and dispersed to make sure they were sporadically placed around the world. That way their energy could be used in the Aquarian Age when it was time for human ascension."

I was stunned by what she was saying. Her story seemed fantastical, and yet I felt deeply connected to it and recognized her words as truth. I remembered reading that we are now living in the Aquarian Age, and this is the time of ascension and awakening.

"So you mean the quartz here in the ocean are from Atlantis?"

"Believe what you will, but yes, that is what I believe."

Maria could tell I was a little confused about ascension. She explained that the word describes what happens when you awaken to your truth and have a spiritual awakening—your energy begins to ascend. She suggested I take the path from the cliffs down to the dark, jagged quartz rocks and cleanse and charge my crystals in the healing water and utilize the sacred energy.

Before I left, she gave me a tiny, heart shaped rose quartz and said it would help me to attract love into my life.

"My intuition, and a gift," she said. "I can tell this one also wants to be with you."

I took her advice and followed the steep path down to the ocean. It was a little scary as the waves pounded those dark, glistening rocks. I laid my crystals in a small shallow cove nearby. As I dipped my feet in the water, I was moved to tears feeling all the beauty and peace that surrounded me. I didn't know why, but I felt at home.

Claire and I met up for lunch at a patio overlooking the ocean, and I showed her my new "friends" I had just purchased.

"Oh, cool! I LOVE crystals," she said. "I can't wait to check out that store. If I can fit it into my busy schedule."

I was so happy to have Claire in my life. She was the perfect friend to travel with, and we'd grown closer during our week of pampering and enlightenment.

"I was just reading the book, *Angels of Abundance* by Doreen Virtue," she said, "and it's really interesting. She talks about ways to attract your heart's desires through thoughts, affirmations, and visualizations. I was laughing to myself thinking as much time as I spend in the car, I may not be able to visualize, but I can dang sure affirm my butt off!"

"Wow, this really is like a spirit camp," I teased.

"More like spirit boot camp." We laughed at how full our schedules had been with yoga classes, personal growth lectures, spa appointments, and meals.

That afternoon I had an ayurvedic treatment, where after a massage, hot oil was poured over my head and in my hair. I laid on the table full of gratitude for this treatment and for this place. I felt like I was in a bubble of pure euphoria.

After the massage the therapist told me, "This oil is from India, and it is considered to be special healing and spiritual oil. Pay attention to your thoughts during this part."

He put a pan at the back of my head to catch any drips, then took the bowl of heated oil and poured it directly onto my third eye. It felt soothing and warm. He then poured the oil all over my head. The music seemed to get louder and more intense, and I felt as if I was going into a trance. An omnipresent feeling of grace and bliss overwhelmed me. The therapist poured another bowl of the soothing oil over my forehead in the same spot directly between my eyebrows, but this time I began to see something in my mind's eye. I wondered for a second if my eyes were open, and then I realized I had a blindfold on to protect my eyes from the oil.

I saw myself as a small child, and Lucas was there too, but he was my brother in this vision. We lived in what seemed like a prison, a tall stone building with concrete floors. Our room was tiny and cold and dark. We were both malnourished, and I wasn't doing well. I sensed this was a time when women weren't treated with any regard; no one cared if I ate, breathed, or lived another day. No one other than Lucas. He loved me dearly, and we were very close.

The next thing I saw was him burying me. I saw my small body; I was still just a child. I knew that Lucas lived that life never truly being able to recover my loss. I also saw how I lingered over him in the clouds, staying with him until he had also passed over. I didn't want to leave him. I wanted to stay by his side and offer him any divine help that I could. I wondered if this was the history Papa Jack was talking about when he said Lucas and I had been together in a past life.

After the session, the therapist helped me up and gave me a tissue to dry my eyes. I wasn't even aware that I was crying, because I was so focused on my vision.

"How was your experience, ma'am?" he asked. "Did you have any visions?"

"Um, actually yes, I did, and I thought it was um . . . interesting, really touching . . . actually."

"This is definitely one of our more spiritual spa treatments, and that tends to happen a lot. Enjoy the rest of your stay." He escorted me out.

To celebrate our last evening at the resort, Claire and I dressed up and splurged on dinner at the fancy sushi bar. We shared some of the highlights of our visit. For Claire it was the hike to the top of the mountain and the Reiki work. "I also met the sweetest woman in my yoga class today. She is a medium, and we had a great connection. I might book a reading with her."

Just then an older woman with blonde, silky hair and a warm smile strolled into the dining area.

"Hey Annie," Claire called out. "What a coincidence, I was just telling Sam about meeting you today."

"Hello Claire, and you must be Sam," she said, glancing in my direction. "You girls know there are no such things as coincidence. I actually was looking for you both. I felt compelled to leave these with you." She handed Claire and I each one of her cards. "You all have a lovely dinner," she said and walked off.

We looked at each other and burst into laughter, shaking our heads.

"You will not believe what happened to me today," I said. I decided to test the water, and I told her about the spa treatment I had with the oil. I explained the way I slipped into the trance and felt an overwhelming sense of bliss.

"You had a spirit orgasm," she exclaimed. "I'm jealous."

We both sat there cracking up and giggling about how exciting it was to have a spirit orgasm.

"I also had a past life vision," I said, suddenly feeling shy. "I don't want to talk too much about it, but it concerned me and Lucas."

Like a true friend, she didn't press me for details. Instead she simply said, "I think that happens with some of the people in our lives. Maybe that explains why it was so intense between the two of you."

We had the best conversation over dinner. Both of us sensed that an important shift was taking place; so many people were opening up and showing interest in angels, meditation, and just loving in general. It was like Annie had just said: there is no such thing as a coincidence. Instead there were synchronicities every which way we turned.

"Let's have a toast," I said, and raised my glass of sparkling mineral water. "To love and friendship."

"And to our future adventures and to definitely coming back to Agape!" said Claire.

Chapter 18

When I was sixteen and still dealing with the fallout of my parent's divorce, my mom sent me away to a counseling rehab for two weeks. It worried her that three years after their divorce I was still so upset and still blaming myself. Initially, I hated the counseling, but by the second week I felt safe, and most importantly, understood. I no longer felt like I was to blame for all my parent's problems. I was actually reluctant to come home.

I felt the same way when I arrived back home after my days at Agape. I'd felt safe in that environment. Angels, crystals, spirits, talk of third eyes, and a crazy handsome man who beat me—gently—with feathers, seemed normal. Visions of myself and Lucas from lifetimes ago actually made sense. But in my condo, with dirty dishes piling up in the sink, I felt low. I doubted I could carry all my newfound wisdom into my life. Then I remembered Jimmy suggesting I listen to the first part of Hiro's recording. I popped it into the CD player, grabbed a green juice, and settled in to listen to his insights.

Hiro started by telling me that I would never digest all of this in one sitting. I was to listen and take what resonated with me, because each time I listened something different would be revealed and understood. That made sense. I looked up the dates of the new moon for the next several months then plugged reminders into my phone on the correlating days. LISTEN TO HIRO'S RECORDING.

He started the reading by explaining the four energies or elements. Fire, which is spirit. Water, which is feelings and emotions. Air, which is the mind and mental aspects. Earth, which is our bodies and the physical aspects.

He then said, "We all have lived dozens or more, maybe hundreds or thousands of lifetimes, depending on where we are in relation to the evolution of our own soul. We are all doing an experiment here on earth to see if we can learn to live and make choices out of love. Samantha, you are here to help with this transition and to teach about love. Love is what every living thing on the planet is looking for, living for, and craving."

He told me that once I had mastered the practice of self-love, I would begin to teach it to others. "You have massive potential in this lifetime and can be a major force for good if you veer down the right path. You have several fortunate aspects in your chart. You even have a couple of transits that mirror Deepak Chopra's chart."

I wasn't sure who Deepak was so I added that to my list of things to research. Hiro then went on to describe me as playful, excitable, impatient, bored easily, impulsive, and someone who liked to have a lot of fun. I was a little shocked about how dead on he was.

"You will be at your best in this lifetime when you have a crusade, when you find something you believe in and are willing to fight for. You should always be expanding the horizon of your personal truth, my friend. It will behoove you to be fanatical and obsessed with finding your truth. Your job is very simple in this lifetime. It's to find your truth and learn to love and accept yourself fully just as you are. Then to share your truth and push others to find their own. You can do this. You will lead the way and boldly go where others do not dare to go.

"Yoga and meditation will be key for you, and if you go deep into these practices you will see visions sent to you from the Divine. You want to live in a spirit of empathy and compassion for everything that lives and breathes—all animals, trees, plants, and people."

I shivered as I remembered Bridget telling me the same thing and also reading about it in *The Seat of the Soul*. I made a mental note to keep empathy and compassion at the forefront of my mind. I was glad I had joined the yoga studio. I already noticed a difference in the way I was feeling just by going to yoga on the regs.

"You are here to come to the realization that you are a spirit temporarily living in a human body," he said. "You will help others become aware that the same is true for them. It will be key for you to hone in on self-love versus self-hatred. Love is the greatest power that we humans have available to us. Loving and adoring ourselves is extremely powerful and can change the vibrations on this planet."

I loved hearing Hiro's voice. I remembered how nervous I'd been driving up the mountain in Sedona and the excitable way he spun around that rickety house as he spoke to me. Taking his advice, I stopped the recording—I'd heard all I needed for now. I opened my laptop and googled Deepak Chopra. I was stunned. He had done amazing things for the planet. Was this really my potential?

I started pacing back and forth. I felt so energized, as if I'd had five shots of espresso. After hearing all of Hiro's encouragement, I realized there was a common theme. Jimmy, Bridget, Hiro, Ted, Papa Jack, Archangel Raphael, and Archangel Michael had all spoken about my unique contribution to humanity and my importance. Although it was hard for me to grasp, I couldn't keep denying the fact this is what all the humans and angels were telling me. If so many different sources were giving me the same message, it had to be true.

My phone dinged with an incoming text. Lucas!

Sam, what gives?? Where are you??

Along with the phone message, he'd texted me while I was at Agape. And now this one. I'd ignored them, but now I thought why not see him? The Demon Brigade couldn't take me down when I felt so confident. I was sure Lucas had heard stories about how my life had fallen apart after the breakup. Now it was time for him to see how well I was doing. I texted him back.

I'm back. Guess where I've been? If you buy me dinner tomorrow night I'll totes tell you.

He responded immediately *Sure!! Tex Mex?*

7? I'm already hungry xo

See ya then

No xo? Already I felt annoyed. I reminded myself to breathe. This was not a date, this was a chance for Lucas to see Samantha Kingston happy, content, and moving on with her life.

For my dinner with Lucas, I wore the dress I'd bought at Agape, and I put the smallest amethyst crystal in my bag for good luck. Perhaps we could actually be friends. I walked into the restaurant and saw him sitting across the room, but he wasn't alone. He jumped up and ran over to give me a hug.

"I'm so glad you came to meet me," he said. "I wasn't sure if you were going to come after it took you days to text me back." He grabbed my hand and eagerly pulled me to his table.

"Um, I thought I was just meeting you."

Damon didn't even bother to look up.

"Well, hey Damon . . . aren't you going to say hello?"

Lucas looked hurt that the first thing I did was snap at his brother. I sat there in a sulk and ordered a skinny margarita, while Lucas and Damon slipped back into their habit of talking about inside jokes. When the server brought our drinks I chugged half of mine and then stood up.

"You know what guys? I have better things to do with my time." I grabbed my bag and left before the food arrived.

Driving home I thought it was their loss. I had to keep my focus on all that I needed to accomplish. I was done dealing with Lucas and for sure with Damon. I'm special and divinely protected. What was I thinking even going there?

The next day, I ran into Ashley, one of my good friends from college, at the grocery store.

"Hey Ashley. What's up?"

"Just grabbing some food. What have you been doing? Did you get another job?"

I shook my head. *Please, I don't need another job; I've got important work to do. But then you wouldn't understand.* "Ummm, not yet," I said.

"Well, keep in touch. I would love to get together sometime." She left and walked toward her car.

When I got home, I decided it was time to let Anna know what was going on with me. I was a little nervous about telling her though, because I was scared what Bill would do if he found out. She would never tell him, but still, he was so manipulative and had ways of finding out just about anything. After that visit from him and Aunt Mary, when I sensed exactly what he was thinking about me—*get rid of her!*—I knew to proceed with caution. But I missed Anna, and my gut told me I could trust her to keep my secret. From what I had been reading, I'd learned that psychic abilities are passed down family lines. The aunt who'd been banished from the family had obviously been an intuitive. My gut told me there was a good possibility that Anna was too.

When I called her I got her voicemail. Then something odd happened. I felt as if I blacked out. One second I was in the kitchen about to leave her a message, and the next thing I knew I was sitting on the couch staring into space and my phone was off. *Hmmm, that is weird. I'll just text her instead,* I thought.

Hey Anna, call me asap. I have something major to tell you.

I then walked out on the deck with a book that Bridget had suggested, *A Return to Love,"* by Marianne Williamson. I read all afternoon and into the night. When I was finished, I had such a hunger for more wisdom, that I downloaded an Eckhart Tolle book. I also ordered several other books by Wayne Dyer, Deepak Chopra, and Louise Hay for overnight delivery.

I read and read nonstop. I had boundless energy. It was as if my body had been taken over and put on autopilot as words poured into me. Time felt really weird too—hours zoomed by and then other moments seemed to happen in slow motion. At one point, I put down one of the books because I literally felt wave after wave of chills enter by body and then slowly depart.

When I wasn't reading, I got lost in the internet—spirit guides, animal totems, chem trails, negative ions, vortexes, ascension symptoms. There was so much to learn about. I read crazy and preposterous stuff about spiritual awakenings, and I wondered if I had made a mistake jumping into all this so quickly. There was so much I didn't know, and I had no idea how to understand what was real and what wasn't.

At some point—day, night, I barely knew—Rose knocked on the door and announced she was coming in. "Sam, are you still at it?" she asked as she walked in. "You haven't come out of this cave in three days. What are you reading anyway?"

I tried to answer but couldn't. I panicked. Cold sweat clung to the back of my neck. How could I not have absorbed anything? I'd been holed up for days and days. What had I been doing?

She grabbed a small mirror off my wall and held it up to me. I barely recognized myself I was so unkempt. I snapped at her to put the mirror down and get out.

She looked appalled. "I never thought I would say this, but maybe your mom is right. Maybe you do need some help."

"What? You have been talking to my mom? You need to leave, now!" I shouted.

She left, and I huddled in a fetal position on the couch in a crying fit. These tears were filled with pain and sorrow and felt as if they came from ancient and deep wounds. Another hour passed. I had almost sobbed myself to the point of exhaustion, and now I lay on the couch trying to understand what had triggered the obsession with the books. I still couldn't believe I had retained nothing of what I'd read. My phone rang, and I flipped it over to see the caller ID. At last, it was Anna!

"Sam, are you okay? I lost my phone and I just found it. Your message sounded awful."

My heart dropped. "What message?"

"You left me a message ranting on about how I needed to get over to your house as you needed me there stat."

"Oh gosh, I don't know what happened. To be honest, I don't remember saying that." I then recalled that I'd thought I'd blacked out. "I do have some things I need to tell you, though. I am nervous to say them, so I am just going to get it out before I lose my nerve. I have been having a spiritual awakening, and some pretty crazy stuff has been happening to me. All of it is really good, and I know it will work out okay, but it is scary and crazy right now, and I feel so alone." As I spoke I felt myself getting lighter and less and less in control. And then I blacked out again.

"Oh no, what just happened?" I said as I came to.

"Sam, whoa, what is going on?"

"I don't know. I just blacked out again."

"You mean you don't remember what you just said to me?"

"No, what did I say?"

"You were screaming in a really low pitched voice, and you said 'I have a lot of psychic ability, and the world is changing. It's time to wake up and quit living this illusion of a life. If not, you and your dad are going to die. Our family is powerful, and we have lineage that needs to be carried forthright. You need to wake up now, Anna!'"

"Oh my gosh, I did not say that!"

"Calm down," she said in a firm but gentle voice.

"Whatever you heard just now wasn't me. Something, and I am not sure what, is literally coming into my body. I am so sorry, and I don't even know what I just said to you, but I know it wasn't good. Please, please promise me you will not tell your parents about this. I know they are worried I will screw up your dad's reelection. They also have my mom convinced that I need be on lock down. Please promise you won't mention it to any of them," I begged.

Anna snorted, and I imagined her rolling her eyes. "Dad's being paranoid, don't worry about him. I won't say anything, but I have to admit I'm worried about you. What the heck is going on?"

I hesitated, wondering how much I should reveal. In hearing what I'd said to her, I realized I had probably allowed the Demon Brigade to get inside my body and take over, yet again. Although I'd been excited about revealing my discoveries to my cousin just moments before, I didn't know if I could now.

"I promise I'll tell you when the time is right. But I don't think this is it."

"What are you talking about? You just said you were going to tell me everything! Sam, you're scaring me. I'm gonna come over."

"No!" I yelled. "Seriously, I don't think that's a good idea."

"Are you kidding me? You sound like you're falling apart over there!"

I racked my brain for a solution. "You know what? I have a therapist I've been talking to. I'm going to call her right now. She's been amazing, and I'm sure she'll have some advice for me. I promise to be in touch soon. I love you."

I ended that call, and as I dialed Bridget's number I heard a knock on my door.

"Sam? Are you home?"

I dropped the phone and ran to open the door. There stood my guide, the woman who I could entrust with my life. The only one who really understood what I was going through. "Bridget? You've come to my house."

She stepped inside and wrapped her arms around me as I began to sob.

"Just get it out dear. Just let whatever you are releasing come out."

After crying in her arms for a few minutes, I looked up at her warm face. "How did you know to come? I'm so happy to see you."

"I just sensed you were in trouble and needed me. First thing, I want you to stomp your feet on the ground as hard as you can. Now!"

I trusted Bridget, so I stomped away on the floor.

"Then put both hands on your belly and take ten long, deep, slow breaths in and out."

I breathed long and deep, and to my surprise I began to feel calmer.

"That is a grounding technique and an invaluable tool. I'm wondering though, Samantha, has your ego been getting in your way?"

"What do you mean?"

"I mean have you been acting like the curious, adventurous, and loving Sam that we both know you are, or have you been allowing your ego to pump you up with thoughts that you are better than everyone and that you are unstoppable?"

I stood there frozen, as I knew that was exactly what I had done. "Well, I guess maybe I did do that a little," I said, not wanting to admit the full truth to her.

"This is all a process," she said, "and a major part is to stay humble. When we let our egos run the show, we open the door and invite the Demon Brigade to come in and use our body. This work isn't about feeding our egos, and in fact when we do that, it can be dangerous."

"It was dreadful, Bridget. I blacked out and said cruel things to my cousin. My body felt so weird, and I can't remember anything that has happened to me over the past three days. Seriously. I read the entire book that you suggested, and I tried to tell my friend Rose what it was about this morning, and I couldn't remember one word. And then on the internet I read all this crazy stuff about people who get to a point where they do not need food and they do not age and they meditate for five hours a day and that sounds awful."

"Calm down. The more you react to all this the more you feed the negativity. First of all, things are moving quickly with you, so grounding is going to be very important."

"But what does that even mean? I had never heard of grounding until you had me do it." I remembered that one of the crystals I really liked and bought at Agape was supposed to be good for grounding.

"When you ground yourself you align your energy with the earth's core. You are aware of the now and remain in the present moment. You don't allow your mind to drift off. When you are ungrounded your soul is not in your body, and that's why you were not remembering things. Don't be scared, this is part of the learning experience."

"It's a little hard to not be scared."

"Let's give you specific things to do this week, and we will see if it helps. Get your journal."

We sat at my dining table, and I wrote down her suggestions

"First, you need to get a serious meditation practice down. No more random meditations, and no more meditating in bed."

"But I like meditating in bed. It's so comfortable."

"Go ahead and continue, but know you will probably remain ungrounded."

"Okay, I'll get out of bed to meditate." I felt a little exasperated with her but knew she was right. According to her plan, I was to use a simple mantra that I liked when I meditated.

Another grounding technique was to go outside and put my feet in the dirt or grass. I was to envision the earth's warm, loving energy coming up through my feet, going up my legs, through my heart, and lassoing around my head. Then I was to picture it coming down the back of my neck, through my heart again, and going back to my feet. She also told me to eat root vegetables and to buy a grounding crystal.

I stopped her mid-sentence. I ran upstairs to my closet and grabbed the pointy smoky quartz. "You mean like this?" I said with a smile when I returned. I was happy I had known what I needed before I even needed it.

She applauded me and confirmed that was exactly what I needed. She suggested I hold it in my hand when I was meditating or anytime I was feeling out of sorts or ungrounded. She also gave me some black tourmaline that she said would help with both protection and grounding.

"Try your best to stay present in everything you are doing," she said. "It's probably best that you stay off the internet for a while until you are stronger. I think your ego was making you want to search for more and more information, and in this way you were feeding the Brigade."

"Yes, I agree," I said with a sigh.

"Finally, there is no nice way to say this—this place is a wreck."

As if for the first time, I saw the dirty dishes in the sink, the pile of used tea bags, my yoga clothes scattered across the floor, and the bags of recycling piling up.

"It is critical you have a nice living space and a welcoming and loving energy in here," she said. "Consider trying out feng shui. My instincts told me you might need this." She reached into her large shoulder bag and pulled out a book. "You're transforming your inner world, let's see what you can do with your environment. Your home energy can be very healing if you set it up to support you."

Chapter 19

I decided to take the next week slow and dedicate it to self-love. I knew I needed to take a break from my obsession with reading and online searching. So programs on OWN, Oprah's network, were my only indulgences. I also sensed I was losing Rose, and that terrified me. She was my best friend, and I needed to get myself together.

The grounding work produced fantastic results. I carried my smoky quartz or black tourmaline with me at all times—in my pocket, in my purse, and sometimes I even wore the crystals in my bra. I know it sounds silly, but it really worked. I stomped my feet on the regs—loudly in my condo and once even in the natural food store when I felt freaked out with indecision as I stared at the flower remedies. I put my hands on my belly and breathed deep and chose one called Joy Juice. I figured I couldn't go wrong with that. I was grateful to know what was happening and how to control it if I began again to feel as though I was leaving my body.

Every morning I did a ten minute meditation right after I woke up, repeating the mantra om over and over in my head. Bridget had explained this was the universal mantra to open your heart. I went outside a few times a day and practiced pulling the earth's energy into my body and feeling the sunlight soaking into my skin. I decided to plant some flowers, as I had read that gardening could help to ground you as well.

Finally, I studied up on feng shui and was on a mission to get my place in perfect order. I wanted to make it my sanctuary. I bought some cherry red paint for my front door. I absolutely loved the way it popped next to the white brick. I bought a beautiful flowing water feature for the deck. I'd used up my sage from Sedona, so I purchased another bundle, along with some palo santo sticks, and I burned them throughout the condo. I bought several beautiful candles and more crystals—I was beginning to discover a girl could never have too many crystals.

I spent one blissful evening creating a beautiful vision board. In the center of the board I placed a picture of the most serene and beautiful beach house with wraparound windows. I could even see my home office overlooking the beach and the water—although I didn't yet know what I would be doing in that office. I added a picture of Jimmy Fallon, because I love him and think he is hysterical, and it's my dream to one day be on his show. I decided to put a picture of Oprah on there as well for inspiration, to show me what was possible. I added other pictures of places I wanted to visit, and then I added personal photos. One of me, one of my mom, and one of my dad—I missed them both—and one of me and Rose. I wanted to hold space for them and for their happiness as well as for my own.

Then I cut out the words Abundance, Friends, Fun, Laughter, Romance, and Joy and placed them in the empty spaces that were left. I stepped back. Was I finished? No, I needed a few more. Trust. Patience. Forgiveness.

The next day, I was out planting purple pansies for abundance, and Rose pulled up. For the first time I felt nervous about talking to her.

"Hey Sam," she said, as she walked toward me. "Red door, huh?"

Rose had been visiting her new boyfriend who lived out of town. I felt grateful for the timing as it gave me time alone. I knew she had been upset by my erratic behavior.

"I love it," I said. "What do you think?" Then, before she even had a chance to answer, I blurted out, "Please forgive me. I don't know what got into me, and I'm so sorry for the way I behaved last week."

She looked down and took a deep breath. "It's okay. I didn't like seeing you like that. But I'll admit you look great today and really happy."

"Thank you." I stood and gave her a big hug. "I loaded up on delish snacks and some cool eats from Whole Foods. Want to come over tonight? We could cook together and have a dance party?"

"Sounds perfect Shawdy," she said with a smile. "Oh, and yes, I love the red door. It looks really cheery."

That night we cooked and laughed and reminisced about so many funny stories. I still wasn't ready to tell her everything, so I was glad she didn't question me. After dinner we rocked out to T Swift and then watched some funny reruns of GIRLS. It felt so fun to be doing normal things and to give myself a break. Her birthday was just two days away, so we made plans for a last minute birthday dinner celebration.

"How about La Lune et Le Soleil?" I suggested.

"We'll never get a resie, the place is so hot right now. Well, actually knowing you."

Rose was always amazed at how I was able to do things she thought were impossible. When we were on the party circuit going out to clubs there would be long lines wrapped around for blocks, and I was always able to get us in with a quick wink and a smile at whoever was running the VIP line. Anytime we were looking for hotels, I would always find the most amazing deals at the best luxury spots. Things sort of worked out the way I wanted, because I just knew they would.

"Don't doubt my skills, I'm feeling lucky," I said as I switched on my phone and went to their website. "Told ya! We've got a table for the crew at eight on Saturday."

"I should have known. Of course you would be able to do it."

The next morning I walked for three miles, as my body still wasn't allowing me to do exhaustive cardio exercise. So I got a massage and finished planting the rest of the flowers. I went inside to relax and heard a knock on the door. Rose was off with her guy, and Anna was busy with her kids. Bill and Mary? Ugh, that would really ruin my day.

I opened the door, and my heart skipped a beat. Lucas stood there with a big bouquet of lilies. His eyes were bloodshot, and it looked like he hadn't shaved since I fled that awful dinner when I was so short and rude with him and Damon.

"I miss you so much," he said. "Can I please come in?"

"Wow, this is a surprise. How are you?" I said gingerly.

"Honestly, not good. Can I come in?"

"Yes," I said, doing my best to hold back my tears.

He stepped inside and looked around. "Where's Honey? I have really missed her too."

"She got hit by a car shortly after we broke up."

"I wish I had known. I'm so sorry."

"Really? Would you have called? Would it have changed anything?"

"I messed up, and I can see it now. I want another chance." He paced the room. "I was trying to act tough at dinner, as if I didn't need you. That is why I had Damon come, because I knew it would make me stronger if he was there."

"But he doesn't make you stronger. Don't you see that?"

He turned, and I could see how angry he was. How dare I criticize his brother. I remembered how crushed I was when I overheard Damon and him talking once. Damon was telling him there was no need to rush things, and that he had much better things he needed to be spending his money on then buying me a diamond ring.

"How do you think it made me feel," I asked, "when you told me you had to decide if you wanted to buy me an engagement ring or buy yourself a new car?"

"You have never had to worry about money, because you have always been so good at your job. Not everyone can land their dream job after only one year of college. It didn't come that easy for me, and I actually had to go to college and work. I still wasn't doing as well as you were. How do you think that made me feel?"

"I am not going to apologize for my success. Besides, if it makes you feel any better, I'm not working now. I decided to take some time off." I didn't want him to know that I actually got fired. "If your brother hadn't been dominating our conversation the other night, maybe some of this stuff would have come up and —"

"Whoa, since when. You loved that job, it was made for you."

"I used to think that, but I don't any more. A lot has changed."

We stood there in silence, on opposite sides of my kitchen. He walked over to me. "Sam, I still love you. I think about you all the time. I miss our games, S-bear."

My stomach dropped at the sound of his words. I remembered how deeply in love we once were. We had created our own secret language with pet nicknames for each other.

"Hey S-bear. I double totes love you so much," he'd say and my heart would melt.

"Hey L-bear. I triple totes love you."

"Totes love you more." And then he'd come closer for a kiss.

We'd spend hours on the couch in my condo or down in his basement laughing at things that might not seem funny to anyone else but were hilarious to us. Despite our many issues, he did show me what it was like to be in love. Now he stood in front of me asking for another chance.

"I would be lying if I didn't say I missed all of that too," I said. "I really did think we would end up together. But I told you before, I want to be with someone who chooses to put me first. You don't make any decisions on your own without checking in with your brother, and I can't live like that. I am taking this as a sign from the universe that it's time for both of us to move on. Besides, even though I have missed the good times, I have been relieved not to have to deal with the constant fighting. Don't you agree?"

"I just don't know if I will ever love anyone the way I love you."

You will, you just think that now because of our soul contract.

"I felt that way at first too. But I am optimistic we can both be happier, and that we can both find matches that are better suited for us. I am happy that you came by, and you will always hold a special place in my heart, but for now I really need to just be alone."

"Stop it. All this moving on talk. I don't buy it. Why don't you just come out and say there's someone else." He tossed the flowers into my trashcan.

"Lucas! I am going through a lot, and I have realized that I don't even know how to love myself. I am spending some time getting to know myself and learning about self-love. There is no one else."

"Yeah, right. You hate to be alone for even one night. I'm tired of hearing your lies." For the first time since walking in, he took inventory of my place. "Since when do you have so many plants? What is that smell? Are you burning incense? What in the hell is this thing?" He walked over to the corner of the room and pointed at my vision board.

"I don't have to explain anything to you." I hated how I suddenly felt embarrassed for the way I changed my condo. I loved my home, it was my sanctuary now.

"You know what? Forget I ever came over here."

"Please don't leave like this."

He slammed the door on his way out. Seconds later he was peeling out of the parking lot.

I stood there watching him drive away, and I knew one thing was for sure. Lucas was not the guy for me. Even though he and I would always have a connection, I felt immense relief at finally having closure on the decision I had made to move on.

Chapter 20

I ran a salt bath, lit candles, and selected one of the CDs that I picked up at Agape. I sank into the soothing water and prayed. *Dear God, please help me to forgive Lucas. I release him. I surrender.* All of a sudden, I started to see spots of lights appearing just in front of the mirror. I feared the Brigade was up to their tricks, but the presence of the lights felt loving and gentle. Within seconds an extraordinary image of a beautiful and sexy woman formed in the mirror.

"I am here to let you know it is time for your next power spot," she said in a sultry voice.

"I'm in the bathtub. Why do you guys always come around when I am naked? It makes me really uncomfortable."

I moved the bubbles around in the tub making sure I was covered. By now she had stepped out of the mirror. Her silver, floor length dress floated around her as she stood beside the sink.

"Fair enough, finish enjoying your bath. Just know that this journey may begin before you go to sleep or maybe even during your sleep. We are taking you on a soul journey, and you will get what you need to continue on your path. Also, I want to congratulate you for not taking that easy road to get back with Lucas. Many women would not have been strong enough to walk away from that situation, so congratulations for trusting your intuition."

"What is your name?" I asked.

"I am Isis, Goddess of Magic, Life, and Feminine Power. I am on your divine team of support. I am here to help infuse and awaken your divine goddess energy and gifts."

Sounds pretty awesome!

"It's nice to meet you," I said. "But I have to be honest. Even though I know deep down all this stuff really is happening, it's hard for me not to think I am going crazy, and it's hard for me not to have any friends to talk about these things with."

"I understand, and we can help you with this if you will simply ask us. You should start each day with a morning prayer asking for everything you want and need for support in living your divine mission. If you ask us daily to bring you a human support system in the form of friends, then you will get that—with a little bit of patience."

I was happy to see such a beautiful and loving woman here to help me. I also wanted a clear explanation, and so I made sure to ask her before she vanished, "What do you guys mean when you say divine mission?"

She perched on my wicker laundry hamper and rearranged her stunning gown. "Before you come here you pick a purpose, something to accomplish during your earthly experience. After you choose your purpose, you go on to pick your genes and the family that will best serve you. When you start living your purpose in a human body, then you are fulfilling your divine mission."

"You mean I picked my Uncle Bill? You've got to be kidding." I sat up with a splash.

She laughed. "It will all be revealed in due time. Just know you are loved, supported, and protected. Try your best to connect to anything that makes you feel like a queen. Wear beautiful clothes and continue this beautiful bath time ritual and anything that makes you feel goddess like.

"What is the point of that?"

"It will help you embrace the beauty energy from within. You will be able to channel your inner goddess energy by connecting with these types of things. I need to be going, but get some rest and I will see you soon. By the way, I do like the way you added these feminine touches to the bathroom, especially those antique perfume bottles on the shelf. Just perfect."

Then she turned and disappeared through the mirror as if it was a door.

A visitor from the spirit realm who also compliments me on my bathroom décor? Could life get any stranger? I snuggled up in my pink, fluffy robe ready for a relaxing evening at home, when all of a sudden I felt another crying fit coming on. This had been happening on and off for months. I'd finally learned it was best to surrender to the tears and allow them to flow through me. Sometimes they would last for five minutes and sometimes for an hour. During this particular crying session, I felt the urge to get on my knees on my bathmat.

"Why is all of this happening to me?" I glanced up and shouted in between sobs.

I didn't want to be the weird girl with all these crazy supernatural friends. I didn't understand what was happening to me. I was scared, and even though I had frequent visitors from "the other side," I felt more alone than ever. The Rocket Blast with Jimmy had relieved me of many of my backaches, however the nausea was still on and off. On top of that, with the recent crying episodes—these releases as Bridget called them—I felt harsh stabs of pain in the center of my heart. I'm not sure how long I cried for, but finally I managed to peel myself off the floor and climb into bed.

"Please send me some love and some answers in my dreams," I whispered before falling asleep.

The next thing I knew I was in a dark jungle that didn't seem the least bit familiar to me. My feet sank deep in quicksand-like mud, and I could hear the howls of an animal. Fear welled up in my chest. My right leg started itching and then my left. Mosquitoes were going to town on both of my legs. That was all the motivation I needed to get myself the heck out of this place.

It took all my strength to pull my left foot out of the quicksand. Out of nowhere, an elderly gentleman in a long purple robe with a golden cloak gently took my hands and helped me out of the sand. Quick as wink, I stood with him on a series of wide, uneven stone steps in the middle of a jungle clearing. It was daytime now, and sunlight filtered through enormous trees laced with emerald green vines.

"Whoa, what just happened?" I asked.

"You passed a test. I was only allowed to save you if you first tried to save yourself. Welcome to Peru, Samantha."

"Wow, I have never been to Peru. This place is truly beautiful," I said, doing my best to embrace all of this. I felt so happy that I wasn't waist deep in the quicksand.

"My name is Melchizedek. I am the master of unified consciousness, and I am going to escort you through the cleansing and make sure you are taken care of."

"What cleansing? And it is okay if I just call you Mel?" I knew I would butcher his name.

"Of course, Samantha. You have taken on a lot in your lifetime. Words are powerful, and when used a certain way, they can cause toxins to build up in your cellular memory and tissues. You have started releasing and clearing some of this on your own, and Jimmy helped with some, but you need more help so you can . . . well, get on with things more quickly."

Two men walked up to us wearing only leaves as clothing to cover their goods. Each one reached for one of my arms, and followed by Mel, they guided me down the steps to a path that led deeper into the jungle, past ancient stone monuments and distant mountains. We got to a stream, and the two men scurried around as though they were on a scavenger hunt.

Obviously, I don't really have a choice in the situation.

"They are getting ready to do the cleansing ritual before you drink the *ayahuasca*," Mel said. "It will take them a little bit to get set up, so do you have any questions for me?

"Of course I have questions. What in the heck is *ayahuasca*? Do I have to do this?"

"It is a plant-based drink capable of inducing altered states of consciousness. Let me assure you that we would only do this if you were ready. It can be a bit of a strong cleansing, but you will be well prepared. The shamans and myself are setting the intention that you clear anything blocking light for you, and that you clear any negative toxins or demons that you have picked up along the way. We will all be here with you, holding the space and making sure you are protected. You do not have to do it, but it is highly advised, as this is your third power spot. There is no moving on until you have had the necessary cleansing."

"I have another question," I said. "I want to understand what the physical symptoms I have been having are. My back aches all the way from my tailbone to my neck, I am constantly having crying fits, I feel tingling sensations throughout my body, and my eyes have been stinging and burning. I wake up every night at almost the same time, I get headaches galore, I am often dizzy and think I have vertigo, and I am also having chest pains. What is all of this, and why is it happening?"

"It sounds like you have a variety of things going on. I am not sure I can explain them all to you right now, but I can tackle a few. Often when humans spiritually awaken their spine is sore, because that is the line along which the chakras are and where they open up. This should only be temporary. You are having some of the symptoms of ascension.

"Waking up in the middle of the night is a common theme of people opening up, as this may be the only time your angels can get your attention. They're trying to tell you something. Often, if you write in your journal for a few minutes, you will get their message and then can go back to sleep. They could also be trying to tell you something based on the time you are waking up. Look up the angel meaning of that number to find out." He chuckled, allowing me to see his personality a bit.

"Your eyes are burning," he continued, "because they are readjusting to the things you will be able to see once this process is over. You can see us now when we come to you with messages, but once you are further through this process, you will be able to tune in whenever you want to and ask us questions. Finally, in regard to your crying fits, unfortunately this is also part of human healing. We have to dredge up our pain and consciously feel it in order to let it go. It happens differently for each person, but it appears tears are a way through which you heal and release."

"Well, I must have been doing an awful lot of healing then," I said, feeling quite flabbergasted by his answers.

"You are doing beautifully, Samantha. A human awakening isn't an easy task, otherwise everyone would be doing it and human evolution would have already taken place hundreds of years ago. Stay strong and know you are on the right path."

"What do you mean exactly when you say an awakening isn't an easy task?"

"When we wake up and become aware of who we really are, we have to pass tests in order to prove our trust and our faith. We have to go against logic and trust what we know and believe in our hearts to be true. Often, we have to go against beliefs we have known and carried all our lives, and this can be traumatizing. When awakening, you have to trust yourself and trust your feelings. It's tough not to trust what the logical mind says or what you have known to be true your entire life.

"We have to look our fear straight in the face, and tell it that it no longer has power over us; that we are now in the driver's seat. It takes a lot of strength and courage to do all this, and I must say, as per usual, you are doing exceptionally well."

He gave me an encouraging pat on the back. I needed that, because it sounded like I was just in the beginning phases of what might be a long road to awakening. Mel walked me over to the stream, and with a snap of his fingers I was wearing my favorite bright yellow bikini.

"Hey! How did you do that?"

"All these questions." He smiled and handed me off to the two shaman men who had led me down the path earlier. Now they were accompanied by five Peruvian dudes who all had musical instruments. The musicians started to play, and I was instantly moved by their talent and soothed by the music and the sound of the stream. The two shamans shook branches covered in leaves up and down my body, both front and back. They filled two bamboo bowls with water from the stream, and then blew on them so the water hit my stomach and my back in sync.

"Easy does it, fellas." I just knew their spit was mixed in with the water on my body.

The men then played some sort of fake sword game, stabbing their branches above my head while chanting something I had definitely never heard before. I sat patiently, ready to get this cleansing thing over with, while I watched them do their performance right above my head.

Finally, one of the men brought over a cup and put it to my mouth for me to drink. I hesitated and looked over at Mel. He nodded me to proceed. "Go ahead," he said. "This is where the magic happens."

The drink tasted absolutely disgusting, and I was shocked I was able to down it without spitting it out.

"Gross! A little bit of a warning would have been nice." I shot daggers at Mel.

"Trust me, you would never have gone through with it if you had been warned. You can thank me later."

"Now what?" I was ready to get out of this place ASAP.

"Now we wait."

I sat there for at least thirty minutes thinking this was a total waste of time. The music was still going, so I did my best to enjoy it. Then in my mind's eye, I saw myself standing in the middle of a lush green field filled with white lilies and yellow butterflies. I could smell the fragrance of jasmine trailing along a white fence to my left. I felt a tap on my shoulder and turned around. A man with a dark beard and the sweetest loving smile stood before me. Close to his right stood the most angelic looking woman. She wore a simple blue dress with a white lace headband and headdress, while he had on a white robe. Both of them radiated pure love.

"Are you Jesus and Mary?" I asked, recognizing them from Sunday School classes I attended as a child.

"We are so proud of you," said Jesus in a soft, reassuring tone. "We have been with you, looking out for you, your entire life. We have been waiting for this day."

Now I know it might seem presumptuous to be quizzing Jesus, but every time an angel or guide showed up and said, "We're here for you. All you need to do is reach out," I felt pissed off. "If you guys are with me all the time, then why am I in so much pain? Why is the Brigade still messing with me?"

"Unfortunately, it is part of the human process," said Jesus. "You have to learn to fight off the demons yourself and to not let your ego take over. Otherwise, it will allow them to come in and use your body for dark instead of light."

"That would have been nice to know a few weeks ago." I rolled my eyes.

Mary chimed in. "Samantha, you are doing great. I will give you a clue that will help you. Your mind is so much more powerful than you think. In the human world, what you see in front of you is simply a manifestation of what you think you deserve or what you are attracting. The key to having a smooth transition when you are spiritually awakening is to focus on the good and on love. You see, you get what you focus on. If you let fear take over and you spend your time focusing on fear, ego, or the demons, then that is what you will get more of. If you can focus on the divine and our love, then you get more of that. It is really that simple."

I have to say Jesus and Mary were really cool. It felt so comfortable and so natural to be interacting with them, and I almost felt guilty for not spending more time in church.

"We are honored to escort you to our traveling tunnel of healing light," said Jesus. "The only rule of the tunnel is no talking, so you can be fully present and experience the feelings and the healing powers." He pointed to a corner of the field where the softest pulsating circle of white light grew larger and larger.

"It is time," Mary said softly.

Jesus cradled my left hand, and Mary intertwined her soft fingers through the fingers on my right hand. We slowly walked toward the tunnel of white light. When we reached the entrance, they each embraced me and gently kissed me on my forehead. My eyes filled with tears. I could feel the utter love surrounding me and comforting me, and I thanked them for their help and support.

With my bare feet I felt the loving energy rise up and circulate throughout my entire body as I entered the light. Thousands of little cherubs lined the tunnel and showered me with a golden healing dust. They pointed me to stand on a yellow box in the tunnel. I stepped up on the box, and it felt like a vacuum going in through my crown and sucking away debris from my entire body. I stood frozen in time here, until they waved me off the box. The cherub closest to me was about three feet tall, with baby wings that reached a foot and a half over each of her shoulders. She had beautiful, bright blue eyes, soft pink lips, and pale pink skin. My heart was officially cracked wide open. I stopped just to feel the goodness and the beauty, and I wished I could have stayed in that tunnel for eternity.

But all of a sudden I was on a beach. I felt the warmth of the sand and the ocean breeze exciting every cell on my skin. I looked to the left and saw glistening blue water that went on for miles. Lush green mountains rose up in the distance. Close to shore, the most beautiful man I had ever seen swam toward me and rose up out of the ocean. I was shaking and my stomach filled with butterflies, as he walked toward me. He cradled my face with his hands and leaned in to give me the most amazing gentle and loving kiss.

He held my hand and said, "I love you, Sam. I am so happy to have finally found you."

I swooned, and the most exquisite aching tenderness filled my heart. Apparently, this dreamboat was my boyfriend. I felt the love between us, and it was the love I grew up reading about and dreaming about in fairy tales. This was the love I longed and hoped for, and I had been praying for it on a daily basis. This was what Bridget had been predicting was coming my way.

Next thing I knew, I was standing on top of one of those green mountains overlooking a deep blue ocean with a white and golden castle behind me. The love of my life stood beside me. I looked to my right and realized we were surrounded by the Divine and by angels. My entire family was there, including Anna's parents, and everyone looked so peaceful and happy. My vision expanded to include people in lands faraway, all of them seeing love within themselves and each other.

After what seemed like hours of silent and peaceful bliss and communication with the Divine, this magnificent and gorgeous man—my ultimate love—looked at me and said, "You are on your way. It won't be much longer now. Until then, remember I am here, and I love you, and it's only a matter of time until we are reunited."

I sank to my knees and golden tears poured out of me, tears of loss and gratitude. I melted into the sea, into the sun. I spun through eons and then opened my eyes.

"Mel!" I gasped.

But before I could reach for his hand, I started to projectile vomit. Out of nowhere, the shamans came running to my side with buckets. I puked and puked until I couldn't puke anymore. Throughout this purging I sensed darker visions—vague images that eluded me. I could feel movement around my belly. There was something still inside me, something wanting release.

"You didn't tell me this was going to happen," I moaned.

I leaned over the bucket as something vile and potent filled my throat. I felt as if a snake were writhing inside me. The projectile vomit continued for another fifteen minutes or so, before I collapsed onto the muddy ground in a ball, sobbing. I had always hated to throw up. This was literally like my worst nightmare coming true.

After a couple more hours of darker visions and continued puking which had now become dry heaving, Mel got down on his knees to come to my level. He softly rubbed my back. My stomach and organs were sore. They had literally been rung out. I was exhausted, light headed, and dizzy.

"You are finished now," he said. "I know it was painful, and for that I am sorry. There's no easy way to clear you, so this had to be done. We were here holding space for you, so the healing should be pretty much done. There is still a chance you will experience a bit more of a release later on. Focus on the vision you had earlier, because that is a picture of what your future looks like—as long as you follow through with your divine mission."

I glared up at him. As if I could even think of remembering that right now.

"A woman will be serving as your earthly divine travel agent," he said. "She will help get you where you need to be for your next few power spots. You will find her in perfect timing."

He helped me up off the ground.

"After this do you really think I want to continue on with all this craziness?" I said.

"This was a necessary evil, and you will feel differently tomorrow, trust me." He patted me on the back.

I snored so loudly I woke myself up with a start. I was in my warm, cozy bed. What a relief to be out of the dream. I glanced at the clock—it was four in the afternoon—I'd slept for at least sixteen hours. I needed to get ready for Rose's birthday celebration at La Lune et Le Soleil. I jumped out of bed and noticed I was wearing the same bright yellow bikini from the dream. I shuddered. How weird was that? I must have been sleepwalking and somehow put it on. I headed for the bathroom and stopped dead in my tracks when

I saw my reflection in the mirror. My face was muddy, and my hair was all tangled and strewn with jasmine flowers.

I found my phone and took a selfie. I needed it as evidence, a reminder for those moments when I doubted my sanity. My visit with the shamans was more than just a dream.

Chapter 21

I opened my eyes to see sunlight filtering in through the kitchen window. Every muscle, every bone in my body ached. I was curled up in a ball in front of my altar. I lay there, not moving, as I recalled how Rose's birthday celebration had gone from a joyous event to an evening where I was fighting for my life. I remembered the strange, bitter taste in my throat and my vision blurring as we toasted Rose; the lame excuse I gave Ashley for my abrupt departure; the desperate ride back in the taxi; and the hideous voices that came out of me once I stumbled into my condo. I felt unclean and violated. I'd been in the grip of a demon possession.

"Thanks a lot angels," I muttered.

And then I heard that whisper in my head. *You won, Sam. It's over. The worst is behind you. You did it! We are all so proud of you. You were so brave.*

I felt wiped out, but after a few minutes I managed to get to the phone and call Bridget. I knew I needed a session, and it seemed she knew it too, because for the second time she was just about to drive over to my condo. That's what happens when you're intuitive. You always just sort of know things . . . *Sam's in trouble! She fought a demon! She needs a session!*

When Bridget arrived she made me a cup of tea. She rubbed my shoulders and arms and legs with a healing oil that smelled sweetly pungent. We did a minute of grounding exercises, and then she asked me to tell her exactly what happened, starting with Peru.

I filled her in on the journey and told her about the a*yahuasca.* She made an awful face when I said the word—apparently she'd done it too.

"In real life or a dream?" I asked.

She chuckled. "You'll soon realize that the veil between dreams and what we call reality is tissue thin."

"Obviously," I said with a touch of sarcasm.

But that didn't put a dent in Bridget's loving support. "Go on," she said.

But I didn't want to go on. I had had enough for a while. "Can't I just quit? Can't I say enough, this is as far as I go, and so what if I don't fulfill my purpose?"

"You can quit, as you put it, anytime you want to. Do you think you'll be happy if you do that?"

"I don't know. I feel like I should be getting stronger, clearer. I suppose I am, but it's still hard. The whole trip to Peru was so crazy. Was it real or not? And then the business at Rose's birthday... I swear, I felt like I was fighting for my life with that demon possession."

"On the phone you told me about the voice in your head saying you had won, and that the worst was over. Wouldn't it be a waste of all you have accomplished to quit now?"

I guess she was right. I did realize that I couldn't ever go back to the way I used to be even if I wanted to. I decided to continue.

"After I woke up from my time with the shamans," I said, "all I wanted was to feel normal and have a break from all the craziness. The timing was perfect, because it was Rose's birthday dinner."

She looked at me with sympathy, as if she already knew what I was going to tell her. I explained how I couldn't even make it through dinner and how horrific it felt to have a demon fighting with my body; how disgusting it was to hear its wretched words come out of my mouth.

"Then," I continued, "as if it wasn't bad enough already, the demon started screaming at me in a dark and scary voice within my head." I finished telling her about the trauma my body underwent during the exorcism.

"I just . . . I mean . . . I need to understand all this a little bit better. I have an idea of what happened, because I sensed this thing inside me toward the end of whatever happened in Peru. But I need some validation and more of an explanation."

She closed her eyes and softly said a prayer. She sat there in silence, I guess listening to whomever she was talking to in her head. Then she took a deep breath and looked at me.

"I can give you the answers you are looking for," she said. "You came here with such a bright light, and because of that it appears you were attacked in your mother's womb by a large and aggressive demonic energy."

"Ugh! What do you mean?"

"It was a shaman type of dark energy. It's nature is to attach to powerful beings that carry a lot of light. Your mother also has a large light, and the demon knew that if it pounced too hard you would sacrifice yourself to save her. As a fetus you wanted to protect your mother, not only for her sake but also to protect her womb so that you would come into this world."

Holy crap, this is a lot to digest.

"When this type of demon finds a fetus willing to protect, it will usually attach right away. It looks like the demon pounced and attached the instant it had a chance too. Your mother became vulnerable because she was afraid of something."

"What was my mom afraid of?" I asked.

"It appears that in her mind she associated psychic powers with evilness and being crazy. She knew these abilities were in her family, and she wanted nothing to do with them. It appears that someone was trying to call her out on her psychic lineage, and your mother didn't want to be an outcast like her aunt who had agreed to take on the abilities."

"But why would Mom not want to open up her abilities?" I asked, really confused.

"Times have changed, but even today a lot of this energy work seems woo woo. Back then it was even more so. People wanted to steer clear of it for fear of not being accepted."

"When you put it that way it makes sense. I have been scared to tell my friends what has been going on, and obviously my family isn't at all on board."

"You had been living with this demon your entire life," she said. "It was so big and fierce that it made you forget your truth. It told you that you weren't good enough for things that are your birthright."

As she said this my heart sank, and I felt nauseous.

"You mean I have been carrying that nasty demon around in my body since birth?"

"Yes, because it could serve as a test to see if you could still find love and a joy filled life while being that exposed to darker energy. People who have these attachments really know and understand darker energy."

"I don't understand what you mean. I thought I had a pretty happy and good life up until recently."

"You have, Sam. This particular demon could only try to run you toward darkness. You were strong enough so you could fight it. It appears the Demon Brigade was watching you when you were sent here and has been trying to stop you from fulfilling your mission. The deep cleansing work you did with the shamans in Peru tried to bring forth the release of this thing out of your body. But it was so strong it held on for dear life, and that is why it didn't come out in Peru. However, you did a great job protecting yourself, because you released it last night after Rose's party."

"This seems so awful. Is it normal?"

"It is more normal than you think. Our world is mostly unconscious right now. Most people are unaware of how the darker energies can overcome us. It is so easy to beat them if we are aware they exist, and then we must be aware of all the love and light that exists from God, the universe, and the beautiful enlightened helpers.

"It is an honor to be in a body," she continued. "Five times as many souls exist as there are bodies, yet they all want to come to earth. Only select souls are chosen to do so. Earth is like a school for our souls. We know what we are getting into before we come here.

"There exists a beautiful and exquisite building that is like a library of everyone who has ever lived. It contains all the lives and their histories plus all the life lessons we can choose from. When we are given the chance to choose a body we go into this building. We meet with our Divine Angels to decide on our life lessons. Once we have looked at the options and have their guidance, we enter this beautiful, universal library alone. We pick the seven karmic lessons we would like to learn for the betterment and evolution of our soul." She spoke with confidence, as if this was common knowledge.

She then went on to explain that we actually pick our genes, our IQ, our race, gender, and family. Then we conspire with the universe as to what will best challenge and fit our needs to learn our life lessons.

"The test is to see if we can go down to earth, forget everything we have known for all of history and all our previous lifetimes, be conditioned by our families and by society, and still remember that despite the difficulty of the lessons, we are all one, that all of humanity, ourselves, and God are one. We choose to test ourselves and see if we can get rid of the limiting belief system with which we have been taught and conditioned to learn. We try to enter into an empowering and limitless belief system."

"Are you making this up?" I asked. "How did you learn all of this?" I wondered how in the world I would ever understand everything.

"No," she giggled. "I know it is overwhelming, but think about it. Think of all that has happened to you and how it is all coming together. You wanted to come here, to this planet, and do all of this. Don't you see? This is the moment you were looking forward to in your planning stages for your life. You knew if you could just get to this point, you could achieve your goals for your soul's evolution. This is it Sam. This is happening now for you."

Mind blown, head spinning again. Just when I thought I couldn't be stunned any further, it had happened again.

"Come back to me," she said, noticing I was out in space. "There is more information your angels want you to know. They are telling me you can heal yourself with crystals. But I see you already know that—look at your altar."

With a huge grin, she went over to my alter filled with crystals. "Ah, these are beautiful."

I joined her and filled her in on my experience at Agape in the crystal shop. I had even bought the book, *The Crystal Bible,* so I could learn more. I reassured her that I had been using the grounding crystals as well. Kneeling down in front of the altar, I touched each of the beauties again, to feel their energy. "I bathed them in the ocean water before I came back from Agape. That trip was so magical. How long have you owned your casita?"

She didn't answer, and when I turned to her, I could tell she was having another "conversation" in her head. She nodded, closed her eyes briefly, and then said, "So you are also clear on the fact that you are an empath."

"Apparently so. I found out when I was writing on the way to Agape. I also asked Jimmy about it during the Rocket Blast."

"Jimmy—of course, his treatments are the best. Okay, it's critical you understand this means your body is like a sponge to other people's energy. You soak everything up. I understand you had a protection ritual done at Agape, but you still need to protect your energy. You also need to clean and balance your chakras daily. You should continue to use black tourmaline to protect your energy, and you will soon get a message on how to balance your chakras directly from the Divine.

"When we come here," she said, "we all have a purpose. But when we start to live our purpose and extend it to the greater good of all, it then becomes a divine mission. These are tips that will help you begin your divine mission.

"You are here as a teacher and a healer. You need to understand how to use and protect your energy in order to serve your mission. It is coming through loud and clear that your mission is now, your time is now. All of these tips will also help ease the physical symptoms you have been having. You should try to spend time in nature and be sure to stay in a love vibration. Only do things you enjoy."

She then toured my condo noticing all the changes I'd made thanks to her feng shui book. "This makes me so happy, Sam. You have made your home a sanctuary. This will help lift your frequency and help you grow spiritually." She gave me a huge hug. "Congratulations, this is going to be fun."

With that she whisked out of my apartment.

I stood there, alone. I believed everything Bridget had told me. I also sensed that my struggles were far from over.

Chapter 22

The Demon Brigade

Sneeth, Skanky, and the Brigade huddled around a big screen by their scum pond pulling out Sam's old lives. The torture scenes were their favorites—a roar went up from this hideous crew whenever they saw Sam wincing in pain. They loathed her, recognizing her as one of the elite from Atlantis, and they longed to take her down. Her last several lives on earth weren't happy times, and usually she was persecuted as she attempted to carry out her sacred and divine missions.

"The one with the witch hunt!" the junior demons cried." Please please, let's see that again!"

"Which one?" Sneeth said with a leer. He twisted the hair coming out of his ear as his minions groveled at his feet. "The one where she and her two buddies are burned at the stake together for their witchery? Or how about the one where we sent the whole town after her, the one where she is stoned to death?"

The ugly cries of cruel delight grew louder until that life flashed on the screen. That time Sam was hated and betrayed by almost everyone she loved. Although she only used white magic and wanted to help the world, she was an outcast and lived a solitary life. The Brigade got bored when they watched the scenes where the people in her town were desperate and allowed her to help them. The people she helped pleaded with her not to tell anyone what she had done, because they would in turn be persecuted. Of course, she agreed to and honored their requests.

During these scenes of compassion, the Brigade chattered amongst themselves. They threw rocks at the screen and dipped their fingers into the scum pond and licked them clean.

"Pay attention. Now we are getting to the good part," Skanky growled.

The demons hawked lugies and laughed hysterically, as tears streamed down her cheeks. Even when Sam was being tied up so they could stone her to death, she spoke words of love. She was able to see the good in everyone, and to understand that people only treated her that way because they were buried so deep in fear.

Thick ropes bound her ankles together. A pair of dirty hands wrapped another rope around her waist.

"Man, this was the best. We got her good in that lifetime," said Sneeth with a snarl.

The demons sat back and kicked up their hairy feet. They laughed loudly at Sam's winces of pain, their bellies bouncing up and down. They murmured with happiness when the final rope secured her to the stake. Their eyes grew wide with delight, as the first sharp stone left a razor-like slash across her cheek.

Suddenly, the images on the screen froze. The demons jumped in agitation. Several of them rushed towards Sneeth, shrieking their displeasure.

"More!" they hollered.

"SHUT UP!" Sneeth roared.

A silence fell upon the stinking, restlessly shifting crowd.

Sneeth turned to Skanky. "Did you see it?"

"Uh, see what? The look on her terrified, young face?" Skanky asked.

"No you moron." Sneeth started the images again, this time in slow motion. "Look at the main perpetrator. Look at who is throwing the biggest stones. Look at who is hurling then with all his might."

Skanky peered at the screen. "Dunno. Who is it?"

"I don't know why I even fool with you, you idiot! It is her Uncle Bill. He hated her just as much in that lifetime and for the same reason. We need to keep a close watch on him. If we get inside him, we can use him to take her down."

"Good idea boss." Skanky nodded eagerly.

Sneeth was not convinced. He kicked at his skeletal henchman who slithered just out of reach.

"I'm on it!" Skanky shrieked. "I promise, boss. You won't be disappointed."

Chapter 23

After Bridget left my condo, I decided to take her suggestion and spend more time in nature. I drove an hour and a half up to the mountains. I wished I had Honey with me. Man, did I need her love about now. I felt so alone, and I needed support. I wanted to tell Anna or Rose what was going on, but I didn't want them to think I was crazy.

I parked at the end of a gravel road where the trailhead was clearly marked with a big green sign. Within ten minutes I was alone in nature. I tried to settle into the moment and enjoy the wild flowers and the birds, but my mind was elsewhere. It seemed the more "information" I received and the closer I got to my path, the more questions I had.

What does being a teacher and a healer mean?

What am I supposed to do with all of this?

How could I have lived with a demon inside me all this time and not even have known it?

"Don't be so hard on yourself, Sam," said the ghost man who had appeared out of nowhere, grinning. "You can call me Ted."

"I guess you got tired of me thinking of you as ghost man," I muttered.

"The demonic energy you carried has got you freaked out, hasn't it? You're going through a lot, but you should know a big part of self-love is learning not to be so hard on yourself. Trust me when I say that you are doing amazing. When I was in your shoes, I got buried in the fear. Instead of recognizing the demons voices as not being me, I allowed them to take over.

"Having to fight off the Brigade is part of the learning that takes place on this planet, for now anyway," he said. "The goal is to get as many people as possible to become aware of what's going on so we can take the Brigade out. It will shift everyone toward love and away from fear."

"How do you shift out of fear? My fear seems to be increasing."

"Buddy . . . a big part of the test while we are here is to trust and surrender to the divine. Think of the love, grace, and support you feel each time you have been in the presence of one of the Angels, Goddesses, or Ascended Masters. Each time you are scared or have doubt, focus on that and feel the love. The Brigade will not stand a chance. Be proud of yourself too, for all the courage you have displayed. When I was alive, I wasn't very good to anyone around me. In fact, I was awful." He looked down at his feet.

"Don't feel bad," I said. "I'm sure there was a reason." I could tell he felt ashamed, and I didn't like seeing him upset. He had always been so kind and chipper with me.

"I'm doing everything in my power to amend the mistakes I made," he said. "You can call on me for anything. I am here for you, I promise. Try not to be scared, and trust that all your angels have your back."

"Thank you," I said. "I know I grumble about the way you guys show up at the most unexpected times, but I need and enjoy the messages and reassurance."

His face lit up, and I was reminded again how being acknowledged feels so good.

"So can you not get some other clothes? I'm growing a little weary of that *blah zeh* outfit of yours," I said with a wink.

"Oh, you want to get smart. Let's play hide and seek then." Poof! He was gone, just as quickly as he had appeared.

"I'll get you next time," I called out.

Feeling relieved and not so alone, I continued hiking and drinking in the cool mountain air. In the late afternoon I finally looped back to my car.

As I opened my car door, I had the unsettling feeling that I shouldn't drive. But it was getting dark, and what else could I do? Walk back home? I got in, locked the doors, and headed home in the fading light. The narrow road seemed eerily quiet. I told myself of course, it's a weekday, no one drives up here to hike. I drove with care, paying attention to the twists and turns, when suddenly the lights of a huge Mac truck swept rapidly up the mountain. I thought he was going to lose control and tumble down the side. The headlights disappeared from view, and then as I rounded a sharp corner the truck came barreling toward me taking up both lanes. I had nowhere to turn. I laid on the horn and screamed for it to stop. My heart almost shot out of my chest. I was going to be pulverized by this truck.

The familiar voice in my head spoke with more urgency than ever before. *Hold on tight, and do not move. KNOW that you are safe!*

I closed my eyes and held on tight waiting for impact. Instead, I had this weird swooping feeling in my gut. I peeked one eye open only to see that my car was literally flying above the truck that continued at its insane speed. While I was in the air, I had a vision of Uncle Bill in the driver's seat, his face twisted with malice as he came at me. Seconds later I was back on the road. With a pounding heart, I pulled to a stop, jumped out, and looked up the road. No lights in sight, just the sound of crickets chirping their nightly chorus. I wept with relief, leaning against my car, waiting for my hands to stop shaking so I could continue on my way.

A cool breeze stirred the trees behind me, and I turned to see the most beautiful being wearing a lacey, light turquoise gown. Her white wings were exceptionally large and covered in drops of iridescent pink. Two small deer stood on her right, and a dove perched on one outstretched arm. At her feet sat a dog.

"Honey!" I gasped. My beautiful dog, wagging her tail next to an angel. I dropped to my knees to pet her, but the angel gently stopped me.

"Hello, Samantha. I am Archangel Ariel, and I am sorry we had to intervene like that with the truck, but there was no other way to save you."

"You mean you picked my car up? How is that even possible?"

"One of my specialties is divine magic," she said. "After all, what do you think it means to be divinely protected darling?"

"Ummm . . . I hadn't really thought about it. I guess you do have a point. Oh please, can I pet Honey?"

"I am sorry, but you cannot touch her. I wanted to bring her though, because she is now also assisting in your healing. She has a message for you. She wants me to tell you that she misses being with you, and she is doing everything she can to help you from over here. She is also insisting that I warn you about the Brigade and how they have a hold on your Uncle Bill."

"Oh, trust me, I have already been warned."

"We want you to understand the gravity of this situation. Uncle Bill is unconsciously working with them, and they are feeding his animosity toward you. Since you were on my watch when the truck came for you, I was able to step in and save you. I am so happy to meet you, Samantha. Please know that we always have your back."

Her words started to sink in, and the vision I'd had as the car soared over the truck now made stomach churning sense. "So my uncle was seriously trying to kill me just then?"

"Unfortunately, yes," she said. "You need to steer clear of him as best you can. We have to go now, but we will be with you from afar the entire way home. Just drive safely, and get some rest when you get there."

Tears streamed down my face as I looked at Honey. She wagged her tail and woofed softly.

"Honey, sweet baby girl, thank you for all the love and happiness you brought me over the years. I miss you so much, and I am sorry that I never got to give you a proper goodbye. I hope to see you again soon."

"She knows all of this and says she isn't going anywhere," Ariel assured me. "Goodbye, Samantha. Please know that you are adored and loved and that everyone is so proud of you."

Whoosh—Ariel soared into the night sky with her animal posse.

Ted was right, the angels really do have my back, I thought as I cranked my car and flicked on the headlights. I had been saved once again, but the news that Bill was so vindictive took much of the glory away.

I can't believe that Uncle Bill would actually go through with something like this. How am I going to make it through this alive? That man always gets what he wants.

I trembled the entire drive home.

Chapter 24

After my angel assisted my escape on the mountain, I worked on strengthening my energy every morning. I imagined bright white light flowing from the top of my head down through my spine and clearing out my chakras. I then imagined myself inside a bright white bubble with a green light surrounding it and followed by a purple light. I noticed if I did this the way my angels had taught me, my days went much smoother. The practice helped me release some of my fears that Uncle Bill was on a death hunt for me.

After what went down at Rose's birthday party, I realized I needed to make an appearance with my friends again. If not, they would think I had gone crazy. Uncle Bill was so manipulative, I worried he'd find a way to use them against me. Besides, I felt lonely. I missed hanging with Ashley, Jacob, and Sara. I proposed we meet at Fontaine's that Thursday, and they all agreed.

"Act normal, act normal," I whispered to myself as I entered the restaurant. "Don't be talking about angels and demons and chakras." But what was normal? Maybe I was the new normal? Did I really want to spend an hour catching up on reality shows or gossiping or talking about the awful stuff happening in the news? We sat down, and I already wished I was at home reading or meditating. I felt calmer since Rose's birthday dinner, and I still loved my friends, so I decided to share some of my new interests with them.

"Have you guys ever watched Super Soul Sunday?"

"Super what?" asked Ashley.

"It's a show that Oprah hosts—Sundays at ten in the morning. Each week she has guests who talk about ways to get in touch with your truth and with your higher self. Last week it was a repeat of Maya Angelou's visit, and I was honestly moved to tears."

"Ten on a Sunday? That is waaay too early," said Sara.

"We miss you, Sam," said Jacob. "We were worried about you after last time. That stomach bug sounded horrible. But come on, have some fun with us! When are you going to start drinking mind erasers with us again?"

"You guys, I have been through a lot with Lucas, Honey, and then losing my job," I said. "I'm starting to see things a little differently."

"That's fine," said Sara. "But it looks to me like you still think you're a victim. Start dating." She was full of advice as usual. "And get another job. Sitting alone in your condo is such a cop out. Come on. Have some fun with us already."

I didn't respond, and Sara ordered another round of Red Bull and vodkas. I don't know why it bothered me so much, but I didn't want my friends to think I was wacko or cray cray. It was hard enough for me to deal with all this on my own. But as I sat there listening to them being so judgmental toward our other friends and gossiping about what they thought was best for them, I realized that the people I used to be friends with, and the things I used to do, were no longer of interest to me. I wasn't judging Sara and Jacob and Ashley, but I had definitely moved on from my old life. There was no turning back now.

When we finished dinner, I decided to go home and not join them as they headed downstairs to do more drinking at Highland Tap. I'd just bought *Spirit Junkie* by Gabrielle Bernstein, and I couldn't wait to read it. When I got home I made a cup of herbal tea, rubbed on some frankincense, my new fave essential oil, and flipped through the chapters. My eyes were immediately drawn to chapter nine, "Spirit Became My Boyfriend."

Oh my God, that is where I am right now. I'm not alone!

In that moment, I again had the feeling that the universe supported me. Spirit had become my boyfriend, and I was seriously in love. And when you're in love you have to tell someone. Anna! She was the one person I knew who would understand my journey.

I texted her. *Hey Anna. I am ready to tell you everything that has been going on with me. Can you come over tomorrow please?*

Yes! She replied. *I've missed you! See you tomorrow. I have a few stories of my own.*

I picked up Gabby Bernstein's book again, and because it was such a beautiful evening, I went outside to the porch. Guess who was there—Papa Jack, one of my friendly ghosts.

"Hey, baby doll!"

"Hey, Papa Jack!" I was actually excited to see him. He reminded me so much of my dad, and in that moment I wished my dad lived closer and didn't have to travel so often.

"You have had a lot going on, huh?" he asked.

"That is the understatement of the year, Papa." I sighed.

"Well, I just wanted to let you know that in the human and egoic world everyone perceives imagination as your own, but in reality imagination is just internal communication with the Divine."

"Whoa, can you say that again?"

"I know you have been wondering if you are crazy or making this all up, and I wanted to let you know that you aren't, obviously, or we wouldn't be having this conversation." He grinned. "Part of the human experience is to communicate with the Divine through your imagination. As humans, we think it is our own selves, because in our ego based world we do anything we can to separate our selves. That is just the way society functions, and it is what everyone believes. But the truth is that any imagination is Divine communication."

"Wow, that is interesting." I couldn't help but smile. Who'd have ever thought I'd be having this kind of conversation with a dead grandparent?

"Listen sugar, you have got to understand that having these abilities and gifts is in your DNA. You inherited this from both sides of your family."

Papa Jack's words confirmed what I had been reading about inheriting psychic ability. I just didn't realize the extent to which it ran through my lineage.

He motioned for me to sit beside him on my wicker couch. "I have so much regret from my life, because I chose to bury my pain and fear with alcohol. Now I have so much gratitude for the opportunity to assist you. Not only are you helping me to grow and evolve, but you are allowing me to live vicariously through you."

"Thanks, Papa Jack."

"I also want you to know that I always tried to be a good father to your dad. You don't know much about the situation, but my liver gave out. Instead of facing my demons, the way you are so bravely doing, I buried myself deep in fear and turned to alcohol. My family and my children gave me more joy then they will ever know. Now isn't the time, but when your dad is ready, tell him that he filled me with joy."

"I will. He has fond memories of you. I can tell by the way he talks about you. You died when he was so young, that he doesn't remember much."

"Sugar, I want you to understand more about your lineage. It's extremely powerful. You picked your parents because together they could pass on the genes you needed to be able to see the future and to communicate with the Divine. In fact, the aunt your mom mentioned on the phone is still alive. Your Uncle Bill despised her so much, he threatened her life if she did not disappear. He tried to get her to shut down her abilities, but she wouldn't do it. She knew they were God given gifts, and she was determined to stand in her truth."

"Where did she go, and what has she been doing all these years? If Mom and Dad have these abilities, then why don't they see you the way I do?"

"Because they, like most people in today's world, have clogged their psychic channels with fear and other blocks. What we eat, our thoughts, our expectations, the energy of the spaces we live in, so many things can block us. Most importantly, you have to be aware and willing to feel your pain. You must allow your pain to heal to fully open up your divine channels. Your great aunt is somewhere living her divine mission."

"But surely you know where she is. Can't you—I don't know—fly around and find out?"

Papa Jack chuckled. "The spirit world doesn't work that way. I'm just a messenger. I want you to be aware though, so you can understand your family history better."

"I was just teasing with ya. So is it true that everyone can do this? I mean, can everyone in a human body actually communicate with the Divine?"

"In a sense, yes. Everyone has a sixth sense, meaning his or her intuition. What varies, depending on karma and your goals for this lifetime, is the depth in which you can take on these abilities."

"I think I sort of understand. But when is the shift going to happen? It doesn't feel like many people are ready to be exposed to this sort of thing right now."

"It will happen sooner than you think, and it will all be in perfect divine timing. I have to get going. Know that I love you, and I am treasuring our conversations and time together." He leaned over and gave me kiss on the forehead.

"Good bye, Papa Jack. I love you, and this is fun to get to know you."

He disappeared with a wave and a smile.

I picked up my book, turned off the porch lights, and went inside. I shook my head as I went upstairs. *I certainly never knew I could have feelings so strong and so loving for my dead grandfather.*

Chapter 25

The next morning, I heard a knock on the door and ran downstairs. Anna! I couldn't wait to tell her what had been going on with me. I flung open the door, and to my surprise, there stood Mrs. Warren, my mysterious and aloof neighbor. She wore her normal sleek grey bun and soft pink lipstick.

Oh, no. Busted. Surely she'd seen the few flowers I still pinched from her garden for Honey's grave.

"Hi, Mrs. Warren. Um, can I help you with something?"

"Good morning, Samantha. Please do call me Jane."

She peered around me into my condo. She sniffed. "Sage. I do love that scent."

"I got it in Sedona," I said with a grin.

"A magical place."

This was the first time I'd had more than a passing hello with her. Her eyes were a sparkling green, and I really wasn't sure of her age. I'd thought she was an older woman, maybe in her sixties, but she had a glow about her skin that made her seem ageless.

She sighed and pulled a manila envelope out of her bag. I could tell she was stalling. What on earth was going on?

"Samantha, I am going to go ahead and get right to the point. My mission in life is to assist others on their divine missions. I am an intuitive healer, but I am also a travel agent. I have been getting messages that I am to assist you."

"What?" I said and burst out laughing.

She looked a bit startled, and I quickly explained. "I can't believe this. I totally love to travel, and here you are telling me that you're going to help me. I see angels every day, and now there is a real life human—I mean a wonderful lady—stopping by my door to offer help."

She chuckled. "This is what happens when you align with your purpose, my dear. I am here to assist you to some of your power spots. You are going to have so much fun. In this envelope is everything you will need. The smaller, purple envelopes are dated so you know when to open them. Now listen, this is key. Do not open anything before you are supposed to, as that could interrupt the flow of how this should unfold."

"Do you want to come in?" I said. "I have some questions."

"That is very sweet, but I really can't. I will give you my cell in case you need me or have any troubles with your travels. Although I highly doubt you will, as everything is set up perfectly." She handed me the manila envelope.

I stood there trying to digest what had just happened. "By the way, the red door is beautiful."

As she drove off in her purple Mini Cooper, Anna pulled up. I ran back inside and put the envelope in a drawer, because I definitely didn't know how I was going to explain that to Anna.

"Hey, Sam." Anna walked in and wrapped her arms around me. "You look great. You have a glow about you."

I had read about how you get a natural glow of beauty about you when you start living your truth. I was so glad to hear Anna compliment me, as it was the motivation and validation I needed.

"I'm so happy to finally be able to talk to you about what has been going on with me," I said.

"I am so curious. Please do tell."

I poured us some fruit-infused water and led her to the porch. "Okay, I know this is all going to sound really crazy, so just bear with me. Do you remember a while back when we had a conversation about human evolution? You said you didn't know much about it, but you had a gut feeling that we are living in the tribulation times."

"Yes, totally."

"Good, so I have been reading about this. It turns out that the planets are aligned in a unique way right now, and the energy frequency we usually live in has been lifted. We humans have an opportunity to tap into our sixth sense and make a major shift for positivity in the world. It is complicated to explain. Am I making any sense?"

Anna grabbed my hand and squeezed it tight. "You sure are, and I have things to tell you. All these weird moments of synchronicity keep happening to me. Yesterday I was at the Pizza Shack picking up lunch for the kids, and I saw three people dressed in costumes from Alice in Wonderland. It was bizarre, because just that morning I'd been reading the book with my daughter. These people were so friendly and started chatting me up. I asked them to take a picture with me, because I knew the kids would love it. They told me they were in town for the psychic fair, just down the block, and asked me to check it out with them. The pizzas were going to be another twenty minutes, so I figured why not."

"Oh my gosh, Anna, this is hilarious."

"Well, to make a long story short, I somehow ended up in a tent with a lady in her twenties who said she was born able to read people's energy. She told me I had massive potential in this lifetime, and then she mentioned this shift you are talking about. She didn't give me many details, but she said she could see tension between me and my father."

"Uh oh. What is going on with you and your dad? I thought it was just me he was upset with." And then an even worse thought came to mind. *Surely he wouldn't be going after his own daughter.*

"Ugh, don't get me started," she said. "He is on his high horse about this dang election. I am so tired of him thinking that everyone in the world is out to stalk his family and take him down. He needs to relax and get over himself."

"I couldn't agree more."

"Anyway, the lady at the fair said it was critical for me not to react to him when he has an anger fit. She said I need to understand that whether it is him or anyone else, when someone yells or acts out toward me it is actually just a reflection of how they feel about themselves. She told me to notice when this happens and to remember her words, that I shouldn't take things personally anymore. Then she said she was doing an energy healing and clearing on me. I could feel this rush of energy leaving my body."

Relief flooded through me. "I have been going through something similar and have been exposed to so much."

"I could tell that day on the phone something was really off with you, but your words resonated with me when you said I had psychic ability. I don't know why, because I would never have thought of that."

"I have been seeing and talking to Papa Jack, my dad's dead father." Tears came to my eyes as I said this. I could feel him right there in the room with us.

"What? How? Are you sure?"

"I don't know how. It just sort of happened one day. Yes, I am sure, because I can see him when we are talking. He has been by a few times, and I have also communicated with angels and some other pretty far out things too. I felt like I was going insane at times, but now I'm getting used to it. I have a sort of coach that has been helping me through this transition in my life, as I have no idea what the new rules are or what to expect."

A look of concern crossed Anna's face. "Please tell me you have not mentioned this to your parents or mine. My dad will have you locked up in an institution if he gets wind of this. I hate to say that about my own dad, but honestly, this campaigning has made him power hungry. He'll do anything to win."

Umm, you don't know the half of it, Anna. Your father is actually trying to kill me, but he wants the family to think he just wants me locked up.

I decided it would definitely not be in Anna's best interest to share this information with her. She looked so sad as she spoke of her father. I promised Anna I'd stay clear of him. I told her that I too thought he seemed changed—and not for the better—when he showed up at my doorway unannounced a few weeks ago.

She then spoke of how venomous he sounded when he spoke of his aunt, our great aunt. "He won't even tell me her name or how she died." Her face lit up. "I know what you need to do. Call your mom and at least pretend to have a normal job interview or something. That way they'll back off and leave you alone."

"That's a great idea. I will come up with a plan."

She had to leave to get back to her kids but gave me a huge hug first.

"Thank you, Anna. I love you too. To be honest, I am so relieved, as I wasn't sure how you were going to react to all this." I squeezed her tight and once again felt that flood of relief and gratitude for her unconditional love and support.

After Anna left I wanted to clear my head, so I walked into the forest behind the condo and sat in the presence of the trees and the birds. I leaned against the wide oak tree right beside Honey's grave and cried tears of gratitude. Even though I didn't tell Anna everything, to just be able to tell her I had been communicating with angels and dead people, and for her not to wince, made me feel so loved and supported.

I settled into meditation, focusing on my breath. The wind picked up and got stronger and stronger. I opened my eyes to see a giant, blurry ball of fuchsia and red light flying toward me.

Within a flash the ball of light turned into a funnel like a tornado, but the wind had stilled and the tornado oozed happiness and love. As I looked up in awe, the funnel transformed into the most beautiful mystical angel. Her silvery long hair was gathered into a braid that reached her hips. She wore an oversized silk fuchsia gown with diamonds dripping off the end of each of her sleeves. She held a crystal ball in one hand and wore a smile that looked like she knew how to get into trouble.

"How are you, beloved?" The words slid out of her mouth like butter.

"Do you want the generic 'I'm okay' answer or something more complex?" These surprise angel visits always caught me off guard. I couldn't help being cocky. Besides, I'd learnt that it was fun to tease a celestial being.

"Sassy Sam. A girl after my own heart." She gave me a devilish smile—at least for an angel—and then looked into her crystal ball. "Wow, I am seeing a bright future for you."

"That's what everyone keeps telling me."

"Forget what everyone says, how do you feel? What do you believe in your heart and in your core to be true?"

"I actually believe it, although sometimes I'm not sure why."

"Ah ha! Because you are learning to listen to your inner wisdom. Bravo." She gave me a soft and slow round of applause.

"Let me guess," I said with a smirk. "You are here with a critical message for me?"

"You think?" She threw my attitude right back at me. Then her face softened into the most loving smile. "I am Archangel Uriel, and I am here because you need to do healing work from a past life before you can move forward on your journey. You see, you and Lucas have been together for three previous lifetimes."

"What? I thought I had only one past life with him. Do you have to have more lives to have a soul contract with someone?" I wondered when in the heck I was ever going to understand all this.

"Easy, Sam. I am going to give you a divine download so you can see for yourself what it is you need to know to heal for now. You may find more out in time, but this is what you need to know for the healing today."

Archangel Uriel explained that angels often give us information we need to keep moving forward on our journey. "If you hear ringing in your ears that's a sign you have been given a divine download.

But this time I will give it to you via touch." She leaned in close and touched the crown of my head.

Instantly, I was transported back to the early 1800s. Green fields, a river, narrow muddy dirt roads, and small homes with plumes of smoke rising out of the chimneys. I sensed I was married to Lucas, but it wasn't a joyful time. I felt the presence of a harsh, domineering woman, Lucas's mother. I gasped, because I realized that she and Damon were one and the same. I then saw myself going around the town and neighboring ones rescuing abused and abandoned children. Many of them were girls cast out to live on the streets. I saw myself sitting at a wooden table: Lucas's mother was pointing at me and yelling about how much embarrassment I brought to the family. I didn't really care what she thought though, I knew I had a mission, and I was determined to follow through with it.

I came back to the present time under the oak tree and said to Uriel, "I don't understand. What does all that mean?"

"In that particular lifetime you were married to Lucas, and he had his twin brother now as his mother then. The pattern between you and his mother in that lifetime is similar to the one between you and Damon in this lifetime. In the past life, you married Lucas young, and you were always together. You were very powerful, and your powers in that lifetime made Lucas feel small. His mother could see that, and she didn't like you. She thought you were not good for her son."

I had another flashback to the past life: Lucas and his mom were sitting outside on some stones in front of a fire, and I heard her say to Lucas, "You need to leave her. You deserve better." Lucas stared gloomily at the fire. He didn't want to admit to his mother that he loved me dearly, and that he was simply intimidated by my sense of purpose. Along with rescuing children, I was a no holds barred ballbuster for the women's movement. Lucas had gotten a banker's job so he could support our family, but I wanted to give most of the money to charity to establish orphanages.

"Although you were doing a good service," said Uriel, "many people didn't like it, because you were causing an uproar in society. Lucas's mother thought it was appalling and embarrassing. You and Lucas had a tumultuous love affair in that life, the same way you did in this life. A lot of high highs and low lows. Damon dislikes you so intensely because he carries within the tension from past lifetimes with you. He is terrified of losing his brother in this life time. Lucas feels the pull bleeding through to this lifetime, as well. That is why it was so hard for him to commit to you and to put you first."

"Holy moley. I felt that tension so strongly in the vision. As crazy as all this sounds, I know you are telling me the truth. It is so sad. How often does this happen? Are we all walking around unaware of our connections to others from past lifetimes?"

"All the time. It is part of your learning experience to see what happens and how you will fair under different circumstances. The good news for you is you noticed the tension, and you knew to listen to your gut and move on. The healing today is not actually between you and Lucas, but between you and Damon. It is for both of your higher selves. You do not want to walk away from this causing any further damage with him."

"Okay, so what do I need to do?"

"You need to write a letter to Damon and tell him you never had bad intentions. Tell him how much you loved Lucas, and how all you really wanted was love and happiness for the two of you. Tell him you didn't understand why he didn't like you. Clearly state that you understand now and that you forgive him."

"I don't think it will go over very well if I give him a letter like that."

"Oh, oops, I left out a crucial detail," she said with a giggle. "You don't need to give him the letter. In fact, you will want to burn it afterward. It's just a healing ritual so you both can let go of this and move forward. It is sort of like you are taking care of unfinished business from hundreds of years ago."

"I'm on it. That letter will be written tonight."

"Smart thinking. You got this, my dear. Stay strong and brave." She blew me a kiss and went back into the funnel of love. It floated off in the same blurry ball of light she had shown up in.

I went inside to grab a pen, some paper, and a match. As I opened the drawer, I couldn't believe I had almost forgotten about my new travel agent friend and that I had directions for my next power spot.

I had better write this letter so I can see what is in store for me next!

Chapter 26

Inside the plain brown manila envelope that Jane had given me, I found three smaller purple envelopes with my name written on the front of each in elegant calligraphy: SAMANTHA KINGSTON. Remembering her instructions, I carefully opened the one with today's date. I pulled out a plane ticket and a white note card with several sentences written in emerald green ink.

> Dear Samantha,
>
> I am so excited to have the privilege to be assisting you. Your next power spot is somewhere in Croatia and will be revealed to you when the time is right. There are no specific instructions. It's time for you to tune in and trust your intuition. Do whatever sounds good and feels good to you at that moment. Be sure to take the other envelopes with you, as your travels will continue on after you have reached your fourth power spot. There will be a man in Split holding a sign with your name on it. I do hope you enjoy traveling business class. And don't forget to pack your favorite bikini and sunscreen, and be ready for an adventure!
>
> Much Love,
> Jane

Wow, I couldn't believe how the world was unfolding for me. Just a few days earlier, while searching "coolest island vacations in the world," I'd seen photos of Hvar, Croatia, and I had noticed that you fly into Split to get there. Did Jane have a camera in my condo? Maybe she'd accessed my computer. I chuckled at the thought of sweet Jane being a hacker. No, this was angel power and divine intervention. She was connected, and boy was she tapping in.

I texted Claire who was working in Seattle with clients all month.

> *Croatia! I'm going tomorrow.*
> *Lucky!!! Pack me in your suitcase!!*
> *Next time!* ☺

The flight from Atlanta took fourteen hours with a change of planes in Frankfurt, where I ate way too many chocolates. I spent time wondering about my mission and the purpose of this trip. Then I flashed back to Hiro—funny Hiro leaping around his rickety mountain home telling me to have fun.

Could it really be as simple as that?

Maybe it was. I opened a new journal I'd brought along for the trip and wrote in bold letters at the top:

POWER SPOTS AND THE LESSONS

Power spot 1. Sedona - I learned that I can see angels, and that one of my missions in this lifetime it is to have fun. I also learned that I have a beautiful protective shield to protect me from any negative spirits coming in attaching to me! Halleluiah! In Sedona it became clear that there is so much more to life than meets the eye.

Power spot 2. Agape - Jimmy was able to clear away old toxins and some of the cellular memory that had tainted my body. I learned that I'm an empath. I had my first past life vision, and I learned about the magical world of crystals and their powers.

Power spot 3. Peru - Mel helped me understand what it means to ascend, and why I have been having unusual physical symptoms. He taught me the importance of how you get what you focus on. So in order to move forward, put all your energy and attention on your dreams and what you want to happen. This is where I began to understand that a lot of this is a mind game.

After landing in Split, I went straight to baggage claim and got my bag. I walked out and saw a nice young gentlemen with a sign that said, "Come with me, Samantha Kingston J." A funny way of putting it. But I did like the smiley face; it seemed to be a trademark of my angel team.

"Hello, I'm Samantha. Do you speak English?"

"Hello, beautiful. Welcome," he said with a charming grin. "Yes, follow me, and let me help you with your bag."

We walked to his van, and he told me we had an hour's drive to get to the speedboat. I felt like I was in a James Bond movie. "Sounds good to me," I said.

The town was quiet, and when we drove into the countryside I caught glimpses of the piercing blue sea. We eventually pulled up to a harbor, where I saw a huge speedboat with a line of people waiting to get on board. The driver took my bag up the steep gangway and onto the boat. Once everyone was settled, we sped off across the sea. The coastline was jagged with green mountains jutting out to create little islands throughout the Adriatic.

When we docked at Hvar I couldn't believe this was my stop. The small and ancient town had marble streets and walls from the thirteenth century. It looked even cooler in real life than it did in the pics I had seen online. I checked into my hotel and got a room with floor to ceiling windows that opened up to a view of the bay studded with luxury yachts and smaller fishing boats. I drank in the fresh air, and a cool breeze brushed lightly across my skin. One thing was for sure, I was digging this place already.

I spent the first day walking the border of the island. I loved the way the water clashed against the white stone and how so many buildings resembled Romanian palaces. Locals smiled at me, and I browsed the open air market where I bought a pair of oversized circular shell earrings and a tiny bottle of lavender. In a café overlooking the harbor, I enjoyed fresh mussels and a homemade strawberry tart drizzled with chocolate. I even treated myself to a glass of red wine, since I hadn't had any in so long.

Walking home after dinner, I passed more outdoor cafes where people were drinking and eating and laughing. Music floated into the wide stone street. One particular beat grabbed my attention. I couldn't understand the words, but I felt drawn to the energy coming from what seemed to be a dive bar with a fun atmosphere. I couldn't help myself. I sashayed right in and started dancing on the dance floor. Some local men were dancing too, and they seemed pretty harmless. Besides, I trusted my instincts. Every bone in my body said, "Girl, you gotta dance!"

Two other girls joined me soon after. "Ciao bella!" said one of them as she shimmied to the beat. "Hahaha, we loved the way you pranced right in and took over the dance floor. We love to party, let's have some fun!" We danced and laughed for several songs.

"Hey, do y'all want to walk outside and cool down?" I asked.

"Yeah, what is your name?" asked the brunette with curls and a porcelain face.

"Samantha. And you?"

"I'm Adriana, and this is Fina," said the chubbier blonde with a big smile.

These two girls had the best energy. They told me they were from Italy, and they led bike tours all over Croatia and Europe. It was cool to see how joyful they were and how much they loved their work. After another hour or so of dancing with the girls, I realized how exhausted I was.

"Thank you for such a fun night and for entertaining me," I said.

"It was our pleasure, bella. Don't forget to go to Dubrovnik and check out the kayaking. You can kayak around the stone city walls, and it's absolutely amazing."

"Sure thing," I said. It sounded awesome, but I was well aware of the fact I wasn't the one making the decisions for what I was doing or where I was going. I would let my adventures simply unfold. I fell asleep listening to the waves lapping against the stone walls and was officially in heaven.

The next morning I enjoyed the beautiful spread of fresh fruit and the omelet bar at the hotel. The waitress served me a decaf cappuccino with a heart in the foam—delicious. I didn't have any idea what I was supposed to do other than listen to my gut and look out for signs. I overheard the couple next to me talking about a hiking path that led to a fortress at the top of the island. It sounded great and fun too. That was sign enough for me.

After breakfast, I walked to the end of the main town and found the path the man had been referring to. The path began with a long row of stairs heading to the top of the stone city. When I finished with the steps, I started up the hiking trail. It was steep, and I stopped often to catch my breath and enjoy the stunning views. I was on an island out in the middle of nowhere in the Adriatic, and in every direction were other islands rising out of the blue sea.

When I reached the fortress, I explored its stone terraces and rooms. I even went briefly into the dungeon, a cold, dank place that totally gave me the creeps; especially when I remembered the warning I'd received about the Brigade and how they would continue to search for ways to undermine me. With relief, I made my way back into the sunshine. Cannons jutted out from the ledges, and of course, the views were even more spectacular then on the way up. I sat on the terrace, uncertain about what to do next. I wasn't getting any guidance or feeling about where to go. I racked my brain to think if I had missed any signs.

Next thing I knew, I felt a tap on my shoulder. I turned around to see it was Jesus. "Yikes," I said. "You're in Hvar. You do get around!"

He laughed and gave me a kiss on my forehead. "Hello, Samantha dear. I am glad to see that you are enjoying yourself and having fun while on your adventure."

I felt a little guilty. I'd been out partying all night. Should I have been praying? "Are you serious or kidding?" I asked.

"I am serious. Part of the experience here on earth is to have fun and enjoy all that this life and this body have to offer. It is important to honor your body's needs and to respect and take care of it. But it is also important to enjoy food, dancing, fun, and life."

Well, that is awesome news, I thought. I was a little shocked to hear these words coming out of Jesus's mouth though, I will admit.

He looked just the same as he did in my dream, or whatever that was, when I traveled to Peru. I could feel his familiar, massive, loving presence.

"I have to admit, Jesus. I am really happy to see you."

"I am glad to hear that. I spend a lot of time overseeing that you are taken care of."

"Thank you very much," I said with enthusiasm. "So what's next? Is this my fourth power spot?"

"It is close, but you are not there yet. We figured if you were going to travel this far, you might as well experience some of the beautiful places in this part of the world. You will be escorted from here tomorrow and will be heading toward Dubrovnik. Be sure to open the envelope from Jane with tomorrow's date on it so you will know what to do."

"Awesome," I said, as I remembered the fun Italian girls telling me I would love it there.

"I can't tell you how proud I am of you for making these tough choices," he said. "Actually, your whole Divine team is so proud of you. I know it's not been easy. You are doing a marvelous job of trusting your gut and following our guidance, so be sure to keep it up and stay strong."

"Thank you, it means a lot to me. I need continued encouragement, so please keep it up. You are right, this isn't easy at all. I find myself in my head a lot, telling myself that all this isn't real. Tell me, Jesus, what would you do?" I said, now that I knew I could have fun with him.

"Touché, my dear. When you have doubts, remember it's your ego trying to trip you up. The best thing to do is to witness your ego, and say this isn't me. I know what is real. I know the Divine loves me. So that is what Jesus would do." He chuckled. "You can also write down, 'My ego is telling me this isn't real, but I know what I am experiencing and that it is real.' The ego will do its best to say you aren't good enough, or in this particular case that you are making things up. The more you grow on a spiritual level, the louder the ego gets. Remember to trust your heart and not your head."

I was so happy to hear him say these words. I hadn't understood why I kept having these thoughts. In my heart I knew all this was real, but yet the fear and doubt continued to trickle in.

"Thank you for explaining what Jesus would do. I will try your suggestions."

"I must be going now. Please know you are loved and adored." And he vanished into thin air.

I walked onto the ledge with the cannons, taking one last look of this gorgeous view. I smiled thinking of what could possibly unfold tomorrow.

Chapter 27

The next morning, I carefully opened the next purple envelope. Jane's instructions were simple, written in her now familiar looping script.

> Dear Samantha,
>
> This morning a car will arrive at the hotel to take you to the ferry for a short trip to the mainland. A car will be waiting for you at the other end for the drive to Dubrovnik. Enjoy the day and remember to always trust your intuition.
>
> Much Love,
> Jane

I sat on the patio, cherishing my cappuccino, and waited for my ride. The driver didn't speak English, so the hotel concierge handed me off to him and gave him directions to where I was heading. The view on the drive over continued to be as ridiculously gorgeous as all the views I had seen thus far. More lush green trees and stone cities followed by beautiful vistas of deep blue water. We took a narrow road with steep cliff drops to the sea below. I held my breath, wondering if we were going to fall off the side of the mountain every time the driver barreled around a curve. After a couple of hours of this we arrived at a dock, and I was happy to be getting out of that van.

The driver grabbed my bag and pointed to a sign that said *Trajekt.*

Well, that is real helpful, I thought. I walked up to the window by the sign and handed the woman my passport.

"Ah, Samantha, I wondered when you would be arriving," she said politely. "Here is your ticket. A driver will meet you on the other side. Here comes the boat now."

I turned and saw a large ferry pull up. The sun was out, and I was glad to feel its warmth. I took a seat on the top deck, and the ride turned out to be smooth and easy. A crowd of locals was gathered at our destination, and I had no idea who was picking me up. I looked all over for a sign with my name and the trademark smiley face. When the crowd dispersed, I saw a gruff man standing with his arms crossed in front of a white van. He was the only one still waiting for a passenger, so this had to be my ride. I walked over, not sure what else to do.

"I'm Samantha."

He just stood there looking at me. Then he grabbed my bag and put it in the back of his car. "No Engliese," he mumbled and motioned me to get in.

Was this my driver? He had to be. Everything had worked smoothly up until now. I got in and buckled up. I was about to ask him how long the drive would be when I remembered, no Engliese. Eventually I spotted a road sign that said, *Dubrovnik 280 KM.*

Oh boy, I have got a while. I might as well do some reading, I thought. I opened *The Four Agreements* and settled in for a long trip. I'm not sure how long I'd been reading, but when the car slowed I was startled to see a sign that said, *Welcome to Bosnia and Herzegovina.*

"Umm, excuse me sir. Why are we heading into Bosnia?"

My heart began to pound and the nerves in my stomach couldn't be ignored. I shouldn't have gotten into the car with this man.

He drove on in silence until we reached what appeared to be a passport check. There, several militia men with machine guns strapped across their chests, raised their hands for the car to stop.

As we pulled up my driver commanded, "Passport, now!"

I hesitated, not knowing what to do or who to trust. I wanted out of this car, and I did not want to go to Bosnia with this man. But I also didn't want to cause suspicion by jumping out of the car in front of these dudes wearing machine guns as jewelry. I remembered Bridget telling me to check in with myself when I was in doubt.

"If you can take a deep breath, go into your heart, and ask yourself, you will get the answer you need," she had assured me.

I took her advice, shut my eyes, and did my best to still my racing heart. Clear as day I heard the voice in my head say, *Stay in the car, and then look for the first exit strategy as soon as you get away from this border crossing.*

I handed my passport to the driver, who then handed it to one of the men at the border.

"*Ohh, Americki? Lijep!*" I heard as the men laughed and passed around my passport.

Dear God, please get me through this safely!

After a few minutes, the guard brought back my passport and waved us through. I was somewhat relieved, but I still wanted to get the heck out of this car with this man who I no longer trusted. I was racking my brain thinking of what to do, when I saw a truck full of chickens stopped in the road in front of us, blocking traffic both ways.

The driver mumbled under his breath. Then he got out of the car, slammed the door, and walked over to the truck. Before I could blink, I heard, "Sam, this way and fast."

To my astonishment, I saw Ted, my ghost man, at the passenger window.

"Oh Ted, I have never been so happy to see you."

"Shhh," he said. "I grabbed your luggage. Now follow me."

He snuck me around to the other side of the chicken truck, where I saw the same beat up white Chevy from the dream I had of Ted telling me I was getting my wake up call. I hopped into the front passenger seat.

"Buckle up. We are going to haul tail," he said with a grin.

"Thank you so much. I was really scared. I honestly thought I might be locked up in a Bosnian prison. Was that the Brigade again?"

"Yes, unfortunately they kidnapped your regular driver and sent one of their own as a replacement. I have no idea what they had planned for you, but we are tripling your divine support now. We'll follow them around too, so this shouldn't be an issue any more. Just keep in mind that we will only ever have you with friendly looking people. We have decided to take further precautions as well. From now on do not go anywhere with anyone while you are traveling unless you can see a light in their mouth."

"Oh, you mean like the one I saw in the man's mouth in Target?"

"Yep. Exactly."

He whizzed around several back roads as we made our escape. Before going through passport control again, he had me hide in the trunk in case any of the guards were working with the Brigade. A half a mile back into Croatia, he pulled over so I could get out. I sobbed with a crazy mix of fear and relief.

"Hey, buddy," he spoke in a soothing tone. "Congrats on facing your fears. It takes a lot of strength, willpower, trust, and courage. So I want to commend you."

"Thank you. That means a lot, and you are right that none of this is easy. Why am I so emotional all the time?"

"It's part of the healing process. You have to allow what isn't serving you to come up so you can release it. Often the easiest way to release emotions is through tears and just feeling whatever is going on inside." He ruefully shook his head. "Perhaps if I'd let myself cry more often when I was . . . ah, never mind . . . ."

By the time we reached my beautiful hotel overlooking the bay in Dubrovnik, I'd calmed down, and my usual excitement at traveling had returned. Besides, it was seriously cool arriving in this classic American car.

"Okay, here is the deal," he said. "Drop your bags off in your room and put on your bathing suit. Considering what just happened, I am going to escort you to your power spot."

"Cool! You know I'm always happy to have you around to take care of me, and you're even kind of fun now too!" I teased.

The hotel porter raised his eyebrows as he opened the trunk for my luggage. I couldn't help but giggle as he probably wondered what a beat up old car was doing pulling into this fancy hotel.

Chapter 28

I checked in, took a quick look around my spacious room with its satiny sheets and huge marble tub, and then slipped into my new bikini, a pair of shorts, and a tee. I hurried back downstairs to meet up with Ted, my new bestie and travel buddy.

"Come on," he said. "It's this way. We go through the city walls and down to the marina."

He pointed to a huge stone drawbridge that led into one of the most magical cities I had ever seen. Dubrovnik is wrapped in tall, white stone walls, and on this particular day with the April sun high in the sky, they were glistening, as if touched by angels. We entered an open air square where fountains with ornately carved lion heads spilled water into tiered bowls, adding their gentle music to the balmy spring air. Alcoves filled with statues of saints and mystical beasts caught my eye. We turned into a narrow alley with a vaulted stone roof and chiseled steps. I ran my hand along the smooth stone walls surrounding us. I felt like I was dipping back in time, touching the lives and loves of centuries past. I was simply in awe.

Eventually, the alley opened up into a wide, open air, stone walkway, and we joined a growing crowd of other sightseers. As we walked down to the marina, Ted grabbed my hand, and I was surprised how real he felt. Once we got to the dock, he waved to a heavy set bald man dressed in crisp white pants and shirt. He wore a white captain's cap with gold braid, and as soon as he smiled I saw the light in his mouth. It was similar to the one I had seen in the man's mouth in Target, but this light was all green.

"Do you see what you are looking for now?" asked Ted.

"Thanks, I got it."

I gave him a hug and thanked him for saving me, and then I followed the captain to a sleek speedboat tied up to the dock.

"Where are we going?" I asked, as he held out his hand to help me aboard.

"That is up to you. We can go to the white sandy beaches. We can go island hopping, or we can go check out the grotto in the middle of the ocean."

"Can we do all of them?"

"I am afraid not. You must make a choice."

He untied the mooring rope and navigated his way out of the harbor. I remembered the instructions in Jane's envelope. I was to trust my inner guidance. My first instinct was to head to the grotto. I mean, how cool would it be to swim in a cave in the middle of the Adriatic? Then I started second guessing myself and thought maybe I should visit the white sandy beach.

"Captain, I'm having a hard time deciding."

"Go with your gut. What was your first instinct?" he solemnly asked.

"To go to the grotto."

"It sounds like you have made your choice. Do I have permission to proceed?"

"You sure do."

He revved the motor, and we skimmed over the waves. He took me the long way to show me some of the other islands and the white sandy beaches. When he pointed out the beaches, I was glad I hadn't chosen them. The sand wasn't really that white, especially when compared to the beautiful white beaches in the gulf of Florida.

Some distance out in the Adriatic, we approached a tiny, solitary, craggy island. He slowed the engine and circled the island. On the far side he stopped in front of a small opening in the rock. I doubted I could even fit my head through it.

"Is that it?" I asked, hoping he was going to say no.

"Yes it is. You will love it when you get inside. The light from the sun gleams off the water, and it is quite a magnificent sight."

"You mean, you aren't going to come with me?"

"This journey is about learning to do things for yourself. Now go on," he said firmly and pointed to the cave.

"That water looks awfully cold."

"It is, but your body will adjust quickly."

I felt queasy and on the verge of tears. Maybe I could just skip this part. "We're out really deep. Isn't this where sharks live? I'm not sure this is a good idea."

"You're frightened," he said.

Well, duh. Of course I was.

He thought for a moment, then said, "If you take too long to choose you will end up with the leftovers."

"What?"

"It's one of our Croatian proverbs."

I wanted to say, I'm fine with leftovers! But I knew what he meant. Of course I did. I had an opportunity to trust, to take one more step along my path. I'd seen the light in his mouth. That voice in my head rang clear as a bell. *Sam, you are protected. You will be fine even if it seems scary, I promise. Surrender to the Divine.*

"Are you going to be waiting here for me?"

"Yes, and I will have a stack of warm towels in my hands for you."

The light was back in his mouth. I took that as a sign that I needed to go ahead and jump in.

Oh crap. Here goes nothing…

I stood on the edge of the boat, counted to three, and dove right in. "Oh my gosh! Oh my gosh! This water is freaking cold! This was a terrible idea!" I shrieked.

"Start swimming, and your body will heat up," he yelled. "The faster you get into the cave, the faster this will be over."

You can do this, you got this, swim into the cave, the voice in my head urged.

As I swam toward the cave, I have to admit that it felt utterly exhilarating. It was for sure a once in a lifetime opportunity. Approaching the tiny entrance to the grotto, I couldn't help but be nervous about what sea creatures were in close proximity. I always loved the ocean and water, but I had never been swimming so far out before.

I eased in through the opening and found myself in a mystical, dreamy blue grotto. The sunlight glistening through the tiny hole filled the vast cave with beauty and a sense of peace. I instantly relaxed and swam to a cluster of rocks rising out of the water in the middle of the wide-open cave. I clambered out to rest. I gazed up to see what looked like hundreds of small brown rags hanging from the cave ceiling. Bats! My whole body tensed, and I froze, loosing every ounce of excitement I had just had.

Oh no! Is this another trick from the Brigade?

A loud splashing startled me, and a fin appeared to my left.

Sharks!

Two more fins appeared, and then in perfect symmetry they leapt out of the water and squeaked. Dolphins! I wept with relief. They circled the rock and jumped one after the other, as if they were putting on a show just for me. Feelings of happiness and joy tingled throughout my entire body. After the dolphins played and danced for a while, they formed a small circle in the water directly in front of me. A beautiful woman rose from nowhere in the middle of the circle. Two of the dolphins scooped her up, and she rode on their backs to sit right beside me on the rocks. She had long, pastel pink hair and wore a white bikini with a fiery red cape.

"Hello, Sam. Congratulations darling."

"Wow, you are beautiful. Thank you for that brilliant performance from your friends." I smiled at the dolphins. "But why are you congratulating me?"

"You know why," she said.

And I did. I just needed to claim it for myself. She had congratulated me on overcoming my fear and trusting my intuition. I grinned. "Got it."

"Yes, you do." She smiled, and the dolphins leapt out of the water one more time in formation. "My name is Goddess Amphitrite. I am Queen of the Sea. Water is good for you, Sam. You should frequently visit the water or live close to it if you can. I am here to tell you a little bit about your past. You should know that you haven't been on earth in over two hundred years."

"What do you mean? I thought we all come here over and over to learn different lessons and for the evolution of our soul."

"Yes, that is true. But you see, once you graduate from the school of earth there are thousands of other realms you can progress to. Souls who reach the angelic realms will often volunteer to come to earth as an Earth Angel to help the world with whatever it needs at that time. If a soul can successfully complete a divine mission as an Earth Angel helping to guide the world through crisis, then that soul can skip past a few realms of evolution."

She paused for a moment to hold my gaze. "Being an Earth Angel isn't an easy feat. So if you do it with success, your reward after you transition from earth is tenfold."

Every word she said struck a chord deep within me. "So you are saying I'm an Earth Angel?"

"Yes, that is exactly what I am saying. Isn't it wonderful news?"

I hesitated for a moment at the heaviness of what she was telling me. I knew my life was changing, but this seemed so big, so huge. I was on earth as an angel? Me, a real life angel? I couldn't believe it—it just didn't seem like it could actually be true.

"I do feel honored, and this does feel right to me," I said. "It could be my truth. But it is a little scary, and it's a lot to take in. What does being an Earth Angel mean, exactly?"

"First of all, please know that it is nothing to be scared of. It is an honor. It means you have special magical gifts and powers that you can offer to help save the world."

"You mean I can help with the transition of human evolution?" This message had come up repeatedly, and I was starting to somewhat understand.

"Yes. Exactly. You have a complex mission, and it will be unfolded to you in time. But for now, yes you are getting it. The dolphins say hello, and they want to support you in any way they can. They are one of your spirit animals, and they are happy you loved their dance. Their mission is to make humans feel free and alive and to inspire play-like qualities."

"I am honored to meet them," I said, as one of the dolphins slid right up to me. I ran my hand across its smooth, slippery skin.

"I have something really special for you," she said. In her palm she held the most beautiful, sparkling green emerald on a delicate gold chain.

"Wow, what is it? It is stunning."

"This is an amulet. It was kept hidden in the sea for thousands of years for you. We knew you would need it in this lifetime. If you wear it, it will help protect you. It is from the Atlantean times and will help unlock memories and assist you in remembering all your truth." She attached the necklace around my neck.

"I love it. It's so special. Thank you so much."

"You are doing beautifully, darling. You are on the right path so keep it up. I will be going now, so remember me every time you go for a swim. Try not to stay away from the water for so long."

She looked at me, put her hands together in front of her heart, and bowed her head like we were at yoga together. She then submerged deep within the water, faster than she appeared. I sat on the rock with tears of joy streaming down my face at learning and realizing my truth.

I can't believe it. I really am an Earth Angel. This is so special, and I'm so happy to finally be getting some answers and clarity. Bridget was right; my future really is bright and truly limitless!

Chapter 29

I jumped out of bed with a little extra pep the next morning. I was so happy to have a free day in Dubrovnik to explore its charms. I wandered throughout the walled city and visited unique shops, until it was time to join the kayak tour I had set up per the recommendation of the Italian girls I had met in Hvar.

I marveled at the beauty once again as I made my way along the outside of the stone city walls and headed to the water. The steps were pretty steep, and I paid close attention so as not to bust my tail. Still I almost tripped on the last few steps. Blame it on being totally distracted by the ridiculously handsome dude who caught my eye.

"Samantha?"

He had wavy hair, beautiful, dark skin, and he strutted toward me with a wide smile.

"Yup, you can call me Sam," I said, giggling like a schoolgirl.

"I am Dominik, and I am your tour guide for today." His eyes, full of laughter, grew squinty because his smile was so big. "We have a group of twelve." He gestured to the people gathered around the sleek red kayaks. "But I am curious. Are you here alone?"

Suddenly I felt shy. "Ummm, yes I am."

"Perfect. You can ride with me in my kayak. I get lonely when I have to ride by myself."

Once we were outfitted with lifejackets and given a few basic instructions, Dominik led us on a leisurely paddle beneath and around the city walls. Swallows swooped above us, darting into their nests in the limestone cliffs. The walls were absolutely beautiful and adorned with statues and emblems. Once we got around the walls, we pulled up to another grotto. However, this one was wide open and in a shallow stretch of water. We pulled our kayaks onto a pebbly beach. Dominick and the other tour guides got lunch out for the group, which included several college students touring Europe and a couple on their honeymoon.

Then Dominik decided to show off and took a few guys to the top of the cliff to do cliff diving. I'll admit, I was impressed.

As I was eating my lunch, Dominik came over and sat right beside me, his skin still glistening wet from his swim.

"So Sam, you are quite beautiful, I must say."

I instantly blushed and giggled. I was in serious schoolgirl mode again. Since being on this spiritual path, I seemed to have lost all my cool with guys.

"Where are you from?"

"I live in Atlanta, Georgia."

"Oh, very nice. I am dying to get to the States soon." He took a bite of his sandwich. "So do you have plans tonight?"

Holy crap, is he asking me on a date?

"Well, I was thinking of eating somewhere within the walls. Why?"

"I wanted to see if you would let me take you to dinner and dancing?"

My stomach dropped, and for the first time in ages butterflies fluttered throughout my belly. "That sounds great," I said. I could feel my cheeks getting pinker by the second. Dominik was so sweet and super hot. He didn't have that macho air that most men who looked like him would have. Instead, he had a warm, loving energy that I was very drawn to. When we finished the tour, Dominik told me where to meet him at eight that evening.

I almost sprinted back up those steep steps, I was so excited. I mentally went through the contents of my suitcase. I must have brought something sexy to wear. Yes, my hot pink dress! At the hotel

I flopped on the bed and managed to still my mind and fluttering heart with a deep breathing meditation. I had had a long few days, and I wanted to get some rest so I would be able to enjoy my date in Dubrovnik.

Slipping into my heels later on, I felt both giddy and grateful. For the first time in months I was doing something that seemed "normal." A date! Again, I silently thanked the Italian girls for recommending this kayak tour. I left the hotel, walked down to the drawbridge, and saw Dominik standing there with a pink rose. He looked in my direction with that gorgeous smile and my heart melted.

"Here you go," he said cheerily and as he tucked the rose behind my ear. "This is for you."

"Thank you so much, Dom. That is so sweet of you." I gave him a kiss on the cheek and lingered in the warmth of his body.

He held out his arm, and I wrapped mine through his. We walked in sync down to the main square in the middle of the city where lanterns swung outside small restaurants and candles flickered on the tables. The sky was a deep royal blue that popped up against the white stonewalls. A band played soft romantic music in the middle of the square.

"So Sam, why are you here?"

"Well, I guess you could say I am doing a little soul searching."

"Dubrovnik is the perfect place. Maybe you will find what you are looking for."

He led me to a tiny café and the perfect table for two overlooking the square. We enjoyed dinner together and laughed, and it was such a pleasure to get to know this man who seemed to only want to find joy in life.

"Do you always lead the kayak tours?" I asked.

"It just depends on what else is going on. I also do wine tours, dirt bike tours, cliff diving tours, and then when the weather is cooler I do snow ski tours as well. What are you doing tomorrow? Do you want to go on a wine tour with me?"

He reached across the table and caressed my hand. My heart sank as I wanted to do this more than anything, but I knew I couldn't.

"I wish. This is my last night here. I have to go tomorrow."

"Then we had better enjoy tonight."

He grabbed my hand and led me to the center of the square where several other couples were dancing. There was a deep familiarity about him, as if we had known each other for longer than a day. Effortlessly we danced together. His heart and mine, a magnetic presence between the two of us from the second we laid eyes on one another.

"You are a great dancer," he said. "You are absolutely gorgeous, and I am having so much fun. I hope you are too."

I wasn't used to being showered with compliments, as Lucas was never one to dole them out.

He kissed me lightly on the cheek and murmured, "I want to show you something."

It was as if he was able to navigate the city walls with his eyes closed. We left the square, and he led me through the maze of stone walls to a quiet, cobblestone alley. He pulled me close, kissing me in a way that I had never been kissed before. It was as if he yearned to be with me and wanted to make sure I knew that. I hungrily kissed him back, lost in the feeling of giddiness and excitement.

"Your skin is so soft," he whispered. He lifted me up and pressed me against the smooth stone walls, and I wrapped my legs around his waist. We could still hear the soft music from the courtyard, and as he kissed my neck I gazed up into the night sky.

"You are the most beautiful girl I have ever seen, and you taste so good. You make my body shake just standing here against you." He ran his hands up and down my body, and I moaned with pleasure. He then gently put my feet back on the ground, and he hovered over me, smiling deep into my eyes. He grabbed both of my hands with one of his and clasped my wrists above my head. He caressed my chin with his other hand, kissing me deeply and passionately.

We must have gotten a little more carried away than either of us realized, because suddenly a large swoosh of water dumped down on our heads.

We staggered back from the wall and looked up to see an ornery old lady sticking her head out of her apartment window, bucket in hand. She shouted the Croatian version of "get a room," and we busted out laughing.

"Sam, did you get wet? Come over here under this awning." He grinned and pulled me close again.

"Luckily for me, I think you got the brunt of it," I said. "My back is a little wet, but I am sure it will dry. Oh my gosh, you are sopping!" I ran my fingers through his soaked brown curls and across his white button up shirt that was now see through.

Now another old lady from across the street shouted something. Wow, we had the whole neighborhood riled up. Laughing crazily, we grabbed hands and ran to a "safer" spot down by the water's edge, where we once again melted into each other's arms. We carried on like that for a few more hours, until I knew it had to come to an end, and I pulled myself away from him. I glanced at my watch. It was four in the morning.

"I need to be going," I whispered.

"Please don't go. I know I only met you, but you are truly the woman of my dreams. It is so rare for me to have an instant connection with someone like this. You are the woman I have been looking and praying for."

"I feel the same way about our connection, but the timing is not great for me right now. Besides, we live on opposite sides of the world. You have my number, so text me and keep in touch."

As I said those words my heart ached. I didn't really want to leave, but I knew I had to. Not that long ago I would have never been able to resist a man like this. But I was a woman on a mission, and I needed to honor that instead of getting side tracked into another relationship.

He pulled me close, gave me yet another deep and passionate kiss, and begged me to stay.

"Honestly, I wish I could. But I really can't." I thought about trying to explain why, but I wondered if he'd understand. Instead, I squeezed him tight one last time and murmured thanks for an amazing and unforgettable night. I opened the door to my hotel, and when I turned around Dominik was still standing there, watching me with both hands in his pockets. He really did make my heart skip a beat.

"One more kiss," he pleaded.

I pursed my lips and blew him a kiss and then dashed up to my room before my resolve broke. A few seconds more, and I might have invited him up. I opened the door and all thoughts of Dominik receded when I saw the purple envelope awaiting me on my bed. I had forgotten that I had put it there before my date.

> *Dear Samantha,*
>
> *You've learned more about trusting your intuition and are making wise choices for your life. Congratulations! I'm also happy to see that you are enjoying yourself and tasting all of the local flavors.* ☺

I smiled at her sense of humor and wondered how in the world she had known what was going to happen.

> *Your driver will be in the lobby at nine in the morning and will take you to the airport for your next adventure.*
>
> *Much Love,*
>
> *Jane*

I realized that an eight hour beauty sleep was out, so I fell into bed to salvage what little sleep time remained. In the hours before dawn I had a dream of what my life could be like with Dominik. I have to say it was appealing, but I still knew there was more for me, and that Dominik wasn't my partner in this lifetime. Although I had an eerie sense that I too had some past life history with him.

Chapter 30

I made it down to the hotel lobby with just minutes to spare. I'd arrived in Ted's beaten up Chevy, and now I was departing in a sleek white Mercedes sedan. We left the walled city and made our way to Dubrovnik's airport, where the driver dropped me off at a huge airplane hangar far from the main terminal. I'd seen the light in the driver's mouth, but still I stood there for a moment with my bags wondering if the Brigade was up to something. What flight was I supposed to take? I hadn't found a boarding pass or seen anything about a reservation in the envelope Jane had given me. It seemed odd. Just then a friendly woman who appeared to be in her mid-forties walked over wearing a sky blue shirt.

"You must be Samantha. Hey, I'm Gail." I saw a light blue light in her mouth. In a weird way it complemented her bright red lipstick.

"Yes, I am," I said, relieved. "Where are we off to?"

"Egypt. You are going to love it, and you are one lucky girl. It isn't often that a plane of this magnitude is chartered for only one person."

"You're kidding, right?"

She glanced down at her clipboard. "Nope. Unless the passenger manifest is wrong. It says here I have one passenger only. Ms. Samantha Kingston, from Atlanta, Georgia."

She led me to the far end of the hangar and pointed outside at a sleek, steel grey jet, as elegant as a Jimmy Choo stiletto.

"Oh, wow!"

"It's a G 5. Top of the line."

An official appeared to stamp my passport, then Gail walked me onto the tarmac to the jet. When we neared it the door slowly opened and the stairs unfolded one by one. She took my hand and escorted me on board.

"Whoa, this IS pretty fancy."

Wide leather seats, a flat screen TV, a vase of white roses? I'd never flown like this; never experienced this level of pampering. And I was heading for Egypt, one of my dream destinations.

"This is real. I'm not dreaming, am I?" I asked Gail.

"It sure is real. I am your pilot today—"

"You're also a pilot?"

"Navy for twenty years. Now I fly corporate and luxury jets."

She then introduced me to Amelia, a young woman about my age in a fitted turquoise dress. She was my personal flight attendant for the journey. "Would you like a mimosa with fresh squeezed orange juice?" she asked.

How could I say no? Gail disappeared into the cockpit, and I took a seat in a leather recliner and sipped my drink. No cheap plastic cup—this was a crystal flute.

I checked my phone for messages. There was one from Dominik.

I miss you already Samantha! Thank you for an amazing night and for some awesome memories! Have a safe trip wherever it is you are going. Oh and are you still wet? J

I couldn't help but laugh. I would never forget that night, especially how it felt to be in a passionate make out session and have a pail of water dumped over my head. I texted back.

Thank you Dominik for making me laugh and smile and feel loved and special, even if it was only for one night.

I then took photos of everything. The seats, the carpeted interior, even Amelia with the bottle of champagne she used to pour my mimosa. I selfied away. I had to document this. Samantha Kingston in a private jet all to herself!

When the plane lifted off the ground, I waved goodbye to Dubrovnik and Dominik. Once we reached cruising altitude, Amelia served me an early lunch of delicious chicken salad with fresh strawberries and pineapple. I was too excited to read, so I simply sat in gratitude. Thank you, thank you, I kept saying to the universe and to my angels.

"Hey, baby girl." The words startled me, but I recognized the voice in a second.

"Hey, Papa Jack."

"You think I'd miss this opportunity to travel with you on a private jet? This is fancy! Here you go, sugar." He handed me a bouquet of orange Gerber daisies. "I want us to have a special symbol. I thought maybe it could be an orange daisy," he said with his crooked smile. "I figured if I gave you some you would never forget. Now I have a way of letting you know if you are on the right path with just the flash of a symbol in your mind's eye."

I arranged the daisies in the vase with the white roses.

"Ah, that's nice," said Papa. He sat down in the plush reclining seat next to me, tilted it, and kicked his feet up. "That was a close one back there in Bosnia. I'm happy that Ted was able to save you. I wished it could have been me, but Ted needed to serve his mission, so I respectfully backed off and allowed him to intervene. You have already helped me so much in my evolution, that it was the right thing to do."

"I know you were there in spirit," I reassured him with a wink.

"I want to tell you that the message you are going to get at the pyramids is key. It may seem tough at first, but know that you can't proceed until you master this trait. A lot of people get stuck on this one, so be sure to pay special attention and listen carefully."

"It seems that every lesson and every tip is key. What gives?"

"It's true. In these awakenings you have to master one thing before you can move on to the next. For you, this is all happening at lightning speed, because the world needs you to fulfill your mission. But you still have to allow the shifts to happen. Your divine team is showing up to give you support and provide you with the energetic vibrational lifts you need for your energy to ascend. But only you can control how you deal with it and how you learn to manage your thoughts and your perception."

"Am I doing something wrong?" I wondered if I may have taken too much time having fun in Croatia.

"No, not all. I just want you to understand how important all of this is. Just because you are in communication with the Divine doesn't mean you don't get to have a life or that you shouldn't be having fun. In fact, it is quite the opposite." He said this as though reading my mind. "You should be having as much fun as possible, as that will also lift your vibration. Part of the reason you came here was to have fun and to inspire others to enjoy life and have fun too."

"Thanks, Papa Jack. You always know just what to say to me."

"Keep up the good work. See you soon, sugar."

He gave me a hug and a high five and disappeared just as Amelia approached with a plate of fine cheeses and fruit. She stopped and did a double take at the vase.

"What's up?" I asked.

"I never noticed the daisies. They are so pretty."

After a few hours we were flying over the Egyptian desert. It looked wrinkled and ancient, and I felt a little nervous. What was the tough lesson that awaited me?

We landed at a private airstrip where a huge Hummer with enormous tires awaited. After another lone official stamped my passport, Gail hopped in the driver's seat and motioned for me to sit beside her.

"You're taking me? This is great!"

We drove several miles alongside the Nile River. I couldn't believe it. This was the Nile from stories in Sunday School. We reached a small dock, and Gail pointed out a group of large boats sitting low in the water. "They used these boats in the 1800s to cruise the Nile. They call them *dahabiyas*. We will be spending one night in the boat with the red and white sails. Just a short trip along the Nile so you can relax before your next adventure."

"How many in our group?" I asked.

She laughed. "Want me to check the clipboard again? Far as I know, you are still the only one on this luxurious adventure."

I practically danced up the gangway, I was so excited. My cabin was decked out in dazzling white furnishings with red and yellow accents. I had floor to ceiling windows that looked out onto the palm tree studded banks of the Nile.

For the rest of the day I lazed on the upper deck, watching scenes of daily life on the Nile. Young boys on donkeys raced each other along the bank and waved at me. Water buffalo cooled themselves in the shallows. It was hot, but a dry heat, and I kept myself refreshed with huge glasses of iced water. I ate dinner under the stars and slept like a princess in my enormous bed.

I woke early the next morning. It felt hotter than the day before, and I was restless. The boat was anchored, and I needed exercise, so I thought why not dive in and take a swim? I threw on my yellow bikini, the same one I wore in Peru, and swan dived into the Nile. Unlike my Croatian escapade in the grotto, this water was balmy. I splashed around, swam to one bank and then back to the other.

I had just made it onto the sand when I saw Gail on deck. She wore a sleek black one piece and was waving at me. I waved back. She grew more agitated, shook her head several times, and pointed to my left. I looked at the riverbank and saw the usual palms and a large fallen tree trunk. Then I froze. *Was that a crocodile?* It was ginormous and ugly as sin with a thick tail, corrugated skin, and irregular teeth jutting out of its long deadly jaws.

I felt dizzy with fear. It appeared to be sleeping, but what if it woke up if I started to move? *Help!* I mouthed silently to Gail as my body filled with panic. She held her finger to her lips and then slipped like a knife into the water and swam without making a single splash. She slowly walked up the bank, took my hand, and just as slowly we slid back into the river for what felt like the longest swim of my life. I wanted to shriek, to swim like crazy, to get back to the boat ASAP! I felt even more terrified when I saw one of the deck hands aiming a rifle at the water. In fact, it looked like he was aiming right at us. Gail held my hand the entire time—I think she swam for both of us. Without saying a word, she somehow got me to slow down, to breathe.

Five feet from the boat, and I wrenched free and scrambled up the ladder to get onboard. Gail quickly joined me. When I looked at the far bank there was no crocodile in sight. *Was I hallucinating?* Then the deck hand lowered the rifle and pointed ten feet beyond the boat to the yellowish eyes, the long pointed snout. As if it knew it had been spotted, it sank beneath the waters.

My stomach dropped as I noticed there were actually five large crocodiles, an entire family. Two other deck hands had also crept up carrying rifles. One of the crocodiles snapped, and I jumped backward on the boat.

I turned to Gail. "If you hadn't been there—" I broke down in sobs, unable to continue.

She held me tight and reassured me that I was fine. "Honey, we are never going to let anything happen to you. You are safe and protected."

As I was hugging Gail, I briefly saw a flash of Archangel Michael. He was floating over her head and held his finger to his mouth motioning me not to saying anything. He gave me a thumbs up, and then I heard his words in my head. *Good work, my dear. You made it out safely.*

As I continued to allow Gail's arms to hold and support me, I felt Archangel Michael filling both of us with his divine, loving grace. I stood there in that moment feeling so much gratitude: gratitude for my mission, for this amazing luxury adventure, and most of all, for all the help and guidance I was receiving. It was true. I really was divinely protected.

Chapter 31

We cruised for another few hours, and I was relieved when the boat finally docked. *Get me on land, pronto!* I was going to have nightmares about those crocodiles for weeks to come. I expected to see our Hummer waiting for us. Instead, we had camels.

"Will they bite? Don't they spit like lamas?" I asked Gail.

She laughed. "Only if they are provoked. Camels are harmless but also a bit uncomfortable until you get used to their gait."

The camels were adorned with the most magnificent saddles made of bright fuchsia, orange, and blue leather and cloth. Both camels wore embroidered headdresses studded with sequins and had a special sense of peace about them. They also had the longest eyelashes I had ever seen.

"To protect them during sand storms," Gail explained. "Which one would you like to ride?"

"Wait. You said sand storms?"

"Relax, Sam. Not at this time of year."

And I bet you thought there would be no crocodiles either!

I was still feeling anxious, when Archangel Michael said to me in my head, *Sam, quit fussing! Everything is in divine order. Now pick a camel and proceed. Shake it off, take it all in, and enjoy the beauty and the wonder.*

I chuckled, because he sounded a little impatient with me. I chose the golden hued camel with the longest eyelashes. With a weird rocking and rolling walk, we set off into the desert.

The sand was the color of my favorite salted caramel ice cream, the sky a dazzling blue. The emptiness of the desert filled me with a peaceful trance. We rode the camels for about an hour, until way in the distance, I saw the pyramids. I knew they must be gigantic up close, because they looked massive from here, and I knew we had a ways to go.

This is so cool, despite my massive scare back there with the crocs. Mom and Dad would absolutely love this and be amazed.

I wished I could openly communicate with my parents about what had been going on with me.

They loved to travel and go on adventures, the same as I did. I knew they would think these places and everything I had discovered were really awesome. Even though Dad was a pilot and had flown to so many different countries, I bet I had seen and done things he never knew existed.

If I could only get to a point where I could be real with them and where maybe they would believe me.

Close to the pyramids we dismounted our camels and left them with a man who tied them up with several others—sort of like valet parking. My instincts told me to explore, and I told Gail to stay put—I'd come back to her in a little while. Despite the crowds, I soon found myself alone at one of the pyramids. Out of the direct sunlight the enormous stone blocks were cool to the touch, and I wondered how they had managed to construct these marvels.

I found an opening and entered. Once my eyes got accustomed to the dim interior, I saw a few different passageways. I had a choice: I could ascend or descend. Spots of light began to blink on the stairs leading upwards. They reminded me of the lights I'd seen blinking in my bathroom mirror at home. The lights grew bigger and more colorful, just as they had done before. Then out of the lights reappeared the beautiful and radiant goddess who had visited me at home when I was in the bathtub.

"Hello, darling. Do you remember me?"

"Isis. Of course I remember you."

She gestured for me to follow her up the stairs and turned with a swish of her gown. As we climbed higher I felt an odd sense of familiarity.

"These are the pyramids of Giza," she said. "They are the oldest of the pyramids and some of the oldest wonders of the ancient world. This pyramid was built for a Divine king and queen, and here are the quarters where they lived."

We'd reached a chamber about halfway up the pyramid. The air here smelled sweeter, and I could make out traces of gold leaf on the walls.

"I know this may sound crazy," I said, "but I have a strong feeling I lived here once."

"It is not crazy at all. You did live here. What else do you remember?"

I closed my eyes, took a deep breath, and tried to relax and focus at the same time. Images flickered through my mind. I remembered living a happy life here and having a wonderful family. I could see myself in my chamber with so many beautiful robes and dresses to choose from. I then saw myself cuddled up on a bed draped with gold finery, and I was happier than ever with my husband who I loved deeply. This image flickered and faded. I steadied myself with more deep breathing, and the vision returned. I saw two young children, and I realized my husband was the same beautiful and stunning man I had seen in my vision in Peru. I could feel the euphoria between us the instant he appeared. My eyes filled with tears. I caught my breath and told Isis what I had just seen.

"Yes! You are doing it. You are tapping into your intuition. You had a past life vision all on your own. Often the happier lives will come back to us first, or they appear if there is a message we need to know."

"I can't believe I was able to do that," I said in utter shock. "What would the message be?"

"Think about it."

I tried to tune in, but nothing came to me. "I'm not sure," I said. "Can't you just tell me? This is all so new."

But she persisted. "You have to learn at some point. You can't receive the message, because you aren't surrendering. You are trying to control what the message is so you are not getting it. Try this. Say 'I fully and completely surrender. Please show me what message you want me to know for my highest and holiest good. Please show me whatcha got.'"

"Okay, here goes." I closed my eyes and surrendered, asking for a clear message. Within seconds I was overcome with tears.

"What is wrong?" She gently rubbed my back.

I couldn't speak, couldn't explain that they were tears of gratitude. Clear as day I saw again the man from my vision in Peru; the same man I had just seen in the vision of my life in ancient Egypt. But this time I got an image of my future. It was in this lifetime—in the months or years to come—and I saw him kneeling down on one knee proposing, professing his undying love and devotion to me.

When I finally stopped crying, I said, "I saw him. I saw the man who is my true love. It felt so real. How can I already have such strong feelings for someone I have never met?"

"Oh Samantha, you have met him. You have spent many, many lifetimes with that man, and he is your true primary soul partner. He is the man you wanted to be with before you reincarnated in this lifetime. He is the man you can truly grow with and be the woman you were meant to be in this lifetime. He is your Prince Charming, darling. Hold this vision close to your heart. It will get you through the tough times. Now you know what your truth is. You just have to get a little farther on your path and to know this will soon be your reality."

"So I should use this vision as encouragement?"

"Exactly. You opened up to that vision, because the two of you lived here in Egypt together, and because you need to see what is possible for you in this lifetime. Listen carefully, you must remember to let go and surrender. You know things will work out beautifully for you. To allow that to happen, you have to fully trust that the Divine is taking care of you and that we angels have your back."

I nodded that I would, but Isis wasn't done. There was one more note of caution.

"When you forget to surrender, you block divine flow. Regardless of what happens or what anyone else says, you must remember this: trust the Divine. No half measures. You will be tested to see if you can feel and believe this even when it doesn't seem possible. Do you understand?"

"I guess. So what you are saying is this was a glimpse of what could be my future if I get through all these tests." I felt encouraged and somewhat scared, but I also wanted to get to this future ASAP.

"Yes. But it is not of what could be, it is what *will* be. It is there—"

Suddenly, out of nowhere, as if there was a hole in the floor, out popped a muscled man. He had wild blond curls, a jeweled headdress, and a most dazzling smile. He also had a sword that he twirled with flourish.

"Well, me darlin' Sam. My name is Lugh, and I want ta remind ya, persistence pays off. Now if you'd only be meditating more, you might hear us more. Know what I mean, lass? Never give up, and call on me if you want help enjoying bountiful abundance."

Poof! He disappeared.

"Whoa! Who was that crazy dude?"

Isis frowned, looking quite annoyed, and I burst out laughing.

He bopped back into my sight "I told ya, the name is Lugh. Seriously, lass, persistence is important. You can't just surrender once and pass that test. No joke. Peace."

"He's Irish," Isis said wearily. "A Celtic god, and a terrible flirt. He's been after me for years—oh, never mind. You see, even we Gods and Goddesses have to work on tolerance."

"He's cool. I kinda like him."

"Well, that's a relief. He thinks if he flashes in and out like that, you will remember his words better and clearer. He means well, I promise." She wrapped an arm around my shoulder and squeezed me tightly. "It's time for you to head back home."

"Okay, but I want to make sure I got the message crystal clear. I need to remember to surrender and to trust and to know that all my dreams are in the process of coming true, as long as I can believe, trust, and surrender. Right?"

"You are a natural." She kissed me on the cheek, and then she led me back to the stairs. I made my way out of the pyramid into the blinding sun. I found Gail waiting. She must not have seen me coming, because she was slouched back against the wall, guzzling water, and it was dripping down her neck.

"Hey, Gail," I said, happy to catch her in an imperfect moment. She immediately stood up straight and wiped her mouth. She tried to act as if nothing was wrong, but I knew it bothered her that I had caught her off guard. To my relief, I also saw our Hummer in the distance.

"Did you find what you needed?" she asked.

"I sure did. Please, please tell me we're going back to the private jet?"

"Hmm. Let me check my clipboard again," she joked.

The flight back to Atlanta was overnight, and I had my very own bed on the plane—with 1200 count sheets. I was sitting in bed, looking at photos on my phone, when someone cleared their throat.

"Hey, kiddo. Mind if I join you for a little bit?"

It was Ted. In new clothes too. Jeans and a royal blue button up with his sleeves rolled three quarter lengths up his arm. He was even wearing Converse tennis shoes.

"Looking good, Ted! I like your style."

"Why thank you." He looked around the plane and whistled slowly. "Hot dang. Papa Jack told me about this jet, and I had to come and see it myself. This is one sweet ride back to the USA."

"Can you sit for a while?" I asked.

He needed no more invitation. He settled into a nearby recliner, tilted it back, and we laughed and joked about how much had changed since that day he first appeared out of nowhere to stop traffic so I could gather my precious Honey out of the street.

Chapter 32

An Angel Revolution

Archangel Michael and Archangel Raphael sat up high in the universe floating on light and love, gazing across a brilliant scattering of stars and other celestial bodies. They had gathered, as angels often do, to review the work still ahead—as long as there was one soul not yet in the light, they were committed to doing all they could to transform the universe. For eons they had worked tirelessly, and now they had intimations of the momentous shift about to come. However, because of free will, there was still so much at play—it needed care, it needed nurturing.

Archangel Michael spread his majestic wings wide to reveal galaxies and planets; so many of them bathed in love. But not planet Earth, not yet. Dazzling visions of other realms shut down, and all he and Rafael could now see was the mist of unhappiness, struggle, and fear still veiling on Earth.

"I thought we were close," said Raphael with disappointment.

Michael leaned forward and peered through the mists. "We are!" he cried. He clapped his wings together, and a softly thunderous roar reverberated across the heavens. The mists on the planet they loved the most started to clear. "Look."

"I see," said Raphael "It *is* time."

They talked excitedly about the hot topics of late, the focus of all their work and angelic intentions: awakening and human evolution, Samantha Kingston, and the rest of the elite team from Atlantis.

"Look at Ariel!" said Michael. "She is so tapped in and has been getting our Divine downloads. The Angel Crusade is happening right on time!" Michael high fived Raphael.

"They truly are extraordinary Earth Angels. I know they have had immense struggles. There were times I wondered how they could withstand the Brigade. But look at them. At some point we should let Ariel, Samantha, and the others know their history."

"Yes we should . . . in due time, Raphy."

Archangels Michael and Raphael called over the rest of the band of Archangels and Ascended Masters—Ganesh, Jesus, Buddha, and the gang—so they could add their divine energy to the transformation on the blue planet. It was happening; it was physically manifesting. Ariel had sent out the energetic call, and the right people were listening and showing up.

"We have to get this to Sam. It will be right on time for her," said Jesus. "Now that she has made it to five of her power spots, she is primed for this next step."

The goddesses showed up now too, all smiles and decked to the nines.

"Samantha has got this," said Isis. "She will know what to do as soon as she sees the sign. It was so lovely to hang with her in Egypt. She makes me want to incarnate and give all this a go again. She is making her kind so proud. The feminine will rise, and we will lift up the planet and bring heaven to Earth once and for all!"

Amphitrite blew kisses to the stars and back. The goddesses were beyond thrilled. They had worked so hard, alongside so many, to raise the divine feminine energy on planet Earth. They wanted unity once and for all. Less "doing, doing, doing," and more RECEIVING!

Chapter 33

Two weeks after returning from Croatia and Egypt, I called Bridget. I felt like a changed person in so many ways. I wasn't freaked out by the pop-up visits from the Divine anymore, and I understood what Bridget had seen when she told me how bright my future was. Now, more than ever, I wanted, I needed, that to be true and to be my reality.

The morning of our meeting I got up early and did my vinyasa practice at home. I'd recently added a headstand. I used the wall, but I knew that in a few weeks I'd be doing them without support. Then I'd move to arm balances. The timer went off after two minutes, and I showered and got ready.

Even though my world had changed drastically, and there was still so much unknown, I had a deep-seated peace in my heart. I knew I was absolutely on the right path. I also was not foolish enough to think I was done with guidance. I still needed all the help I could get.

I skipped into Bridget's studio and gave her a huge hug. I then handed her the tiny bottle of lavender essence I'd bought in Hvar.

"You will not believe what I have been up to," I said.

"Well, I can see it's been a transformative time. I have actually been watching you and keeping up with your energy, so I may know more than you think."

I sat there in stillness for a second, thinking how grateful I was for her presence in my life. I could never have made it this far without her. She had taught me so many key lessons: how to check in with myself and get my own answers, how to stay grounded, how to fight off the Brigade. She was the first to tell me the angels were my guides. She'd been the catalyst for this journey. I doubted I would even have gone to Sedona if she hadn't worked on my chakras after Honey's death. I also reflected on some of the more uncomfortable moments when she had called me out.

During one of my visits a few months ago, she'd asked me to write down my goals, as this was the first step in manifesting the life we desired. After I'd done so, she read them, nodding her head and smiling, until she came to the last one.

"I want to applaud you for taking the time for this work," she had said. "Now let's talk about this last goal. You wrote that you want to go on Oprah's show to teach about self-love within six months. Do you think that is a realistic goal?"

"I don't know. You tell me. Do you think it's realistic that I call on Archangel Michael and ask him to use his divine healing power to clear my headache?"

She frowned and sat silent for a moment. "I have something sort of serious to tell you. Please listen carefully. One of your guides came to me in my meditation this morning with an important message for you."

"Really? That is weird. Why wouldn't they have just told me directly?"

"They have their reasons. I get messages for clients all the time, so it isn't that unusual. The message was this: even though you have been making great progress and you are on the right path, you are not coming from the right place of energy."

"I'm totally confused. What do you mean?"

"Whether you realize it or not, you are still allowing your ego to get in the way. Even though your intentions are good, you aren't coming from your heart space. This is a crucial step to moving forward on your spiritual journey. Do you know that God, the Divine, or whatever you call it, lives in your heart?"

"Sure . . . I mean, I think so. I've read that we are all divine, and that we are all one. Sometimes I feel as if I've experienced this. But I guess I never thought of it that way, as God being within."

"We are all born with a connection to source love," she said. "And we all have a piece of God and the Divine inside our hearts. It is what gives us our intuition. When we tap into the Divine within, we are filled with a sense of peace. We also have free will, and so we get to decide whether or not we tap into this love and connection."

That day several months ago, Bridget had helped me understand how to operate from a heart space instead of my headspace. I still needed help with this, and even now I continued to pray for this guidance in my morning prayer.

> *Dear God,*
> *Please help me operate from a heart space today.*
> *Please help me see others the way you see them. Please*
> *help me see myself the way you see me.*

I watched my patient and loving earthly guide open the lavender and breathe in the scents of Hvar. I briefly thought of Dominik and that magical evening.

"You're blushing," Bridget said. "You had fun didn't you?"

"I sure did."

"And what do you need today?"

"I have several questions, but the most pressing one is what do I need to do to prove to the Divine that I trust them? I have traveled the world chasing my truth, so what in the heck else do I need to do?"

"Yes, you have gone on journeys, but that has been for you to recover the pieces of your soul. At each of those places you picked up a large amount of energy that has allowed you to grow and shift so quickly. I believe what you need to do is to prove your trust in everyday situations and to quit trying to make things happen."

At first I resisted her guidance. I trusted and let go during all of my adventures—Sedona, Mexico, Peru, Croatia, and Egypt. But as I sat there, I realized that I still tried to get my friends and my mom to accept me. Instead of allowing things to flow, I kept needing my friends and family to open up and to understand what I was going through. Maybe if I backed off, they would come around in their own time.

"That does make sense. So what should I do?"

"You can start practicing your rituals. Say affirmations, work with color. I suggest you find a beautiful orange nightgown—not a hot lava orange, but a muted orange—and sleep in it as a sign to the Divine that you are owning where you are going."

"Remind me again of the reason for doing this."

"Writing things down and practicing rituals are both great ways to communicate with the universe. It may seem silly or subtle, but in time you will see that these things create massive shifts. I know you mentioned you wanted to learn to manifest, and rituals will help with that."

"How so?"

"If you want to manifest something, you have to get very clear and very specific. You need to focus your energy on exactly what you want and not on what you don't want. If you list everything and be specific about exactly what you are asking for, then you can do a manifestation ritual. You will be amazed at how quickly you will begin to see your ideas and dreams turn into reality—as long as you believe them to be true before they are realized."

She then suggested I do an exercise called My Perfect Day, where I write down every detail about my perfect day. This worksheet would have words to evoke my dreams and wishes. She said I could read it while looking at my vision board for extra oomph. She also encouraged me to make a gratitude list of all I was thankful for in my life.

"Each night," she said, "before you go to bed, I want you to read that list and be in the energy of gratitude, because that energy helps us to manifest our heart's desires."

"I will try those things as soon as possible. But there's something else. I'm so lonely all the time. I really need a human support system, and right now I only have two friends I can talk to about my experiences—my cousin Anna and Claire. Would it be a good idea to try to manifest this with the ritual you explained?"

"Yes. Exactly."

I left Bridget's, as I usually did, filled with hope and a plan for the next steps. I stopped in at Saks and bought a silky, light orange nightgown. When I got home, I pulled out my journal and made a gratitude list, following Bridget's instructions.

> *I'm grateful for Rose, Anna, Claire, and my new friend Jane that hooked me up with an awesome travel and power spot experience.*
>
> *I am grateful for Papa Jack, Ted, all the archangels, goddesses, and ascended masters.*
>
> *I'm grateful for the sense of peace that is now in my condo, and for all the learning's and exposure I have had to what really is.*

The list went on and on.

I then lit a candle, got down on my knees, and prayed to God that he and my angels would please bring me a support system of like-minded people. If I was going to make this leap into the unknown, then I needed a community that shared my goal of wanting to change the world for good and help make this shift possible for human evolution.

Just as I was finishing up, I heard a knock on the door. I hoped it was Rose, as I wanted to take a chance and share a little about everything that had been going on.

"Coming!"

I opened the door. Ugh. It was Uncle Bill.

"We need to talk." He barged into my condo. "Enough is enough."

"I believe I asked you not to show up here again unless you were invited," I snapped. What I really wanted to yell was, *Murderer!*

He walked into my living room and glared at me. His face was bright red. "What in the heck is going on, and what have you done to Anna? She is on some kind of tangent about being psychic and having special gifts."

I settled my breathing, and once again I had access to his thoughts. He puffed out his chest for the next outburst, and I heard, *You have no idea how hard I have worked to conceal this part of our family history.* It took every ounce of self control not to tell him I knew his deep and dirty secrets.

"I can't believe you would dredge all this up right before the election," he said. "I should have had you committed when I had the chance."

"Why? Do you think I'm going to ruin your chances?"

"Don't you get smart with me, Samantha."

We stood facing each other, Bill with his arms folded, me with my hand in my pocket holding my black tourmaline. I thought about the aunt with the psychic skills. Did she also have to put up with his bullying? I gripped the crystal even tighter.

As if he'd read my mind, he narrowed his eyes and took a step toward me. "Your mother and I had a lunatic aunt, and you remind me of her. She paraded around talking about spirits and dark energies trying to attack her, and she embarrassed the heck out of the family."

"Nope. I didn't know that. Please share with me, Bill, what happened to her?"

"That's none of your business. Right now I want some explanations as to what the hell you think you are doing to my daughter."

I remembered Papa Jack saying the aunt wasn't dead, and I made a mental note to dig deeper and find this woman. I was certain that she and I would get along great.

"Anna and I have a deep friendship. I suggest you keep out of it," I said as calmly as possible.

"You're brainwashing her!" he yelled. "I've been keeping tabs on you, Samantha. I've seen you sitting outside in meditation, and I've seen you having supposed conversations with the air. Have you not noticed how there are extra Vote Bill Shilling signs in this part of town? My guys have been over here all the time. Do not think for a second that I don't know what is going on. It isn't too late, you know. I can still have you locked up in an asylum. I do have the power to do that."

He paced angrily back and forth. It was as if he had been taken over by the Brigade. I stood there struggling to keep my cool. I knew the more I reacted to his rage, the more I would feed the negativity and invite the Brigade in.

"You and Anna have lost your minds," he hissed, coming closer again. "I have also been recording your phone conversations, and I can't believe what you all believe to be reality. Talking about taking a deep breath and thoughts becoming things. How if we focus on love and positivity that is what we will get. I hate to break it to you, but that isn't the way the world works. You are going to get burned, and I refuse to go down with you."

Now my blood was boiling—he was the problem with humanity. People just like him, with stupid beliefs just like his, were the ones holding everyone back from being able to evolve. "I am sure the press would love to know that the mayor has been illegally stalking his niece!" I shot back.

"Don't you dare threaten me. You have no idea what I am capable of."

Oh, but I do . . . like murder.

"It's one thing for you to run off doing all this voodoo, but to involve Anna. What on earth are you thinking?"

He was about to blow, and I wanted to rip his head off. Somehow I managed to send a prayer into the universe. *Angel team! Where are you now? Please come help me!*

And they did. I once again heard that soothing inner voice. *Look at him with empathy and compassion. That is your best defense.*

As much as I didn't want to keep my cool, I knew I needed to do the best I could. "Uncle Bill, please stop. I don't deserve this. I haven't done one wrong thing, and I am not hurting anyone. In fact, I am helping people. I am sorry you do not agree, but I need you to leave now."

As I said this, a swirl of light formed in the room with Archangel Ariel and Honey in the center. Archangel Ariel held a lion shield this time, and she and Honey both were emitting healing green light from their bodies and projecting it onto Bill. My expression must have given something away, because Bill narrowed his eyes in suspicion.

"Why are you looking at me like that?"

Before I could respond, Ariel spoke to me. "Hey, doll. He can't see us, so don't worry. We are sending him healing light to try to shift his perception. We're also sending him love from source. We are allowed to intervene like this, because you asked for our help. He doesn't speak the truth—don't worry. You and Anna are helping your entire family, because as the two of you grow and lift your own vibrations, you are lifting the collective vibration of the family."

At that moment, I heard Honey's words telepathically. "Hey, Sam! I am so proud of you! Stay strong!"

I grinned from ear to ear. *Hey, I just connected with Honey!* Then I realized Bill was bellowing at me.

"Earth to Sam! Are you even listening to me?" He clapped his hands in front of my face.

"Oh sorry. I uh, I got distracted."

"I'm warning you. If you don't leave Anna alone you will be sorry. Mark my words."

He strode out of my condo and slammed the door. Ariel and Honey followed him, and I hoped they gave him that green light for as long as possible.

The force of his rage hit me now, and I burst into tears. I longed for my mom, her comfort and support. I dialed her number, and she listened to my teary recounting of Bill's visit.

"He scares me, Mom. Why does he want to interfere with my friendship with Anna? I'm not doing anything wrong."

"Of course you're not doing anything wrong," she said. "But I do think Bill has a point when it comes to the choices you are making. He's called me several times to talk about this, and I'm glad he has. You weren't there to see what happened to our aunt. She kept talking about love and a higher way, but what happened to her was dark, disturbing. She vanished. You need to understand that these types of things aren't accepted in this world. You will have a long road ahead of you if you decide to go this route. I would never want that way of life for you."

No Mom. Your aunt wasn't crazy. You all just made her think she was.

My heart sank. My mother had always been so supportive and kind, and I couldn't believe she was siding with my uncle. The all too familiar feelings of disappointment and loneliness rose up again.

"But it is a gift," I said. "Why would you not want to help the world?"

"Honestly, honey. What are you going to do to help save the world? I don't know where you got off on the wrong path or who in the world has brainwashed you, but I want my daughter back the way she was before all this mess."

I'd been pacing my condo as I spoke to my mom. Now I stood in front of my altar. I looked at the beautiful array of crystals and angel images, and in that moment I felt a surge of energy.

"Mom, I love you. I'm sorry you feel that way. I need to go."

I hung up the phone and grabbed my laptop. I began to type out the meanest email to Bill, telling him exactly what I thought of his election and his rude and uninvited outburst in my home. Just as I finished typing the nastiest words I could think of, my computer started playing this weird rap music. I listened to rap quite a bit growing up, but lately it wasn't on any of my playlists.

"Stop what you are doing, don't you dare go there, don't you dare go there.

You know better so stop whatcha doin and don't you dare go there . . ."

Those words repeated themselves over and over again, until I finally saw the humor and began to laugh. Sometimes my angels had the goofiest ways of reaching me.

I finally understood that writing that message took me right out of heart space, and so I prayed for help in cooling down and deleted the email. Just then a message appeared in my inbox. I'd received an evite to a gathering called "The Angel Crusade."

I clicked on the link and saw a beautiful woman with a truly magnetic air about her, talking about how this was a time for light workers. "If you feel like you are being called to live your purpose," she said, "and to go deeper within, then this is the place for you."

Oh my God. The manifestation ritual Bridget taught me worked.

I knew that being a light worker and an Earth Angel was basically the same thing. This was a way to find my support system and get connected with other like-minded souls. The Angel Crusade was being held in LA, and it wasn't that far off in time. Within seconds I had signed up for it.

I was half exhausted, half giddy. What a crazy day it had been. I grabbed the bag with my new nightgown in it and went upstairs. I got undressed and took the night gown out. I was so excited to wear it and show the Divine that I was READY! Before I realized what I was doing, I swung the nightgown in circles above my head and screamed, "Owning it! Owning it!" I fell onto the bed laughing hysterically at myself. I swear I heard the Divine clapping for me.

Chapter 34

I slept like an angel in my beautiful orange gown. I woke peacefully, but then memories of Bill's awful visit and the upsetting conversation with my mom intruded. I needed to stay busy, so after my breakfast smoothie and my meditation, I opened up a new book that had just arrived from Amazon, *Animals as Spirit Guides and How to Work With Them*. I turned to the chapter on dolphins.

The dolphin spirit animal represents harmony and balance. Dolphins are also a symbol of protection and of resurrection. They are closely in tune with their instincts and are highly intelligent. The dolphin's playful nature is a reminder that everyone needs to approach life with humor and joy. Usually the dolphin totem is a sign of deep inner strength.

I loved the sound of this, and it lined up with the teachings; including my first meeting with Hiro when he'd told me to have fun. I listened to the recording he'd sent me one more time. Each time I heard something different. Today it was, "Oh my friend, you are here to shine with your sense of humor and to bring joy to this world through your teachings about love."

Afterwards, I went outside to water the flowers I had planted in the front yard.

"Samantha!" a voice called out.

"Jane."

I hadn't seen her since my adventures in Croatia and Egypt, and I hurried over to tell her how fantastic the trip had been. Jane used to always wear large hats and sunglasses and would never make eye contact with anyone. Now she hardly ever had her face covered and was always smiling. I joined her on her patio, but before I could tell her anything she held her a finger to her lip to hush me.

She smiled slyly and said, "I have something for you." She handed me her little garden trowel and her gloves and disappeared inside. They were the cutest blue gloves decorated with tiny yellow butterflies. She reappeared with another purple envelope. "Here you go, sweetie."

"Oh my God. Are you serious? Another trip? Who is paying for all of this? I do have money. I mean, obviously not enough to pay for a private plane, but I can reimburse you for the regular travel expenses."

"No need to worry about it. Just know you are taken care of and enjoy it. Think of it as your birth right."

I liked that. How awesome. Unlimited luxury travel was my birthright. I kissed her on the cheek and ran back to my condo. I opened the envelope and found an e-ticket for a flight to Costa Rica. First class too. I was leaving the next morning. Again, I texted Claire.

What a life! I'm off to Costa Rica tomorrow!

Get outta here! she texted back. *Seriously though, I'm super happy for you!*

That night I packed a small bag and tossed in my favorite yellow bikini. I now considered it my good luck charm.

It was a pretty easy flight, direct and only four or so hours. The flight attendants were great up in first class. I was definitely getting used to this.

After I landed in Costa Rica, a polite driver got me to a ridiculously nice hotel on a narrow peninsula. The lobby was open air, and scarlet and yellow flowers cascaded off covered walkways. My luxury room had a small infinity pool and views of the sea and the lush green mountains. Monkeys watched me from the trees. I strolled the grounds, checking out the other amenities. One side of the peninsula had a long beach with chaise lounges and a volleyball net. I saw paddleboats bobbing in the water. On the other side was another beach with umbrellas, several jet skis in the shallows, and a cabana bar playing music.

Although I was tempted to stop at the cabana for a refreshing cocktail, I was instantly drawn to the jet skis. I hurried back to my room and changed into my bikini. Then I took the steps down to the beach, where I relished the feeling of warm sand between my toes. A bronzed, lean, young man with long black hair stood in the shallow water, checking something on one of the jet skis.

"Hello," I said. "Are you the one offering the jet ski tours?"

He flashed a dazzling smile "Yes, indeed. So do you like dolphins, chica?"

"I love them. They are one of my spirit animals."

"Oh really, you must be fun and playful then." He winked, as if he knew all about spirit animals. "Every day the dolphins remind me to keep a sense of humor about my life. Play and laugh—that is the message they give when they follow us in the water."

"Will I see some today?"

"Let's find out," he said.

I waded into the ocean and climbed onto a jet ski. After a few minutes of instructions, we set off, racing out into the bay and then toward the tip of the peninsula. The salty air whipped through my hair, and I soaked in the warmth of the sun. After a few minutes of riding fast, the guide slowed down and we maneuvered the jet skis closer to a rocky point.

"Look, do you see there?" he said.

A turtle with a beaky, ancient looking head had surfaced.

"Wow! It's huge."

"It's actually two of them. It is mating season," he said with a large grin. "See the female beneath him?"

"What? I don't understa— Oh, I didn't know turtles mated doggie style," I said, trying to throw the guide off his guard.

"Touché, you are a funny Americana. Now let's go find some dolphins."

We glided over the water and played with the waves off each other's jet skis, and before long an entire family of dolphins joined us. They too were playing with the waves from the jet skis, and then they began to play with us. It was one of the coolest things I had ever done. I would look to my left and see five fins, and then one or two of them would jump out of the water and do a spin.

After about an hour, the guide suggested we head back. He revved his throttle and set off for the beach. I lingered for a moment saying goodbye to the dolphins. I caught my breath.

No, it couldn't be . . .

I was sure it was though. The most beautiful creature was swimming alongside of me. It was undeniable. Her tail fins were bright turquoise, and she had the most beautiful indigo seashells covering her breasts. She had long golden curls that were almost as long as her fins. She glided even closer to me and made sure to get my attention by playfully splashing me with her tail. She rolled over to float on her back, smiled as she blew me a kiss, and then dived deep and disappeared.

I felt connected to her in an instant, and I was so happy to have had the magical experience of actually getting to see a real live mermaid. *I knew they existed,* I thought with a smile. I remembered a documentary I had seen about mermaids and if they were myths or not.

Back on shore, I thanked the guide for the adventure. I ate scrumptious fish tacos for dinner and fell asleep to the sound of waves caressing the beach. I slept so late the breakfast menu was no longer being served at the resort's main dining room. Fortunately, one of the staff made me a delicious smoothie, and I feasted on an entire fresh pineapple. I was up for adventure, and a hike seemed like just the thing to do. The concierge wasn't around, but I grabbed a map and headed for the forest. Driving here the day before, I'd seen a sign for a trail that looped through the rain forest. Soon I felt as if I were deep in the wilderness. I heard monkeys in the distance and saw green iguanas, brilliantly colored birds, and even a toucan.

After about an hour, I arrived at a fork in the path. I frowned. This was supposed to be a loop that would lead me back to the beach. I pulled out the map to see how to get back to the hotel.

Crap, I grabbed the wrong map.

I looked at the dense tropical vegetation. *Were there jaguars in Costa Rica? What about poisonous snakes?*

"Anyone there?" I said in a shaky voice. "Angels? Come on, Papa Jack or Ted. Hello? Can one of you please show up to help me?"

No one showed up, and I wondered how I'd get back to civilization, let alone the hotel.

"Guides, this is not funny," I said, feeling quite alarmed.

Still no divine intervention. Nothing but trees covered in vines and the earthy smell of the forest. And a funny looking red bird sitting on a branch a few feet away. It had black feet and a long hooked black beak, and it cocked its head to the left and to the right as if sizing me up. It hopped to a closer branch and then fluttered a few feet down the path to the left.

I stared at the map again, and the bird landed on a branch right next to me. It whistled like a kettle about to boil, and I burst out laughing.

"You want me to follow you?"

Again, it flew a few feet away and stood in the middle of the path that veered to the left. It had to be a sign. I followed it, and for the next ten minutes it fluttered and then stopped, fluttered and then stopped. It led me along the path, until I climbed a hill and reached a house on a cliff overlooking the sea. The bird gave its funny boiling-kettle whistle one more time and flew away.

I stared at the house with its Buddha statues in the garden and wind chimes ringing out in the salty breeze.

Think, Samantha. How do you feel? Does this feel like a trick from the Brigade? Or is this a sign you should knock and ask for help?

Bridget had been helping me to constantly check in with myself and see how I was feeling and to use my intuition that way. I had figured out when I was connected to my intuition, I usually felt good and at peace. I stared at the door and noticed that it felt welcoming and inviting, the same way Bridget's door had seemed to me.

Here goes nothing.

I walked up and rang the large golden bell beside the door. *Why not?* The sign above it read *Ring Me*. After waiting for a few minutes, I didn't think anyone was going to come. I sighed, at least I could see the hotel from here. I walked to the edge of the cliff to see if there was a trail heading down to the beach. It looked steep and too rocky, so I decided to retrace my steps through the forest. If I got lost again maybe the kettle bird would show up. Just then the door opened a crack, and a petite woman dressed in white and wearing some sort of white turban stepped out.

"Hello, you are just in time," she said. "We are all out back about to start class."

"I'm sorry, you must have me confused with someone. I got lost, but I can see the hotel now so I'll head back down."

"I am Geeshka," she said. "I don't have you confused with anyone. I have to believe you have been led here to take Kundalini yoga with us."

At first I thought she was joking, and then I realized this woman was dead serious. "Kunda what?" I asked.

She smiled from ear to ear and had a magnificent presence and loving, warm glow about her. "Kundalini is a special healing type of yoga. It focuses on self awareness and delivering an experience of your highest consciousness. I can give you a more thorough discussion after class, but we need to get started now. If you would like to join us, we would be honored to have you. Remember, there is no such thing as a coincidence; you must be here for a reason."

I closed my eyes, took a deep breath, and saw in my mind's eye a beautiful orange Gerber daisy. I knew this was a sign from Papa Jack suggesting I proceed.

"I have been doing a lot of yoga lately, but I have never done this before. Is this a beginners class?"

"You will be fine. We will clearly and specifically tell you what to do. Now follow me."

I followed her through the modest but beautiful and immaculately clean house, and I felt an immense sense of peace wash over me. She opened a sliding glass door and led me to the back, where an open deck overlooked the water. I saw two other women in their forties, also wearing flowing white pants and shirts and white turbans. A very tall man with a long beard was in a similar getup. I was grateful to see a young couple closer to my age both wearing t-shirts and shorts.

Geeshka handed me a white fur blanket and said, "Go ahead and lie down and get comfortable."

As I was setting up, I noticed large amethyst crystals arranged on what appeared to be an alter. She had a guitar and a large gong beside her as well. She passed a sheet of paper to everyone and asked us to follow along in the singing. She played music on a stereo, and I recognized the words of the song instantly. It was the song Jimmy had played for me during my Rocket Blast: Long Time Sun. Tears filled my eyes, and I knew there was a deep connection with me and this song.

Geeshka then led us through some crazy activities. She had us flail our hands in the air to the point of exhaustion. We were doing what she called breath of fire, and it was making my insides rumble and seemed to be awakening parts of my body that had been dormant forever. I could feel the energy moving all up and down my spine, and I almost felt as though I was about to leave my body. I had to get up in the middle of it and run to the bathroom, as my body wanted to cleanse itself very quickly. When I came back and sat down, I noticed everyone looked so focused and into this.

"As you flail your hands this time," she said, "do it with intention, almost like you are hitting something and getting rid of any anger you have pent up. Now repeat after me."

I froze and had to regroup. She was barking like a dog.

Is she crazy, like anyone is going to do that?

Boy was I wrong. Within seconds the group was doing as she asked and "repeating" after her, a.k.a. barking.

When in Rome . . . I thought as I took a deep breath and joined in.

After what felt like hours of intense breath work, barking, and making funny movements with my body, Geeshka finally asked us to lie down and go into deep meditation.

Halleluiah, this I can do.

During the meditation she started to bang the gong, and I felt like my head was on another planet for a little while. It was intense, but also weirdly comforting and I liked the feeling. The meditation time flew by, and before long Geeshka had everyone wiggle around and come to a seated position. We sang a closing song, and I couldn't believe what had just happened. I had some wild experiences back in my party days in the beginning of college—experimenting with pills and other illegal substances, searching for that feeling of euphoria and freedom. Now, I'd entered into a profound state of euphoria and bliss simply by doing this crazy style of yoga.

"Sam, how was your experience?" Geeshka asked with the largest smile.

"Delightful." I still felt like I was flying in the clouds.

Who knew you can actually get high on your own energy.

This was amazing. I now knew how to get high on my own supply.

"Okay class, we will have tea for those of you that want to stay and join us for a tea party."

I burst out laughing.

Is she for real? Flailing hands, barking like a dog, chanting random words, a euphoric feeling like no other, and now we go into the kitchen for a tea party?

I honestly didn't want to chitchat with everyone, but I was pretty sure I was too jacked and too high on this love energy to wonder through the forest on my own.

I went into the kitchen to see what was going on, and I couldn't help but giggle, everyone was so lovey dovey and smiley with each other. This kundalini thing wasn't so bad after all. If the kids at school knew how good it felt, they would be doing this all the time. I was sure there would be no moral hangovers, and no one would make any irresponsible decisions while on this loving natural high. Seriously, this was what we should have been doing as a pre-party in college, instead of downing wine and vodka and god knows what else.

After tea a jeep appeared to take us back to the hotel. Apparently, there was a road up here that I had missed. We rumbled back down, and I kept my eye out for my bird friend, but she or he was nowhere in sight. I described the bird to the driver, and he shook his head. He'd never seen such a creature before.

I said goodbye to the other couple at the hotel lobby. I still felt ecstatic, and I longed to sit in meditation and surrender to this crazy love vibration humming throughout my body. I grabbed a pile of towels from my room and took them to some large rocks overlooking a small cove. Smiling about nothing other than the way I felt, I sat down, lowered my gaze, and focused on my breath. Immediately the water in the cove began to ripple in ever widening circles, as if someone had dropped a boulder into the sea. I felt a sudden onrush of air, and an oversized owl swooped right over me and landed on the rock.

"Hey, Sam. 'Member me?"

The owl looked strangely familiar. I remembered a few years earlier I had seen a large owl perched in the oak tree behind my condo. At the time, I couldn't believe my eyes, and I went out to see it closer. After a few minutes, the owl had spread its wings and flown off. I never saw it again, but I would always hear him call, *Whoo-hoo whoo-hoo."* I named him Hoot and sent him love every time I heard him.

"Are you Hoot?"

"Yes. That's cool that you remember me." He did one of those wacky owl moves and rotated his head 360 degrees. "I am also your totem spirit animal. The dolphins don't get all the credit. Listen, pal, I crossed over recently and joined your divine team. I'm here with an important message. The only way through pain is to feel it. In order to heal pain, you have to first feel it. In the human world today, so many of you avoid what you are feeling and bury it. But it will always come back unless you feel it. I made up an easy rhyme for you to remember. 'To heal it, you need to feel it.'" He blinked his enormous eyes.

"So is this why I have been crying and feeling all this overwhelming and unexplained pain lately?"

"Yes, precisely. As long as you are in your human form, you will always have pain, and you will always be learning until your very last breath. But the hardest part for you should be over soon. There is a team on the way that is going to fill you up with divine power. You are going to sit here with me and watch. I'm here so you will not be scared. We have noticed that you are sometimes scared by your abilities. It is important for you to receive this divine power, and that you don't block it with fear.

"You do make me feel pretty comfortable, Hoot."

The next thing I knew, I was floating above my physical body. Archangel Michael, Archangel Raphael, and Jesus were gathered around my body below me. Mother Teresa too. I recognized her in an instant. Her presence radiated pure love and goodness. I saw her holding my left hand and patting it. Tears glistened on my cheeks, as the angel team gently laid me down on my back across the hotel towels. An elephant approached and gently touched my forehead with its trunk

"An elephant? Wow. Who is that?"

"That is Ganesh," said Hoot. "He is the god of wisdom and learning, as well as the remover of obstacles."

Archangels Michael and Raphael knelt beside me and literally cracked open the crown of my head.

Horrified, I looked over at Hoot. "What are they doing?"

"Don't worry. They're just implanting source light into your body. In fact, it is time for you to go back into your body so you can feel this. Listen pal, you are doing great so keep up the good work, and remember you have several football fields of supporters helping you through all this."

I looked down and saw the archangels threading undulating strands of bright white light with golden droplets directly into the top of my cracked open head. The light traveled in a circular motion, down one side of my body and up the other, again and again, faster and faster. Before I realized it, I was back in my body enjoying this euphoric state of being. The pleasure and sense of grace had almost doubled at this point. When I came to I was still lying on my back. I sat up and noticed the wind had calmed down, but the waves were still crashing against the rocks.

Well, I obviously made it to my sixth power spot. I smiled and shook my head at all that had gone down today.

Boy, has my life taken about a million turns in directions I never knew existed or thought were possible.

Chapter 35

The Kundalini class with Geeshka made a lasting impression on me, and I was even more devoted to my yoga practice when I returned to Atlanta. Now when I did warrior one or a sun salutation, I could feel energy shooting out of my hands. I committed to a yoga class every morning, and sometimes I took the gentle yin yoga class at night. If I was having a day where I felt like I had to try extra hard to fight off the Brigade, then a power yoga class always helped to shake off that nasty energy and put me in a better space.

The Brigade were devious and manipulative, so I made sure to check my 'ego flares,' as I called them. About ten days after returning from Costa Rica, I woke up and heard a voice in my head whisper, *It is time to fire Bridget. And it is time for you to move on.*

I flinched. I knew I was supposed to be following divine guidance, but I didn't want to fire her. I didn't understand why this voice, that for the last few months had been only supportive and encouraging and sending me in the right direction, would be telling me to do this. Doubt crept in, and I had second thoughts about my path.

What did it even mean to be an Earth Angel? I'm not sure I want to do this. Who wants to live a lonely life when all their friends are imaginary? Besides, it really scares me to do visualizations on my own. The Brigade keeps such a close watch on me, and I don't want to have one of them inside me ever again.

I got down on my knees at the foot of my bed and prayed to God.

Dear God, I don't know if I can do this. I miss my friends and my old way of life. This has all been so scary, and I don't want to be locked away by my uncle, or to be killed for that matter. I don't know if I am cut out for all this anyway. Maybe it is best you find someone else to do my job for me.

I decided to ignore the voice for now and focus on how excited I was about my lunch date with Anna. We were meeting at a café down the street from the yoga studio that had the most delicious chicken and walnut salad. I couldn't wait to tell her about my adventures and all that I had uncovered. I got there early and ordered a large Green Goddess juice.

"Hey, Sam. Long time no see." Anna gave me a huge hug. It had been way too long since I last saw her.

"I missed you," I said. "How have you been?"

"I am doing well. A little crazy, but well." She drew a deep breath, and I thought, oh no, something is going on with Bill. She sat down at our table.

"Is it Bill?" I asked. "He came to see me—"

She shook her head. "Well, no that is actually a whole different story within itself. You're the only person I can think of to talk to. No one else would understand."

"Go ahead, I am all ears."

"I can't even begin to explain what is going on with me. I have been having visions of my future, and I am hearing voices in my head. I thought it was my imagination, but no, I'm hearing voices too! And then I was sleeping the other night and at 4:11 am—I am not kidding—a spirit or something started tapping my foot and said, 'Anna, your time has come. You need to be meditating so we can communicate with you daily.'"

I felt so relieved listening to her. I wasn't crazy. Or if I was, at least I had a good friend along for the ride. Anna did look a little freaked out about it all, and I remembered how much I had doubted my sanity when my awakening started. "I know exactly what you are talking about. It's feels freaky, doesn't it?" I said.

"Uhhh, yeah. I was like *what the?*!? I mean, I still sometimes think I made up the voices. But it was undeniable. I looked over to see if Chad was awake, and he wasn't. I was glad he wasn't though, because there is no way he would have believed me."

"So what did you do?"

"What do you think I did? I got up and went and sat in meditation."

I burst out laughing, and she did too.

"Seriously," she went on. "I wasn't going to ignore that spirit or whatever it was. I had tried to meditate before, but it's hard with the kids, and I always get interrupted."

"What happened in your meditation?"

"It was eerily quiet for a while, then I heard a voice explaining to me that I was having physical symptoms of a spiritual awakening, and not to be alarmed, and to be assured that I was not sick . . ."

"Have you thought you were sick?"

"Yes. I have been tired as heck, and dizzy and nauseous. I have been to the doctor twice and nada. Anyway, the voice told me that the ringing in my ears was a Divine download. I didn't know what downloading meant, so I asked it to clarify. The explanation I got was that it was my angels transmitting information into my cellular memory, and the ringing was so I would be aware of what was happening."

She was talking so fast, that I didn't have a chance to tell her I had been having the ringing too.

"I have to admit I was pretty freaked out," she said. "I almost got up and went back to bed, but something compelled me to sit for a few more minutes. Soon after, I heard a loud but loving voice tell me I needed to release my focus on external things and surrender and start to live my purpose. Can you believe that?"

I grabbed her hands and squeezed them tightly. Finally, I had a true companion on my journey. "This is fantastic news," I said.

"Fantastic? I'm not so sure about that."

"I know it's alarming at first, because I've been through it. The headaches, the ringing in the ears, blurry vision, plus so much more. You should read *A Seat of the Soul* or *The Celestine Prophecy*. Both books explain human evolution and the major shift that is currently happening on our planet."

The waiter came just then, and we both blurted out that we wanted the chicken salad. I shooed him away—no, we didn't want a glass of wine—and I decided to take even more of a chance with my dear cousin and tell her some of my amazing experiences.

"So here's how crazy my life is these days," I said. "I have been traveling the world going to different places that are apparently my power spots, and I have been meeting the Divine. Also—this is going to sound bizarre—I am now basically besties with Papa Jack. Remember how I told you I had been communicating with him?"

Her eyes widened. "Yeah, I remember. I just didn't realize how serious you were."

"I'm thrilled about what you just told me, because I have been so nervous about telling anyone. I have been really scared about what others will think. Your story made me realize that I'm not the only one having these out there experiences." At that point I stood up, because I had to give Anna a bear hug.

"It's going to be okay, I promise," I whispered in her ear.

She was crying, and I was crying—tears of gratitude. I could help her. Everything I had gone through hadn't been in vain. It dawned on me that I had these experiences so I could share my truth and help others to understand what they were going through. I could help them realize they were not crazy, and all of this was part of human evolution.

"I'm so sorry," she said. "I have been consumed with me and these crazy things happening. I didn't even think to check in on you."

I reassured Anna that I had actually needed time alone to figure everything out and to make decisions for myself about what I believed and what felt right.

"It's so hard not to get swept up into societal conditioning," I said. "I have gone my entire life doing things based on what others expected of me. I thought I needed a successful career doing something that Mom and Dad and everyone would approve of. Even in high school I was doing it. And Lucas—I loved him so much, and I also knew deep down he wasn't the guy for me. Yet I still wanted to marry him, because I thought that was what was expected of me."

She nodded in understanding. "Think how many people live their lives that way. It is kind of sad once you become aware of the truth."

"I know, and it's not like what has happened to me is a switch you can turn on and off. I still worry about what people will think when they find out that I got fired and haven't gotten another job or decided to go back to school. And if I told 'normal' people that I talk to angels and Papa Jack—can you imagine what their response would be? Your dad already thinks I'm insane and wants to have me put away."

Her expression turned somber. I wondered what it was like to have Uncle Bill as a father. Was he ever loving and kind to his family?

"He's equally as pissed at me, if that helps at all," she said. "I have to say this is all so crazy, how did we go our entire lives and never know any of this existed?"

"I have those exact thoughts daily. You know, I have been doing quite a bit of research on all this, and it seems that psychic abilities are inherited. So everyone has some form of intuition or they wouldn't be in a body. However, we come here with varied levels of gifts. If you come here with a lot of gifts or have the capability to tap fully into divine power, then that means you are an evolved soul. You picked a family lineage that would support what you needed to do."

The waiter reappeared with our salads, and I ordered another Green Goddess for myself, and one for Anna. We chatted a bit about my favorite yoga studio. They had a mama and kids class on Saturday mornings, and I told her I thought she would love it.

"You said something earlier about family lineages," she said. "Do you think we inherited these abilities?"

"Yep, that is exactly what I am saying. When your dad barged into my condo last week, he said he thought he had shut this down; that anyone in the family who explored anything like this would be an outcast. And then Papa Jack told me he had passed these abilities on to me. He told me how he regrets that he didn't take the opportunity to use the gifts he had, or to even realize he had these gifts."

"Oh my God, now I get it," she said. "I was eavesdropping on Dad and Mom, and I heard Dad talking about his crazy aunt. He said she used to spin around the room saying there were evil spirits. He said she was an embarrassment to the family, and that she would walk up to them fanning her hands around their bodies saying she was keeping them protected. At the time it didn't make sense, but it does now."

"I'm so happy you are also on this spiritual journey," I said. "I'm nervous, and I'm going to need support to stand up to your father."

"We will tackle him together. You know I'm always here, and right back at you. I am going to need you when Chad tries to divorce me for being totally cray cray."

"Cheers!" I said, and we toasted each other with our green juices.

Now, if it can only go this smooth when I tell Rose, I will be in good shape.

Chapter 36

When I opened the door to my condo early that evening, I was stunned to see what appeared to be an angel sleeping on my couch. I tiptoed over to take a closer look, and yes, it was. His wings were a pale white, and they wrapped around him to form a cocoon. He snored ever so slightly. Well, maybe not a snore, more of a throaty inhalation. I must have laughed louder than I realized, because he jumped up and shivered his wings.

"Shoot," he said. "I can't believe you caught me snoozing." He was tall and wore a woven, off white gown. As he settled his wings, I saw he had a deep purple silk shawl draped over his shoulders, and it matched the wide belt holding his robe. He wore a crown of red roses, and held a golden cane that was also wrapped in red roses.

"I didn't know that angels needed sleep," I said with a giggle.

"Well, uh, we usually don't. Look, can you make me a promise not to tell anyone?" He tapped his fingers together.

"Sure thing. What is your name?"

"My name is Archangel Jeremiel. I am the archangel of inspiration and of motivation. My mission is to assist humans who are attaining spiritual devotion. I can help you when you feel stuck spiritually, or if you need help feeling enthusiastic about your divine mission. Basically, I am here to help you make positive changes in your life."

He was now standing tall, and he nodded solemnly as I listened.

"I am really glad you are here," I said with a deep sigh. "I have been feeling totally off, and I can't put my finger on why. I have been hearing a voice telling me to fire my coach, Bridget. I really don't want to fire her, but I want to follow guidance."

"I am sorry to tell you, but that voice telling you to fire her isn't us," he said softly, and he placed his wide hand on my shoulder.

"What, is it the Brigade? I thought I had gotten rid of them. I am so over this."

"I know, they are sneaky, but you are still agreeing to work with them."

"No, I'm not. After everything I do to take precautions to keep them out, I am insulted that you would even say that." I removed his hand from my shoulder and glared up at him.

"Please do not take offense. This is all a learning experience and a process."

"How? How can I be working with them?" I crossed my arms and tapped my foot.

"We all have choices. With free will you have a choice to work with us or with the Brigade. Although you are protecting your energy and yourself, you haven't demanded that they go away."

Unbelievable! I thought with an eye roll. "Well, that is probably because no one ever told me that. How in the heck was I supposed to know that?"

"Easy tiger, simmer down."

"Please enlighten me master. How do I choose not to work with the Brigade?" I snipped back.

"Feisty, I like it." He circled me as if sizing me up. "Here is the deal, Samantha. Think about what you want and then declare it."

"Okay, so I want to work with light and love and only light and love."

"Presto!" he said, waving his cane as a wand.

"So it is done then?" I asked, still tapping my foot.

"Not quite. You see, if you declare that you choose to work with only light and love, then any time an entity comes to you from the

Brigade, it will be sent to the light. Eventually, they will quit coming as they can foresee their future—as long as you continue to make that choice."

"So how do I do this?"

"Every morning when you wake up, you need to say out loud and with intention, 'I choose to be light and love. I choose to work with only light and only love. Anything that is in me or around me that is not light and love will be sent into the light immediately. Thank you.'"

"That's it? Are you serious?"

"Very serious. Your voice is extremely powerful, and this will help you get back on track and kick the Brigade to the curb. One other thing, you are not going to be able to move forward until you let go of what others think. This is really blocking you and holding you back."

Shoot, I knew there was going to be a catch. "This is a big one, Jeremiel. Both my mom and my uncle have pretty much threatened to disown me if I follow this path. Or at least get me in for a psych eval. I hate the sound of that."

"Listen, they are your family and they love you. They will accept you in time. I know it isn't easy, but you have to do what you feel is right for you in your heart and not what is right for someone else. Otherwise, you are living their truth and not yours. Besides, listen to yourself. You are scared of being an outcast based on the fact you only look at the good in things and choose to believe that only love is real."

I knew he was right, but this was really hard for me to hear. "What about my friends? They are all going to think I am crazy, and that I have lost my mind. Rose, Ashley, Jacob, I haven't been hanging with them at all the way I used to."

"Why do you think that is?"

"I don't know. Probably because it's what I would have thought not long ago if a friend tried to tell me all this stuff."

"One of the biggest mistakes humans make is making assumptions. You will not truly know until you tell them, and remember that what we think is going to happen, is often what does happen. You are a great manifestor, so you should start doing visualizations to manifest what you do want, instead of spending your energy worrying about what you don't want. Don't you see that when you worry about things, you are calling and inviting them into your life."

"Of course I understand that, but it is really hard not to worry."

"Here is a tool that will help you get what you want, as long as your intention is pure and for the highest good. Imagine yourself having these conversations with your friends and family, and imagine them saying exactly what you want to hear. You are only truly lovable when you are fully authentic. You got this kiddo, and remember your divine team has your back."

He gave me a hug. I couldn't help but well up in tears from the comfort of his soft and gentle wings wrapped around my entire body. He was right. Even though I had been brave, and I had traveled the world to learn my truth, it was time for me to fully own myself, to really be me. I realized that the people who really love me will still love me, and the others, well . . . I guess if they can't accept me for me, then I shouldn't be worried about what they think anyway.

I took one more deep breath of the perfume of his wings, they smelled faintly of cinnamon, and then I lifted my head and looked into his gold flecked eyes.

"Thank you so much for all your help. I really needed this tonight. I wasn't sure I wanted to go through with this anymore. In fact, before I bonded with my cousin Anna today, I was sure I wanted to go back to the way things used to be."

"It is normal to have doubts. That is the Brigade's specialty. They want you to doubt yourself and not say yes to your truth and to your powers and gifts. This transformation isn't easy, and you have done a beautiful job. Now get upstairs and get some rest—you need it. It is key that you take care and nurture yourself, especially when you are at a fragile time like this."

Jeremiel walked me upstairs and tucked me into bed. I knew it seemed like something only a child would want, but I have to say I welcomed the comfort and was grateful that he didn't leave me until I was safe and sound in my bed and already dreaming.

The next morning I sat in bed for a while writing in my dream journal. Writing dreams down helped me understand the messages and wisdom I received while I slept. In the first dream, I was back in my childhood backyard sitting on the hill by the red trampoline. The wretched green snake was back, and it was nastier than ever. This time it had huge fangs. It reared up and then slithered toward me with a wide open mouth. Even though I felt scared, I wasn't frantic like I had been before. This time I was armed with knowledge, and I had a plan.

In my dream I shut my eyes and remembered Honey and how she always knew how to cheer me up. Having her loving body nestled up against me in bed always brought a smile to my face. It instantly slowed my heart rate and strengthened my breath. I focused on this thought for as long as I could before I opened my eyes. When I opened them, the snake was about half the size.

Don't stop now, think of another loving memory, said a faint voice in my head.

I was actually a little shocked at how easy it was to slip away into a relaxed state in the presence of this monstrous reptile. I remembered playing on the beach on a family vacation as a child. I could feel my toes in the sand, and Mom and Dad were actually happy together. We were all in the shallow part of the ocean allowing the salt water to soothe our bodies, as we tossed a ball back and forth. I opened my eyes this time, and the snake shrank even more. It was getting smaller and smaller, and the hisses were quieter and less frequent. I swear I even saw confusion in its eyes. When it was about eighteen inches long, its scales started to dissolve. It slithered down the hill

Suzanne Adams

as it changed from green to a soft caramel color, and to my surprise the snake morphed into a bunny rabbit.

The wind gently blew across my face, and the rabbit hopped back up the hill, and said, "You see, when you are afraid of demons and scary things and react to them, you are feeding and fuelling them. You encourage them to come back for more. When you simply go within and be at peace, the demons have no power. No one can take that peace away from you once you have it. Trust, faith, and confidence are your foundation. You can lean on that."

"I think I'm finally getting it," I said, happy to be talking to the rabbit and not the snake.

The other dream was more puzzling. I was out for a jog near Bridget's, and Ted showed up to go jogging with me. I was making fun of him, because he was totally out of shape and lost his breath within seconds. He then asked me to slow down.

"Listen," he said. "I'm not really here to be your running buddy. I have something I need to tell you."

"Yep, Ted, I figured. That's usually how you roll. What's up?"

"I want you to know there is more than meets the eye with someone in your life. I'm not going to tell you who, because I think you can figure it out. Just know there is someone that you have a . . . uh . . . an unexpected connection with."

Before I could respond he vanished.

I added several big question marks in my journal after writing that dream down. An unexpected connection? I had no idea who he was referring to, but knowing the way my life was going these days, I suspected I was in for a surprise.

Chapter 37

It felt like I hadn't had girl time with Rose in eons, and the times I had seen her had been fleeting. Her boyfriend had recently moved to Atlanta, and they always stayed at his place. I called her and suggested we make up for lost time and hang out. She eagerly agreed. It was two days since I had decided to be fully authentic, and I longed to have her support.

"Hey Shawdy, ready to hit the town?" she asked when she saw me.

"You know it sista!" I replied, giving her the tightest hug I could.

We walked to our favorite sushi spot and got our normal table by the chef's counter. Beautiful, bright colored abstract paintings covered the walls. The ceilings were high with cool retro looking crystal chandeliers. We ordered a bottle of sake, some edamame, and our fave appetizer, the yellowtail sashimi.

"I have to say you have a radiant glow about you, and you seem so happy," she said. "I'm not sure what you have been doing, but I will say it must be working for you. You look fantastic."

"I'm thrilled to hear you say that. I have been working hard to get myself on the right path. You witnessed firsthand what a wreck I was."

"I know, I was so worried about you."

"After everything I have been through over the past year, I have been looking within, and I have actually learned quite a bit about myself. I also wanted to tell you about—"

I stopped. Rose's smile had faded, and she looked a little sad.

"What's wrong?" I asked.

"I have been so absent, Sam. I know it, and I want to apologize. But you were shutting me out, and I felt so lonely. Then I met Frank, and he's been so amazing. But you are too. And sitting here with you, I realize how long it has truly been since we have gotten together for girl time."

"Please don't apologize, I totally understand. I mean, I have changed so much, and I honestly needed the space to figure things out on my own. So the timing was actually perfect." I took a deep breath. I was more determined than ever to tell Rose my truth. I remembered the rabbit's words—I could lean on my trust and confidence.

"I don't really know how to say this," I said, "but I have been having encounters with Angels. And, as crazy as this sounds, I have been in communication with my dead grandfather who I never met."

"That doesn't sound that crazy," she said.

I couldn't help but smile. She was trying so hard. "Come on, you can be honest. I know it totally does."

"Okay, well maybe a little." She grinned. "But I know you so well, and I know you wouldn't make anything like that up. I may not be into all of that, but I can't deny how much you've changed. I don't really care what you have been doing, as long as you're happy. Anyone who saw you at your low and then could see you now would be crazy not to support whatever is working for you. You know I will always love you and want you in my life, no matter what."

I felt instant relief when she said those words. It was validating to hear and to know that she would always be there for me.

"You know I'm not the only one who has noticed the positive changes in you," she said. "Frank and I went to dinner with the crew a few weeks ago, and it seems that everyone has seen you in snippets here and there. They all said you're doing really well, and that you seem to have genuinely changed for the better and are on a path of major happiness. We are all so happy for you."

"That means so much to me." I gave her another hug. I was so happy and grateful that my friends no longer considered me a crazy outcast and were able to respect and honor the changes in my life.

"Okay, enough with the sappiness. Let's have some fun," she said as she playfully pushed me away.

"Sounds great."

Over dinner she filled me in on everything I had been missing out on, and I realized not much had changed. Although I still wanted to keep in touch with everyone, I knew my life would never be the same—those days of living far from my truth, of not even knowing I had a path, were gone—and I knew I would never be the same either.

That night when I got home I cried again tears of gratitude. I wasn't sure why they were flowing, but I had learned when emotions flow it is best to let them out.

As I drifted off to sleep, I felt the strangest sensation, a tingling in my ears. I heard a loud *boing*, almost like in a pinball machine game, everything turned blurry, and somehow I sensed that I was now attached to a long silver cord. When my vision cleared, I was looking into the brightest and most beautiful rainbow I had ever seen. Each color seemed to give off a unique vibration, and I was drawn to the purple one. I stepped into the light. It cushioned underneath me and filled me with love and grace and support.

The purple light swelled around me and then whooshed into an undulating funnel that slowly morphed into an odd looking angel. I hate to say this about an angel, but this one was weird. He had purple hair and a long pale face. He seemed incredibly old and carried a sword made of bright golden light.

"Hello, Samantha. I am Archangel Zadkiel, and this is Lady Nada." He gestured to a beautiful, flaxen haired woman who had appeared at his side. "We are going to help you with the last bit of information to complete your soul retrieval and power spot journey."

Lady Nada wore a pastel pink and white gown and held a large pink rose bud. "Hello dear," she said. She spoke with grace and conviction. "I want you to know that I will help you understand your divine power. I will be with you moving forward, as it is crucial you learn to be authentic with the world around you. Being authentic and your true self is the only way to shine and the only way for you to truly follow your path."

"Are you kidding? I am absolutely my true self," I snapped.

"No my dear, not one hundred percent. You have been hiding your discoveries for fear of what others will think, and that is holding you back. This is perfectly normal and understandable, but it is time to release it. I have something that I think will help you."

"And telling Anna and Rose doesn't count?" I asked, feeling quite annoyed that I wasn't getting any credit for that.

"Yes, and kudos to you for doing so. But it's time to start telling others as well."

In a blink I was looking at a gorgeous, red hued fortress on the edge of a desert in India. As I floated down to take a closer look—I was in a large room with windows that opened onto the desert, and I could see golden statues of Hindu deities like Shiva and Ganesh. Brilliantly colored carpets were strewn across a roughly tiled floor. Huge platters piled high with rice and fragrant meats and fruit were set in the center of the room. Plumes of incense rose into the air, and the sound of laughter surrounded me as women and men, children and elders, ate and drank in a joyous celebration.

"Whoa, looks like that crew liked to party," Zadkiel blurted.

Lady Nada shot Zadkiel a glare. She said to me, "Do you know what you are looking at?"

"Is that me and my family?" I asked. Instinctively I knew it to be true, but I felt oddly shy about claiming it.

"Yes. That is it. What else do you see and feel about it?"

"I'm having a happy life. I am fulfilled and with loved ones and our connections with each other are deep and loving. It feels so amazing. I am so happy." I couldn't quite believe it. As I looked at the scene, I could feel emotions rippling through me. "Oh my gosh, my mom is there with me and Papa Jack, Rose, and Anna!"

"That is right. We often travel in soul groups."

"What are soul groups?"

"Oh, sorry. They are souls you have had loving and supportive relationships with. Often soul groups will reincarnate together. In this particular lifetime, you and your family were benevolent rulers. You embodied love, and by your example, you spread happiness far and wide. The people in this desert region loved and respected your family. Your life back then was one of generosity and service to the Divine."

Having this direct experience of the emotions of that life, I felt the truth of her words. It dawned on me then that I had the same potential with my soul family in this lifetime too.

"Do you understand why we wanted to show you this?" asked Zadkiel.

"So I could see what it could be like for me in this lifetime," I said with confidence.

"Yes, and also so you can see the benefits of being authentic and fully releasing what others think of you," said Zadkiel. "When you care about what others think, you give them your power. To live a truly fulfilled and fun life, you have to let go of that and be true to yourself. This is the most common way people get tripped up. The human ego loves it, because it is an easy way to get you off your path. The Brigade always works this aspect to get people to cave in and step away from their divine missions."

It seemed to me that Lady Nada and Zadkiel had a friendly rivalry around sharing their insights, because Lady Nada nudged him out of the way. He took it all in good sport and bowed ever so slightly in her direction.

"Let's go back to your lifetime in India," said Lady Nada. "Take a look at the entire community. Can you sense how happy everyone is? Look at how everyone is working together. They are happy and living in joy. Notice how they understand there isn't a limited amount of abundance. When we understand that then we can all rise together."

Zadkiel lifted his hands, as if he was raising the roof, and laughed.

"All of us seem to be so in love with just our everyday lives," I said. "It's a miracle."

"It is," she said, "and that is exactly what can happen for you and your community in this lifetime if you continue on your path. Everyone will begin to wake up and see there is more to life than meets the human eye."

She glanced at Zadkiel, and he said, "We have a few more things we need to show you." He spoke in a more serious tone of voice. "This may be painful for you, but you need to see."

His voice trailed off, and I was transported back to a life in which I was a witch. It seemed strangely familiar and dark and brutal. Then I realized I'd visited this life while in the trance in Peru. What I saw under the shaman's care was so graphic and painful I had totally forgotten about it until revisiting it again now. I had obviously done my best to block it out of my mind.

I was tied to a stake in front of the entire town. Men, women, and even children were jeering at me and yelling insults. Many of them had stones in their hands and they shook them at me. My arms and legs were slashed and blood was pouring out. Suddenly a sharp stone struck me on the cheek. My instinct was to flinch, but I was tied so tightly I couldn't move.

I remembered seeing a shadow come up to me, and this time the person's energy was unmistakable. I recognized him instantly. The person leading the stoning was Uncle Bill. He was standing the closest to me with the largest and sharpest shards. He was making sure this was a torturous and slow death. One surprising realization was that in that lifetime I had actually slipped out of my body and watched from above as I was stoned to death. It became clear to me that as a soul, if you are having a painful exit, you can slip out of your physical body and watch so as not to have to endure the actual physical pain.

"Oh my gosh," I said. "It was him." Rage welled up in me, bitter in my throat.

"Try to get a good look inside of him and the others throwing stones at you," said Zadkiel. "What are they thinking?"

I needed a minute I was so furious. I hated Bill with every cell in my body. Lady Nada came close, and her gentle energy allowed something to shift. She held me, and I sobbed through a sudden rush of grief. Eventually, I was able to focus on what Zadkiel had asked. It was clear to me that the townspeople, including Bill, were frightened.

"They honestly believed that I was evil and against God," I said. My anger flared again. "That is the most ridiculous thing ever. All I did was try to help and heal every single one of them with my powers. I was the one serving God."

"I know," she said, "but they didn't see it that way. In their minds they were serving justice by getting rid of you. You need to understand this. You and Bill have had several lifetimes when this has been the scenario. You both chose to be family in this lifetime to see if you could grow together on a soul level."

Her words infuriated me, and I stomped like a little kid. "I don't get why would I want to have anything to do with that man."

"You both wanted to see if you could love and accept each other for what you are," she said. "Even if you do not agree with the other's point of view. You also knew you were going to be coming into a family that initially wouldn't be supportive of your psychic abilities, because they would think it was taboo. You wanted this challenge, because you knew you had the power to lift them up. From a soul level, tests with our family members are often the hardest, and they are the hardest lessons to learn."

A light bulb went on when she said that. Now I understood why— apart from Anna—no one in my family supported me, and why I had been so scared to tell them my truth.

"We want to congratulate you," said Zadkiel. "You did it. You stepped away from your family programming all on your own, and it isn't an easy feat. You can soon begin a new supportive relationship with your family."

I was so happy to hear this, because I had missed talking to my mom and dad tremendously.

"If you understand the history between you and Bill," said Zadkiel. "You can try to see him with love."

"Don't you think that is pushing it at this point?" I asked. "Maybe it's a little soon."

"Do you want to grow on a soul level or not?" he said.

"I will try, but it isn't going to be easy."

"We know that."

Next thing I knew, the three of us were observing Uncle Bill and Aunt Mary in this current lifetime. I saw them going into separate bedrooms to sleep. Uncle Bill sat in a chair in his room with his head in his hands. "Why me?" he said. "What did I do that is so wrong? When does the pain stop?"

"What is wrong with him?" I asked. "Why is he so upset?" I'd never seen him like this before.

"Because he is fighting his own demons," said Zadkiel. "He has his own encounters with the Brigade. When he lashes out in anger it has nothing to do with you. He is only acting on the outside how he feels on the inside. He is in pain and has never dealt with his deep issues. He has run from his inner truth his entire life. Sadly, he learnt this as a child; this was his survival mechanism. Now he buries his pain even deeper, and it festers. He doesn't mean to hurt you. In his mind he thinks he is protecting you. He thinks he is doing his job."

"Protecting me by trying to kill me and have me scared for my life?"

"On that particular day, the Brigade had truly taken over his soul. Just remember that he is fighting his own demons, and that you are safe. You are divinely protected so he can't hurt you."

Please help me to see this differently. I choose again, I choose to see this with love, I prayed.

As I stood there overlooking Bill, I was able for a brief moment to actually feel his feelings. Even though I thought his view was totally outlandish, for the first time I was able to see how his twisted mind actually worked. I could see and feel his pain. Most painful for me was the bolt of awareness I received about Bill's relationship with his psychic aunt. As a toddler he had loved her so much, and when his parents denounced her, he was forced to do the same. This act of betrayal scarred him deeply.

"That is so sad," I said. "I never knew he actually had feelings, much less that he was feeling so much pain."

"We know that," said Lady Nada. "That is why we wanted to show you this, so you could know and understand. You haven't forgiven him yet. Until you let go and forgive him, you will be stuck. In order to forgive sometimes we need to understand where the other person is coming from. When we hold onto resentment, we only hurt and punish ourselves. Forgiveness will set you free."

I remembered the lesson Bridget taught me when I was in so much pain about Lucas. Forgiveness had been the key for me if I truly wanted to let him go and move on.

"All people and relationships that come into our lives are lessons and assignments," she said. "The sooner you understand this, the easier it will be for you to look at these lessons as an opportunity to be of service. The more you help and serve others, the more divine power you will have. I think you got a pretty good glimpse of that by seeing and feeling your life in India."

Zadkiel chimed in. "You must nail this, darling. This is one of your big life lessons."

"Remember, forgiveness gives you freedom," Lady Nada said softly.

They both looked at me with adoring eyes. Lady Nada held out the rose bud. As I took it in my hand its petals unfurled, releasing the most heavenly fragrance.

"Congratulations. We can feel that you have shifted your perception," said Lady Nada and disappeared.

"Alright, queen bee," said Zadkiel. "I'll get you back into your body safely now. Remember we are all so happy and proud of you. You have done great work."

That was the last memory I had before waking up all snuggled in my bed the next morning.

A faint trace of rose perfume lingered on my pillow. I breathed it in and realized how momentous the night had been. India! That was my last power spot. I'd made it to all seven. I immediately went to my journal and wrote down the memories and the lessons from my last four power spots. I didn't want to ever forget them.

> *Power spot 4. Croatia - I learned that I am an actual Earth Angel!!!! I learned about dolphins being one of my spirit animals, and I received the most beautiful crystal amulet.*

> *Power spot 5. Egypt - The importance of surrender, and that when you forget that the angels have your back you block divine flow. I had some amazing past life visions, and I also had visions of what this life could be for me.*

> *Power spot 6. Costa Rica - I learned that I LOVE kundalini yoga, and "To heal it, you need to feel it." Thx Hoot!:) I was so grateful for all the beautiful energy the angels implanted in my body there.*

> *Power spot 7. India - The only way for true success is to be truly authentic. When you don't forgive, you are only punishing yourself. Forgiveness will set you free.*

As I finished writing I heard a knock on the door. *A visitor at eight in the morning?* "Coming!" I shouted, and I hurried down the stairs, still in my orange nightgown. I opened the door and couldn't believe my eyes.

"Mom! I'm so happy to see you!"

"Boy, have I missed you too." She squeezed me tightly. "I don't want to let you go. I can't believe how long it has been since I have seen you."

She kissed me several times on each cheek and then took a step back and noticed the amulet that I had gotten in Croatia. I hadn't taken it off since that trip. "Oh my gosh, I love your beautiful necklace."

"Thanks. I love it too. I am so glad you are here. But why didn't you tell me you were coming?"

Her smile vanished. "I don't want to alarm you, Sam, but Bill seriously almost tried to have an intervention with you. He wanted to have you committed. Even though I agreed with where he was coming from, I couldn't stand the thought of you being questioned in a psychiatric ward. I told him to please wait for me so we could do it together, because I knew that was the only way to stop him. My plan was to come talk to you and see if we could get this all straightened out and calm him down."

"Oh, Mom. Thank you so much. I am so happy to have you on my side."

"I may not agree with everything you say or what you are doing, but you are my daughter. I will always love and support you no matter what."

I gave my mom another big, long hug. I never wanted to be estranged from her again.

"So what should we do about Uncle Bill?" I asked. As the words came out of my mouth I winced, remembering his pain in my journey with Lady Nada and Zadkiel. "He is really hurting, and I am not totally sure why. But I know he is."

"Why would you say that?"

One day soon I'd tell Mom some of my angelic encounters, but for now I said, "Let's just call it a hunch. I have decided I want to forgive him for how he has treated me."

"Wow, you are growing up. I am so proud of you. I think if I can get him alone, I can tell him I have been with you and that you seem to be getting back to your old self. That should relax him a little. Besides, he will never be successful at putting you away without my support. So please do not waste another ounce of your energy of worrying about it."

Mom and I had the most amazing afternoon of shopping, bonding, and going to the movies, just like old times. We strolled the quaint streets in the Virginia Highlands and enjoyed an afternoon meal on a patio with the most perfect table in the warm sun. At the end of a perfect afternoon, we headed back to my condo and made plans to meet for a mother-daughter weekend at a spa in the North Carolina Mountains.

Maybe I can have it all in this lifetime. Maybe it can be like my life in India.

Chapter 38

I jumped out of bed, threw on my clothes, grabbed my bag, and drove to the airport all smiles. The weekend of the Angel Crusade was here. I had no idea what to expect, but I held the firm conviction that it was absolutely where I needed to be. When I landed in Los Angeles, I could feel the excitement in the air. I was staying just a block from the venue, and after checking into the hotel I walked over to the conference.

People from all walks of life and all ages where lining up around the block. I walked to the end of the line to take my place, and a beautiful brunette gave me a hug.

"Hey! My name is Sally," she said.

"I'm Julie," said another beaming girl, and she too gave me a hug.

"Sally, so what is your story?" asked Julie.

"I am known as The Angel Lady. I do angel readings, and I do them quite often for celebrities since I live here in LA. My father is a medium, and my mom is psychic, so this is all I have known all my life. I basically channel the archangels all the time. It is so cool to see everyone coming together like this. The angels have been prepping me to get ready for this for years."

"Wow," I said. "That must have been so cool growing up that way."

"Yeah, it was to me anyway, because I accepted my gifts. Not everyone who's grown up with spiritual parents feels that way though."

"I had an aunt who was cast out of the family for her abilities," I said. "So I'm quite new to all of this. It's changed my life though, and I can't wait to see what is next."

"Well then, welcome to living the life of your dreams," said Julie. She reached into her green suede shoulder bag and pulled out a handful of crystal bracelets. "Pick one. It will be a sort of welcome gift from me to you."

"Oh wow. They are all so beautiful that I can't decide." As the words came out of my mouth, one of the light pink ones said, "Pick me." I hopped back, startled, and they both giggled.

"Haha, it's normal for crystals to talk to you," said Julie. "Don't be scared." She handed me the pink bracelet.

When the doors opened, we were ushered into a large common area where we were given time to chat and mingle. Everyone was so open about their missions and their stories.

"I am just a good ol' boy from the south who had a few major losses in my life," said a young man with the sweetest smile to a group of girls who nodded in agreement. "It made me think there has to be more to our lives. I was introduced to *A Course in Miracles,* and it changed the way I view the world. I go around Alabama trying to get my friends to read this book, and they all just tell me to go relax and watch some football. I'm so happy to see how crowded this event is."

I giggled as I overheard him talking and made a mental note to be sure and introduce myself before this thing was over.

"What is your name?" said a tall, thin girl with red wavy hair. She gave me a hug.

"I'm Sam, what about you?"

"My name is Emily. I am stoked to be here."

"So what brings you here?" I asked. I was loving hearing everyone's stories.

"Well, I actually was a pretty bad alcoholic and ended up in a coma and almost died. I came out of it, and now I have learned how to live a fun and sober life. My mission is to teach others here how to do the same. I wrote a book about my story, so you will have to read it and let me know what you think."

We exchanged numbers, and I promised her I'd order her book.

"I don't believe it. Sam? Is that you?"

I turned around. There stood Beth, Claire's friend, who had given me Hiro's information. "Hey, Beth. This is so cool. I didn't expect to see anyone I knew here."

"Neither did I," she said, "but boy am I happy to see you. Isn't this place awesome?"

"Yeah, it is," I said. "How did you end up here?"

"I have been on quite a journey. I met with Hiro several years back—oh yeah, you met with him too, that's right. Anyway, he predicted I would be some sort of spiritual teacher. He told me I had the potential of Hillary Clinton. I almost wrote him off as a kooky Asian guy, but something caught my interest. I read books on awakening and chakras, and it was all going great. But I lost interest and got busy with life. You know how it goes. Then I lost one of my parents and was feeling super unfulfilled in my marriage. I was in a really bad place, living in New York.

"One day I was waiting on the subway platform," she said, "and poof, out of nowhere a scrawny boy with wiry glasses came up to me and handed me his card. He said, 'I'll be expecting your call soon.' I glanced at the card, and when I looked up he was nowhere to be seen. All the card said was, 'Psychic Sean' with his phone number."

My eyes grew wide, as I stood there in awe and got the chills. Even after all that I had been through, I was somehow still shocked at these stories.

"Oh wait, there's more," said Beth. "I mean, I couldn't make this stuff up if I tried. I wasn't sure if I wanted to call Sean, because the whole situation seemed so bizarre. I was baffled and needed a drink, so I went to a martini bar a few hours later. A friend joined me, and while we were chatting a mysterious looking woman with a heavy bust and stunning features walked over and very sweetly said, "I believe this is for you."

She handed me a note in an envelope that said, *Listen to your recording from Hiro and call Sean ASAP. This is not a joke; you are getting your wake up call. Hugs and kisses - LJ (Loving Joy)*

"Needless to say," she continued, "I did what the note said. All sorts of other unusual things began to happen, and here I am. This meeting means the world to me. I felt so alone, and it is so helpful to know there are so many of us going through this together."

"I know what you mean," I said. "I felt exactly the same way, and I was so happy to learn about this too. I wish I would have known, and we could have connected sooner. Come on, let's go get a good seat. It looks like we can go in now."

I grabbed her arm and we went into the banquet room. The tables were draped with bold pink tablecloths and each held a beautiful flower centerpiece. A massive crystal chandelier in the middle of the room scattered flashes of light onto the ceiling and the stage. On the stage a row of the largest and most beautiful crystals I had ever seen refracted subtle rainbow-hued waves of light back into the audience.

The ushers had all of us take our seats, and then I noticed all the archangels and the ascended masters began to gather onstage. I couldn't tell what they were doing, but they all were smiling, and I could feel it in my bones that they were happy with what was going down.

"Oh my gosh, do you see that?" I asked Beth, and pointed to the stage.

"See what?"

"Uh, those crystals," I said, not ready to explain to her that I can see angels.

"Oh yeah, aren't they gorgeous?" she replied. "I love crystals."

I looked around to see if anyone else had noticed the archangels on stage. It seemed as if a handful of other people in the room were able to see them—I could tell by their radiant, knowing smiles. No one was saying anything about it however, so I decided I wouldn't either. The lights went down in the room and lights went up on the stage, and everyone grew quiet. A tall woman with long silky brown hair, the biggest smile, and a truly spectacular aura stepped up to the microphone. This was Ariel, and she was the leader of the crusade.

"Welcome Angel Crusaders!" she belted out. "I cannot express how freaking pumped I am to see all of your beautiful faces! Can you guys believe this? The energy in here is fantastic!"

The crowd went wild with applause and cheers.

"It is with the utmost respect and honor that I welcome you all, fellow Earth Angels. This is a very special time, a time that will go down in history. I put out a special energetic invitation when I launched this meeting, and I am so happy to have you all along for this glorious ride. What we are going to do here together is something we can only do with the power of a group such as this one. Tonight we begin a movement for the fight of love! Whewwww!"

As she spoke, I could see the angels on stage filling her with golden energy. Everyone in the crowd clapped and cheered, and the energy in the room was beyond powerful and uplifting.

"Tonight, my friends, is just the beginning. We have all been called, but you have said yes. You have agreed to show up, and for that you will be rewarded greatly.

"As we can all witness and feel the divine energy in this room, we all know we have A LOT of work to do. And I mean A LOT! We need to take this weekend seriously, and we need to harness the light that we build here in this room. We need to take it home and graciously give it out to our loved ones, our clients, and our communities. Together we will take the Brigade down, one by one.

"This weekend you will learn the tools you need, and you will have the support you all have been longing for. We will call in our ancestors, our angels, and our protectors to fill each and every one of us up with the energy we need to stand up and be authentic and serve our divine missions to fulfill our legacies. Tonight that legacy becomes the legacy of the Angel Crusaders."

Intense chills ran up my spine as the crowd roared. Ariel had such an amazing and contagious energy about her. She was able to show everyone in that room what we could accomplish collectively.

"First," she continued, "I am sure you all are aware of what is happening on the planet right now, but I want to address it so we are all clear. Humans are evolving from a fifth sense personality to a multisensory personality. As human beings, we all have the ability to tap into our intuition and to fuel ourselves with divine love from within our hearts. This isn't an easy feat, and so I commend you for being here. Let me assure you that when you get over the initial hump of the transition, you will begin to live a life beyond your wildest dreams."

The crowd could not get enough of her. It was like we had all been waiting in unison for this meeting to take place. After each sentence, each promise, we broke out with applause and cheers.

"We are all here tonight to learn how to make our lights brighter and to take them and give them to the world around us. Each time we can open a door of enlightenment and awaken someone else to the knowledge of their own divinity within, each time that person becomes aware of their power and connection to the Divine, we are spreading light. The world becomes a brighter and better place. This, my darlings, is how we can shift the world through this transition."

The lights were dimmed and the song "Shine bright like a Diamond" by Rihanna blared through the speakers, and everyone including Ariel rocked out. We were all lifting each other up and making a statement of unity.

Ariel roamed the stage, grinning from ear to ear, and even though I didn't think the energy could get any stronger, it continued to elevate. The more we danced, the more divine angels showed up.

"We are here to learn to surrender to a power that is so much greater then we are. We are here to learn that this is not about us individually, but about us collectively, as one. You will all walk away from this with the knowledge that you need to go and uplift your loved ones, your community, and the world. You will let them know that it is safe for them to shine their own lights.

"Together we will break through the limiting beliefs of fear, and my human angels, we will leave a freaking loving stamp on this world together starting now!"

She lifted her arms, and music and laughter and cheers filled the room.

"Oh my God, she is spectacular!" Beth shouted and looked over at me.

"I know, it's true, she really is." Tears of grace poured down my face. I felt open and so revealed and trusting, as I freely let my emotions flow though me.

Ariel then introduced her guests; a panel of powerhouses who were all well known throughout the spiritual community. They were there to teach us and offer their support. First up was Catherine Cherub, a petite African American with a massive presence. She walked on stage in stiletto heels and skinny jeans, and she oozed happiness and love.

"Hello Angel Crusaders! Let me tell you this group is fierce, this group is powerful, and I am thrilled and excited. I bow to you all for having the gumption to show up for yourselves and for the planet. Whooohooo!" she yelled.

"I am a medium," Catherine continued, "and let me tell you the angel world and the spirit realm are having a par-tay tonight. If you think we are partying here, then you do not even know the half of it. Mother Teresa is here and wants me to channel a message for you? Are you ready?"

The crowd roared. People were standing on their chairs to get a better view of the stage. An overwhelming "Yes!" reverberated from the crowd.

Catherine stood in the center of the stage and took a deep breath, then she closed her eyes. When she opened them she seemed like a different person.

"Beloved ones, I am so proud of the commitment you have taken, and the courage you have shown to be here. If I were living today on this planet, I would want to be in this room with you all.

This is the beginning of a new movement, a movement of grace, love, happiness and joy, hope and inspiration. It is the beginning of heaven coming down to earth. You all came here filled with love. Tonight your angels and deceased loved ones and the archangels and the ascended masters, all of the Divine, are coming through the audience and lifting you up and showering you with divine love and grace. We are implanting into your energy fields divine droplets of love and power to take you where you need to be and to lift you up so you can serve to the highest truth and compassion.

"It is time, beloved ones, it is time. Remember, you have each other now, and you are loved and supported in more ways then you know. Thy will be done."

Catherine closed her eyes, and her head wobbled around for a minute, and then in a blink she was back in her body.

Ariel walked on stage, and they joined hands and lifted their arms and said, "It is time, Angel Crusaders. The time is now!!!!"

I felt like I was flying in that room, but I was still on my feet. I wasn't the only one with tears. Something happened in that room that night. Something more spectacular than any of my spiritual encounters which were already so magnificent. At the Angel Crusade I experienced the power of everyone coming together with the same intention and hope, each one of us ready to rise up and support our fellow Earth Angels. The power of love in that room was unstoppable.

It was a true movement. A movement of grace and love and honor. A movement to teach those we love what life is really about, and how together we can fight off the Brigade one by one and be rid of them once and for all. I had found my posse, I had found my support, and I knew I would never again have to feel the loneliness that had been so prevalent over this transition.

Chapter 39

For another two days I rocked out with my fellow Earth Angels, learning from some of today's best teachers. By Sunday evening, when I said my goodbyes, I was in a state of ecstasy. I had a beautiful new soul family that I would look forward to working with and supporting. And they in turn would do the same for me—I could lean on them. I ate dinner with Beth on Sunday night and then headed back to my hotel. I'd given myself a few extra days in LA as a treat, and the next morning I took a yoga class at a hip studio in Santa Monica that one of the girls at the Angel Crusade had mentioned. I treated myself to a massage, and then I relaxed in a Himalayan salt sauna I had discovered at the spa. It was spectacular.

That afternoon I strolled the streets of LA admiring the avenues of palm trees. I dipped in and out of shops to simply admire objects. I felt no desire to purchase anything—I was living in a state of abundance. At one point I reached a traffic light, but instead of crossing the road I had the powerful impulse to return down the street I had just explored. Halfway back, and I stopped in front of a particular parking meter. I'm not sure why, but I knew to follow my gut.

I froze. *Was I dreaming?* The man who had appeared in several of my visions, my soul mate, was parking his car directly opposite me. He stepped out and noticed me instantly. The connection was magnetic. From my heart, my soul, to his. Our eyes locked. He looked at me with such love, such tenderness and longing, and then he called out, "Well, HELLLLLO!"

I looked to my left and to my right, but cars were coming so fast that I couldn't cross the street quite yet. The energy of his words played inside my aura, and I was filled with an intoxicating feeling of love and familiarity.

This is him! This is the man I have been dreaming about. This is the man I have lived lifetimes with. This is the man that Bridget predicted I would find.

I could feel it in every ounce of my being. From across the street we continued to lock eyes, and it was a connection like no other. An immediate sense of soul recognition and belonging and LOVE.

I heard a gentle male voice within my head saying, *Is it really you?*

I shivered. I could hear his thoughts, and I wondered if he could hear mine.

The light in front of me turned red, and I was finally able to run across the street to join him. Just then a movie theater let out, and a group of paparazzi converged on the corner in pursuit of some celebrity. I'd lost sight of him. He'd disappeared into the crowd.

"Wait!" I shouted. "Oh, please wait!" I couldn't lose this man now, not after all of this.

I panicked. I shoved people aside and tears blurred my vision. The crowd dispersed, and I saw a gruff, familiar looking man. It was the driver who had kidnapped me in Bosnia. He stood beside a black, beaten up BMW with dark tinted windows. On the opposite side of the car, I saw a figure being shoved into the back seat.

"Nooooo!!! Stop!!!"

I was too far away, and before I could do anything or go anywhere the Brigade sped off with the man of my dreams. I stood there in total disbelief, tears streaming down my face. I felt utterly heartbroken. I tried to find a policeman, but then I wondered how would I explain it. I knew the only person who would be able to help me find him and take down the Brigade was Bridget.

I rushed back to the hotel, grabbed my belongings, and headed to the airport as quickly as I could. I jumped on the standby list and luckily grabbed the last seat on the last flight out of LA that evening. I boarded the plane anxious to get to Bridget. She hadn't answered my call which was unusual for her. The flight seemed to last an eternity. I spent most of the time talking to my angels, asking for help, imploring them to please keep safe two of the most important people in my life, Bridget and— I realized I didn't even know his name.

I landed at 5 am, and I couldn't get in my car fast enough. I drove straight to Bridget's and dashed up the path to her cottage. And then I stopped. My stomach caved. Something was wrong. I could feel it energetically. I saw that her door was ajar. I could hear her dog whining in the backyard.

"Bridget?"

There was no response.

"Bridget, are you here? Bridget you are scaring me, what is going on?" I pushed the door open and ran inside. I searched her healing studio and then raced into her private quarters.

"Bridget?"

As my eyes grew accustomed to the dark, I saw her slumped on the floor. I crouched beside her, and then I saw the growing pool of blood on the floor.

"Bridget! What happened?"

"Sam . . . I am glad you are here . . ." She could barely get her words out. She tried to sit up, and when she pulled her hand away from her stomach I saw that her dress was soaked with blood. "The Brigade . . . they got to me . . ."

I pulled out my phone and dialed 911. I gave them the address and then turned my attention to my beloved friend and guide. I cradled her in my arms. I could feel that I was losing her.

"Stay with me," I said. "Don't you dare leave me now."

"Stay strong Sam . . . fight with all your might . . . no matter what."

"Don't talk like that. You are going to be okay. The ambulance is on the way." I stroked her hair, and she gazed at me with absolute love, and then her eyes started to close.

"Promise me . . ." she whispered as she was going in and out of consciousness. She gripped my hand tight. "Say it. Tell me you will fight . . ."

"I promise, Bridget. I promise I will stay strong no matter what, and I will fight. Please don't leave me," I begged, as tears rolled down my face.

Bridget's eyes rolled back into her head, and I felt her heart stop beating.

"NOOOOO!!!" I wailed. "Please, I can't lose you too! Not now!" I cradled my arms around her. I couldn't stop the tears and the convulsive crying. *How am I ever going to make it without her?*

Musings of an Earth Angel

- A course on attracting Happiness and
Freedom into your life!

*Do you find yourself wondering if there is more to life?

*Are you searching for purpose and meaning?

*Do you want to know what your specific and unique life purpose is?

If so please join Suzanne Adams for her digital course: Musings of an Earth Angel- A course on attracting Happiness and Freedom into your life.

Participants of this course will:

- Be given the 5 key steps to Happiness and Freedom!
- Be able to implement the steps and make changes immediately!
- Have instant support, inspiration, community, and access to Suzanne's guidance via her private Facebook group for course participants.
- Understand energy and how your energy and thoughts affect your reality.
- Have all of the tools and understanding to attract more Happiness and Freedom!

You can access more information about the course at:
www.musingsofanearthangel.com/attract-happiness

Thank you so much for joining Samantha Kingston on her journey! Don't forget that you can spread the word about love and compassion and MOAEA by using #MOAEAsnippets across your favorite social media sites.

You can tag Samantha and she will be honored to share your posts!

Samantha Kingston loves social media and would love to interact with you!
You can find her at:

Instagram: @musingsofanearthangel
Facebook: Musings of an Earth Angel FB page
Twitter: @musingsofanEA
She is also blogging at: musingsofanearthangel.com/blog

Printed in the United States
By Bookmasters